MORTAL REMAINS

a novel by

Jason Andrew Bond

KIMURA
PUBLISHING

ISBN-10: 0615693946
ISBN-13: 978-0615693941

Front cover photo copyright © 2012 Paul Ransome,
www.PaulRansomePhotography.com
Back cover photo copyright © 2012 Rolffimages, www.dreamstime.com
Gold font texture copyright © 2012 Clearviewstock, www.dreamstime.com

Consultant for cover layout – Todd Krummenacher

For more about the author, future novels, and events please visit:

www.JasonAndrewBond.com

ACKNOWLEDGMENTS

I'd like to begin by thanking my editor, Leanne Sype of Pen to Paper Communications. Her invaluable guidance has made the experience of finalizing Mortal Remains much more enjoyable than previous projects. I also owe sincere thanks to my beta readers Katrina, Pat, Ray, Rocky, and Russell. Their final observations were critical for a final polishing I could not have achieved otherwise. I want to offer special thanks to dive masters Larry Inscore and Jim Brockus who guided me through open water SCUBA certification as part of my research for this novel. Thanks for sharing such a wonderful sport with me. My life is forever changed due to it. I also want to thank Paul Ransome for the perfect photograph and his enthusiasm in its inclusion in this project. Finally, I owe immense thanks to the person who sees all my writing before anyone else. Sol Stein wrote that you can't trust your loved ones to give an honest opinion on your work because they won't fully perceive its flaws. It isn't so with her. If she hates it, she hates it and tells me so. She has the pulse though, and I've learned to listen carefully to her thoughts, no matter how painful to hear. I have to credit her with cleaning up a great many fissures in my writing, and for that and so many other reasons, I dedicate this book...

...to my best friend and wife,

Lindsey.

Thanks for sharing your life with me.

TO THE READER

In Spring 2011 I was lying awake for a third straight night with insomnia. I can't say why; nothing was troubling me. I simply couldn't sleep. As I stared at the ceiling, a National Geographic special I had watched months earlier on blue holes in and around the Bahamas wandered into my thoughts.

During the show, divers discover a body hanging from thirty-year-old SCUBA equipment. I found myself turning the memory of that body over and over in my mind, wondering what it would be like to drown in the dark. At that moment, the entirety of *Mortal Remains* poured into my mind as if the muse on hand had lost patience and dumped it from a bucket.

I ran to my office and typed out notes for two hours before going back to bed and finally, blissfully sleeping like the dead. Apparently my muse had been trying to get me to listen for three days and would only let me rest when I had dutifully received the message.

That singular moment would lead me to study topics from Sumerian mythology to the Wolof of Senegal. I would have to travel to the Bahamas for research (I know… poor me) and dive into the cold January depths of Puget Sound (seriously… poor me).

It has taken me a year and a half of almost daily work to complete this. I've put in that effort because I respect your time as a reader and want to offer you something worth reading. My goal throughout has been to create a story people simply cannot put down. Have I achieved that? The answer to that question, of course, lies in your capable hands.

I offer two requests to you as humbly as I can: First, if you should enjoy *Mortal Remains*, please tell others about it. Your recommendations are as important as they are appreciated. Second, if you are so inclined, I would love to hear from you at jasonandrew@jasonandrewbond.com.

In every tyrant's heart there springs in the end this poison, that he cannot trust a friend.

-Aeschylus

PROLOGUE
Abaco Island - Bahamas

Erica Morgan walked in darkness among thin, crooked trees.
What moonlight managed to penetrate the upper canopy settled
on the forest floor in small patches, arcing over her arms and
shoulders as she passed. The scant light left the trees a few
paces away in a black thicket.

As she stepped forward, the end of a stick pressed into the
sole of her foot. Unable to fight his will, which had made a
marionette of her, she brought her weight down. The stick
pierced the skin and grated between the bones, tenting the skin
along the top. Pain lanced up her leg, causing her head to go
light with endorphins. When she brought her foot down again,
the stick shifted.

As she walked, her lungs drew air, and the muscles from
toes to shoulders flexed and relaxed, but she had no control.
Thoughts of her own death preyed on her while her heart beat
in a calm rhythm. With her next step, the base of the stick
broke away, twisting at the length still jammed in her foot.

1

A poisonwood unfolded from the darkness ahead. As she walked by, its lower branches dragged along her neck and arm, catching on her shirt. She feared that the bag, which—slung over her shoulder—carried the weight of her salvation, might become tangled, but the fabric of her shirt pulled taut and ripped open at the side.

Beyond the poisonwood, she passed into a darker area of the forest where the trees faded entirely into blackness. As her eyes gave her less, she became more aware of sounds: her feet shuffling in the dirt, twigs cracking, the breeze filtering through leaves.

Her neck and arm burned where the poisonwood had brushed, yet her thoughts stayed on the pit. She'd stood over it in the daylight, stared down into the depths of the submerged cavern yawning in the forest floor, but in the darkness, she had no idea how far she'd come or how far she still had to go. With any step she might fall. She'd have just a half-heartbeat to feel the wind pick up before hitting the water.

She imagined it crashing around her, soaking and suffocating. She would float face down as the darkness went still, but when he forced the air from her lungs, she would sink into the belly of the earth, down nearly three hundred feet, her ears pressurizing. As she imagined the need for air burning in her lungs, she wondered how he would finish her. Would he force her mouth open, allowing water to pour down her throat, or hold her tight and let her suffocate?

But what came after death troubled her far more. If she failed there would be no tunnel of light, no escape from the bones and flesh. She'd exist down there with him, locked in his dead embrace.

She wasn't going to let that happen. He thought he had her, but he'd misstepped. She wasn't the same woman she'd been even a few days before. She'd killed again earlier tonight, at least led the man to his death, and she wasn't done.

The mineralized scent of cold, stone-leached water tinged the air and grew stronger with each step. Walking out of the trees, she entered a moonlit clearing and saw the tombstone glow of a rock wall. At its base, an uneven void cut a gap out of the forest floor. She needed to be closer, had to get right to the edge.

CHAPTER 1

Nine Days Earlier—
Palm Beach, FL

Holding a wad of bloody toilet paper over her nose, she looked at her face in the bathroom mirror and saw a small circle stamped into her cheek. Leaning closer she could make out the facets of his diamond ring. She touched the skin under her right eye where it had already begun to darken. It would be eggplant purple in the morning. She wished she could get to the kitchen for ice.

"You know too much about getting punched in the face," she said into the mirror and could no longer look at herself.

Sitting down on the toilet, she looked out of the bathroom, across the master bedroom, to the locked door. Something crashed in the living room downstairs. She took the toilet paper from her nose and stared at the red-soaked wad. Fresh blood ran down into her parted lips. She dropped the wad into the trash can, pulled another streamer of paper from the roll, folded it up, wiped her lips, and pressed it over her nose. The bridge of her nose felt sore but didn't give the sharp pain of being broken.

She heard his Italian shoes ascending the marble staircase, shifting to muted scuffs as he came down the thick-carpeted hallway. Something smacked the door. The loud crack made Erica jump.

That's new.

The nightclub must have been harder on him than she'd guessed.

What could have lit him up so badly? A clash with a younger, stronger thug? Maybe a stripper gave him hell after he stroked her ass.

Whatever it was, Brandon's rage was peaking tonight. The door handle dipped, stopped, and rattled. She stared at the door, stared at its small latch and thin, wooden panels, her belly going cold.

Again, the handle dipped and rattled.

Just on the other side, Brandon said with a growl, "Erica, open the door."

Erica stared at the frail, protective door. When he blew up, he'd punch her, bloody her nose, bruise ribs, but if she could get away, run up the stairs, and lock that door, he'd bluster against it and go. He could have kicked it down any number of times, but he never did.

The door rattled again; then a fist whacked at it. "Open the fucking door, cunt."

That last word made her go still, like a deer waiting to know which way to run from a wolf.

Calm down Brandon. You're supposed to calm down now.

His fist hit the door with a resounding thud, rattling it in its frame.

She looked at the walls of the bathroom, the thin, high window in the shower, up at the head-sized vent, and back to the door.

Another harder hit on the door—and then silence. On her fingertips, Erica felt warm wetness soaking through the toilet paper. She remained still.

A tremendous crack rattled the door, and one of the lower panels split. Her heart pounded blood through her shoulders and neck, stabbing pain into her eye with each beat.

Stay calm. It's going to be okay.

Even as she thought it, she knew it was getting worse. Someday he would cripple her, or—

"Erica!" Fury still laced his voice, but hearing her name instead of 'bitch' or worse made her feel a rush of relief. He was losing steam.

"Open the door," he said, but only anger remained, not the switched-on fire that had ruined her dreams. A moment more of silence; he grumbled something. She stared at the door, and hearing his steps scuff back down the hallway, she let out her breath, only then feeling the dizziness of having held it. The storm had passed.

Sitting on the toilet with the wad of toilet paper at her nose, soaking with her blood, she stared at the door's cracked lower panel. Brandon would leave her alone tonight. He'd sleep in the guestroom, and tomorrow they would both pretend it had never happened.

Her gaze dropped from the panel, and she saw the red stains she'd left across the white carpeting as she'd come into the room, her hand under her nose, cupped full of blood. She'd have to get that cleaned up before he saw it and, with a pair of black eyes, would have to cancel tomorrow's lunch date with

Sarah. Resting her elbows on her knees, she considered the lie she'd have to offer to cover it up.

She knew she should leave him. As she had done so many times before, she imagined packing a bag, going out on the balcony, climbing down the lattice work, and meeting a taxi. It wouldn't be that easy though would it? She had nothing to pay the cab driver with. Her cash, cards, and phone were in her purse, which lay on the kitchen counter. The cops could get it for her, but if she called the police, then what? Stay in a woman's shelter? He had all the money and the pre-nup. She had nothing and wasn't sure she was ready for cots and cockroaches. She looked at the back splash—tile from Venice—and the Waterford Crystal-shrouded lights. She had thought this was everything. She laughed, and a sob cut it short. His rage would pass, and she could go back to avoiding him. She felt ashamed that she was willing to put up with this for a nice house and a Mercedes. She'd had to worry about money every day growing up. Of all the problems she had now, that was no longer one of them. Perhaps his anger would fade as he got older. The drugs and alcohol seemed to be eroding his sex drive, or maybe he had a girl down in Boynton... somewhere anyway. If an affair kept him away from her, she couldn't be happier, as long as he didn't give her an STD. Probably would.

She thought about going home to the hovel her drunkard father lived in on the edge of the Everglades. Imagining him sitting on the porch, his stained cotton shirt worn thin across the belly, she shook her head and looked around at the bathroom again. This was the best she had been able to do. She took the tissue away from her nose and examined it. The air cooled the wetness in her nostrils as she held the tissue ready. The bleeding seemed to have stopped. She tossed the wad into the trash.

Standing, she looked at herself in the mirror. Runnels of blood stains striped the front of her shirt. She pulled the shirt over her head, feeling the blood-dampened fabric drag across her face. Dropping it into the sink, she looked back at herself in the mirror. The thick waves of her blonde hair hung around her face and shoulders in a confused mess. Running her fingers through it, she smoothed it behind her shoulders and pulled it into a pony tail. She turned sideways and looked at herself: athletic shoulders, ample breasts, and a thin waist. She turned a bit more. Great ass. She had everything it took to get herself into just this kind of mess.

"Trophy wife," she said to herself and twisted her face into an oddball expression. She'd have been better off looking like that. How might it have turned out for her if she had? She let her face go slack. With her graceful nose, wide sea-blue eyes framed by long, auburn lashes, and delicate chin, she was beautiful, even with blood smeared across her face. Her beauty had been very important to her in younger years when she believed she had nothing else, but years of rapacious glances, uncomfortable pick up lines, and her husband's unpredictable temper had worn her down. When she looked at herself in the mirror now, she felt not like herself, but a reflection of other's expectations.

If she hadn't had hair that naturally hung in thick, wheat-highlighted locks, if she hadn't had the chest or ass, she wouldn't have registered on Brandon's radar when he came in with advertising orders. As she took them from him, he would have given her a weak smile and walked out without another word. She would have stayed in her small apartment with the view of a back alley and a half-dead palm tree.

"I would have been better off," she said to her reflection. She took a hand towel from the chrome rack, turned on the faucet, let it run until it was good and cold, and wet the towel under the aerated stream. Shutting off the tap, she began dabbing the crusting blood from her upper lip and nostrils.

Thinking back on her studio apartment, she remembered sitting on the window sill with evening coming on. She'd imagine she could see the ocean instead of the sea of worn roof shingles and power lines. She felt lonely and poor those days, but she had something she hadn't had before or since: freedom. It had probably been the pinnacle of her life.

She stared at herself in the mirror. "That's pitiful, Erica."

When she first met Brandon she had found him dramatically handsome, a real leading man with a strong jaw and wickedly beautiful eyes. His dark hair had already begun to pepper with age, and the Hublot watch he wore was worth ten times everything she owned. There had been no question in her heart when he had asked her out; she knew right away he was the one. He had taken her to the Azure Martini. She'd had daydreams about going to restaurants like that, and there she sat among the wealthy, feeling so out of place. But she hadn't hesitated to fall in love with him. As they sat at dinner, she saw them both old, shopping in an exotic place, perhaps for hand blown glass in Venice. He would be such a handsome older man.

She had been so embarrassed by her own poverty that she never allowed him to meet her at her apartment. When he took her to his house, she stood beside the cascading fountain in the center of his cobblestone driveway and stared out the gates and across Ocean Boulevard. There the Atlantic lay, glittering in the sun and stretching off to Europe. At that moment, she thought she was the luckiest woman alive.

"Stupid," she said to herself in the mirror. The hollows under both eyes had already begun to tint purple. She ran more cold water over the towel and pressed it to her eyes. After rinsing the towel, she took it into the bedroom and knelt down in front of the door. She pressed the towel into the first dime-sized drip of blood and then scrubbed at it. When she lifted the towel, she saw that most of the blood had come up, leaving a coppery stain. She'd have to get the carpet cleaner out but wouldn't be able to until morning, after he had left for work.

If he sees the stains...

Kneeling back on her heels, she looked at the cracked door panel, a splinter sticking out at the center. She gripped it between thumb and forefinger and pulled.

The bang was so loud she couldn't make sense of it. The splinter coming out couldn't make that sound. The door flexed from the middle, and the entire frame broke free, bouncing around her, almost walking away as if a pair of feral stilts as the door followed, flying open from the destroyed lock. It cracked to a stop on her knee and sheared away from its hinges, falling toward her. She covered her head, and the door struck her side.

Run.

She dragged herself out from under the door and ran for the closet.

That door doesn't have a lock.

Before she could change directions for the bathroom, he shoved her hard. Her head snapped back, and she felt a sharp pain at the base of her skull. She turned as she fell, landed on her side, and rolled to her back, ready to kick, but he was already on her, shoving her legs down. She tried to claw at him, but he flailed for her wrists, caught them, and shoved them to her sides. He sat on her, muscular thighs pinning her arms. She could barely draw a breath as his weight crushed her belly.

His dark hair had been messed as if he had pulled at it, and a day's stubble mottled his jaw. He glared at her, his eyes wide with switched-on fury. What had brought on that anger didn't matter; he was going to take it out on her. Pressing her feet into the floor, she tried to push him off but only succeeded in knocking him forward. He held out his hands to stop himself, pushed her back down, and slapped her across the face. Before she could shove off the carpet a second time, he slapped her again and again. He began to yell at her, but she could only feel the overwhelming cracks coming across her face, first one side and then the other. She tugged at her arms, desperate to get something between her face and his open palms, but he squeezed his legs to her sides.

His hands kept lifting up and cracking down, back and forth, and her face began to go numb. She felt dizzy, and her stomach clenched, acid burning in her throat. He raised his hand again but didn't hit her, just held it there, hovering over her. "You think you're so damn hot don't you?"

Her voice choking with tears, she said, "No," but knew saying anything was a mistake.

He gripped her neck and leaned down close to her ear. "No, you do. You think you're so much better than everyone else." He reached into his pocket. When his hand came back up, Erica felt metal at her neck, felt the blade bite at her skin.

This is it. He's finally going to kill me.

"You know what I should do?" His voice cracked as unstable grief mixed in with his rage. "I should cut your face off."

She felt the blade bite deeper into her neck. Pushing her skull into the carpeting, she tried to get away from it.

He leaned in closer, his face beside her head, lips whispering at her ear. "No one will want you then. I'll never let another man have you. You understand that?"

She nodded as best as she could with her neck pinned to the floor and the blade at her throat and said in a choked rattle, "I've never… been unfaithful…"

Her face pressurizing with blood and vision tunneling, she gave one last shove, but had no strength left in her legs. She began to slip into the closing tunnel. He released her neck, and blood rushed into her head. As she drew long gasps of breath, he stared at her. She expected him to slap her again, but he only stared, the red anger depressurizing out of his face. His eyes went empty, like the clear sky after a hurricane, pale and silent. It had run its course tonight, and she had survived.

Pushing off the carpet beside her head, he stood and looked at the knife in his hand as if its presence confused him. He folded it, returned it to his pocket, and left the room. Erica rolled to her side and came to her hands and knees. Sitting up, she felt as though she was in a dream, dizzy and disconnected. She crawled into the bathroom, shut and locked the door, and lay against the far wall beside the toilet. Putting the back of her head against the wall, she felt the numbness leaving her face, replaced by burning pain. She expected tears, waited for them, but felt nothing aside from a broad emptiness. In that emptiness she walked back through the last four years of her life—back through the parties and the beatings—back through tonight, and the solution clarified itself to her.

I think I have enough cash… but it has to look like an accident.

A smile drew across her lips.

CHAPTER 2

Erica woke with a start. Brilliant sunlight framed the edges of the window blinds. She looked to his side of the bed and found the duvet smooth, undisturbed through the night. Sitting up, she pushed the covers off her legs but paused when the clatter of something metal being set on tile came through the bathroom door. A drawer slid and thumped closed. She knew she should leave the room—avoid him—and bent her knees to swing her feet to the floor as the bathroom door opened, spilling sunlight into the room.

Brandon walked out, setting a platinum cufflink into his shirtsleeve. He lifted his gray Versace blazer from the valet and put it on. The tailored coat snugged to his broad shoulders as he straightened the lapels. He looked at himself in the cheval mirror in the corner, smoothing the sides of his hair. He side-stepped so he could see her in the glass. He had two days growth on his face, but had shaved away the stubble on his neck. Erica pulled the comforter back over her legs.

"You planning on sleeping all day?" His voice gave no hint of his mood. He usually left her alone after a bad night. This tangent and his neutral tone made Erica feel unsafe. She remained still, glancing at the door. Its frame lay propped up against the wall.

"Hey," he said, holding out his hands, commanding her to speak, his neutrality shifting toward anger.

"No," she said, looking at the muted shape of her legs under the comforter.

"Look…" He walked up to the bedside. As he approached, she wanted to slide away from him but stopped herself.

Stay still. Don't provoke anything.

He continued, "How long are we going to keep this up?"

She said nothing.

He sat down on the edge of the bed and put his hand on the comforter over her thigh. In that position she remembered how romantic he had been their first few months of marriage. Having seen his rage come out at others, she justified that everyone had their flaws, and he had been sweet to her most of the time. Even that had been a lie. He had been a rattlesnake from the start, joking at her expense and being playfully rough—a cruel child masquerading as a man.

"I'm sorry about last night."

Her eyes came up to meet his, and she almost thought she saw regret there. She froze at the sight of it, letting him make the next move.

"You don't believe me."

"I do," she said. She believed he was the greatest asshole she'd ever met. She understood that beneath his fashionable stubble and smooth, expensive fabric lay the soul of a devil, cool and mesmerizing at one moment, abusive and hateful the next.

"It's true. I'm sorry," He ran his hand up the comforter, nearing her groin, "but, you gotta give me space when I've been partyin'. You got me?"

Erica felt anger rising, gripping at her, goading her to lash out, to scream, to claw. Yet she knew well enough where that would lead, so she sat still and said, "I understand. I won't bother you again when you come home late."

"That's not what I'm saying, Curves."

Holy God, not that nickname anymore.

It had been so sexy to her before, to think that a guy who looked like him liked the look of her enough to give her that nickname. Feeling her face flush at the sound of it, not with allurement, but fury, she smiled at it like she was supposed to.

"I'm just saying that you need to be polite. I like to show you off, but that means you have to act high class, like I know you can be, not the Everglades swamp rat you used to be."

Her hands gripped the comforter, fingernails digging in; she imagined the fabric was the flesh of his neck. Exhaling, she said, "Okay. I'm sorry."

"There we are." He leaned forward, took hold of the sides of her face with his smooth hands, and kissed her mouth. She kissed back.

Still holding the sides of her head, he leaned away and looked at her with his coppery, lion-like eyes. "You should get yourself cleaned up and put on some makeup. You'll feel better then. You had a hard night."

If she said anything now, she'd spit the words at him, so she didn't respond, didn't move. He let her head go and stood. Looking down at his lapel, he flicked a bit of lint away and turned and walked to the bedroom door. He opened it and said, "I do love you, Curves. You know that right?"

"I do," she said, fingernails now digging into the meat of her thigh.

You're almost there, Erica. Stay focused, stay strong.

But she felt herself stumble, felt the beat of time as he stood looking at her, and the danger of that gap. Her belly trembled as anger-driven instinct held her back, but her rationality won over, and she said, "I love you too."

He smiled and left the room, his voice becoming more distant as he walked down the hallway. "You should go online and blow some money this morning. That'll help you feel better. Get yourself some earrings or a necklace. No cars though." He laughed at this, and she heard the leather soles of his shoes descending the marble stairs.

Imagining those shoes bending as he walked, she remembered him bragging when he had brought them back from London. She hated those shoes, hated his watches, his suits, his car.

A bullet hole would look great in his shoe, especially if his foot was still in it.

A smile crept across her face as she listened for the garage door to rumble open and then close. When she heard his Mercedes squeal its tires on the curved driveway, she let go of her hold on her anger, and it—along with frustration and embarrassment—overwhelmed her. She sat in the bed holding her face, sobbing. The soreness across the bridge of her nose and around her eye sockets flared up as she cried.

When the sobbing had reduced to silent tears, she let out a trembling sigh and looked back at the broken doorframe propped up on the wall. She took tissues from her nightstand and blew her nose. Looking at the clots of blood in the tissue, she closed her hands around it and dropped her forehead to her knuckles. She felt tears rising up again, but pushed them back down.

No more. It's time to go.

She slid off the bed, walked into the bathroom, dropped the tissue into the trash, and—placing her hands on the counter top—stared at herself in the mirror. The white of her right eye had hemorrhaged red across the outside edge, looking demonic next to the blue iris. The skin around that eye had only a hint of purple, but the left was another matter. There, a dark-purple swath ran in a ragged arc around the socket, trailing off toward her ear. Both sides of her face were red, peppered with tiny, broken capillaries. She lifted her chin and saw, on the pale skin of her neck, the small, red tick from the cut of his knife. As she looked at the cut, the bridge of her nose caught her attention; it seemed slightly enlarged. She touched it with her finger and thumb, pressing side to side.

Not broken.

She thought of Brandon driving along in his Mercedes, probably already riding high on coke. She imagined him pulling in to work, walking into the marina, and giving a self-assured smile to his 19-year-old receptionist, the one who had been runner up for Ms. Florida. Erica stopped herself for fear of what she could imagine them doing and how true it probably was.

Her commitment from the night before floated up in her quiet mind, and she turned it over as she stared at her bruised face. If he died, and if it looked like an accident, she would get everything.

Done.

She turned on the shower and began to undress. She had work to do. Brandon wanted her to spend some money today? Fine. She had no idea how much putting a hit on someone cost, who to approach, or what to say. Then she thought of Rafi, a friend from her first days in the city. Rafi lived at the fringes of the legal world and hated Brandon. That's where she'd start.

CHAPTER 3

She wore sunglasses large enough to cover the bruises around her left eye as she drove north on Broadway up into Riviera Beach. Skillful makeup hid the rest. As she drove, a nervous energy—which seemed to have its source in her belly—made her arms and hands feel light. She felt somewhat ill.

Am I really about to commit a felony? Offer to pay for the murder of my husband?

She remembered being pinned beneath him, thought of his eyes as he slapped her. She let her breath out through clenched teeth.

Yes I am.

Here, north of the posh districts, bare dirt with patches of brown grass made up the lawns in front of the businesses. Chain link fences surrounded the car lots and mechanics' shops. At the base of the fences, weeds cast spindly shadows across cracked asphalt. Many of the businesses in the worn-down strip malls had hand-painted signs with faded, uneven letters.

Rafi's shop is somewhere up here on the right.

She couldn't quite remember which block. Then, realizing where she was, she slowed. A horn honked. She looked into her rear-view mirror and saw a Honda with a cracked windshield. Holding up her hand in apology, she pulled over to the side of the street. As the car passed, the driver—a woman who had seen too many decades of hard sun—extended a blade-like, blue fingernail.

The gesture had little effect on Erica as her eyes had been drawn across the street, over the roof of a convenience store, to the second story of a house. The house's yellow paint had long ago begun its surrender to the elements, flaking away here and there to expose gray wood. A ramshackle staircase hung off its side. So many times she had walked up that staircase tired and disappointed, the unsteady steps creaking under her.

Erica sat in the leather seat of her black Mercedes, the vents blowing cool air over her, and stared at the second story window where she had sat so many nights, watching the sun set through the power lines. On those nights, the smell of lighter fluid-soaked charcoal grills searing lime fish would mingle with music and shouting. She would look out across the rooftops to the darkening sky, which hung over the unseen ocean, and imagine she lived in a house where a perfect lawn bordered a white beach and the cool ocean air drifted across the patio.

She pressed a switch, and the window slid down, thumping to a stop. Inhaling the air, she found only heat, a stale, diesel-fume scent, and the noise of traffic. She closed the window and looked down the street.

Rafi's shop is two or three blocks north of here.

She pulled back onto the street and drove two blocks up. There it was—the center shop in a three-store strip mall. She pulled her car up to the empty curb. The store still had the old turquoise paint, more faded now than it had been four years ago. Some of the roof flashing hung down in a bent arc. The sign above the window in red-painted wooden letters read, without further detail, "ART". Through the dirty glass she could see an empty display case.

Getting out of her car, she walked to the door, which had a single-pane window set in it, the edges smeared with paint. She held her hands up to shield the bright sunlight and saw shelves on the back wall but could make out nothing beyond that. Gripping the worn, brass knob, she twisted it. The knob resisted, and she twisted harder. It popped free and the door pushed inward a quarter inch, catching on the jam. She shoved at the door, and it came free, the weather stripping scraping along the linoleum squares.

Leaning in through the open doorway, she said, "Hello?"

Forlorn sunlight filtered through the windows, filling the shop with heavy heat. The musty scent of old wool caught in her throat. Stepping inside, she shoved the door closed, the glass pane rattling in its frame, and found herself in muffled silence. She took off her sunglasses and hung them off her jeans pocket.

She looked around the empty room. A space on the counter, less worn than the rest, marked where a cash register had been. At the far end of the counter by the wall, she saw a solitary, creased postcard. Walking over to it, she picked it up and unfolded it. A Jackson Pollack print. Turning it over, she found a paragraph on the painter. She looked at the image again, scattered black and white trails of paint on a thicker base of brown and gray streaks.

This thing looks like how I feel.

Setting the postcard down, she thought back to how the shop had looked when it was open.

Not much better.

The register, a worn-down hulk, had still been there, and cheap resin copies of statues from all over the world had lined the shelves. She looked at the floor. Three rusty circles lay imbedded in the linoleum where wire post-card stands had stood. Rafi had kept the real pieces, antiques mostly from the Middle East with questionable import status, in the back storeroom—all obviously gone now.

He probably got shut down.

She imagined Rafi sitting in a resin chair and wearing the bright-orange jumpsuit of a federal prison. She sighed and turned to leave, her eyes passing over the rear wall. She stopped and looked at it again. The book case didn't cover the entire wall. In the middle of the wall, a single, white door broke the even lines of the shelves. It hadn't been white before. It had been a rickety, wooden door. This door had a smooth, metal surface, broken only by the lens of a peep hole the size of a silver dollar.

She stepped through the open pass-through in the front counter and, looking into the curved glass of the peep hole, saw the dim glow of electric light. She touched the door with her fingertips, cool to the touch, air-conditioned. She rapped her knuckles on the door.

"Hello?" she said into the solid surface of the door, "Rafi?"

She knocked again and listened. The silence of the musty, front room blanketed her again. She looked back to the worn counter top, the sunlight, and the clouded windows. Dust motes floated through the light. She looked down at her Tory Burch sandals, Ernest Sewn jeans, and sleeveless Phillip Lim top. She lifted the stem of her Gucci sunglasses from her pocket and stared at them.

"Seriously, Erica?" she said to the empty room. "You're going to hire a hit on Brandon?"

She felt a sob rising up in her chest, pushing its way into her throat. The corners of her mouth curled down beyond her control and her chin pulled tight. Gritting her teeth she snapped the glasses in half. But it didn't stop the feeling, and the sob escaped. She put her hand over her mouth and tears brimmed in her eyes, freefalling from her lashes, past her hands, to the floor. Shaking her head, she drew slow breaths until the feeling passed.

She looked out the fogged shop windows. "What the hell am I going to do?" She looked at the broken sunglasses in her hands.

Now you have no way to cover your eyes.

With a defeated sigh she set the broken sunglasses on the counter and walked to the front door. As her hand touched the doorknob, the white door behind her opened.

She turned and found herself facing a man who wore a black rugby shirt with green and tan stripes around the upper shoulders and a crest on the left breast. He had powerful shoulders and a lean waist. Close cropped hair framed a rugged skull, and his thick eyebrows hung over clear-blue eyes. A scar ran through his left eyebrow, and the ear on that side stuck out, cauliflowered.

He stepped through the door into the space behind the counter, and in a deep voice with a thick Irish accent said, "What did ya want?"

Erica stared at the man in surprised silence. Cool air from the open doorway drifted toward her carrying the scent of sandalwood and gun oil.

23

A muffled voice came from the back room, and the Irishman looked over his shoulder. He looked back at Erica and said, "Out with it."

She said, her voice quiet and unsure, "Does Rafi still own this shop?"

"Wha' shop?"

She looked around at the empty store front and back to the man. "I'm sorry. It's been about four years. Things must have changed since then."

"Yeah."

She turned and grabbed the door handle to leave, and the man said into the back room, "Says she's lookin' for someone called 'Rafi'. Says she knew 'im years back."

Erica yanked on the handle, but the door remained stuck in its jam. Muffled words came from the voice in the back.

The Irishman asked Erica, "You have a name?"

"Erica, but I'll go. I'm sorry to have bothered you." She tugged at the handle, the door slipping another quarter inch in the jam.

The muffled voice from the other room said something, and the Irishman lifted his hand, beckoning to her. "Come back this way, girlie."

She felt a rush of panic telling her to get the hell out of there.

"It's okay," she said. "I'm sorry to have disturbed you." She gave another yank on the door handle, and the door came open. Walking out of the shop and toward her car, she heard charging feet behind her and turned just as the Irishman grabbed her by the upper arm. She tried to twist away from him, but couldn't fight his strength. An old Monte Carlo, its vinyl top mostly cracked away, rolled down the street. The gray haired man at the wheel paid no attention to the store front.

The Irishman grabbed her other arm, forcing her to face away from him, his fingers clamping into the flesh of her biceps. She tried to plant her feet, but he lifted her off the ground and carried her back into the shop. Just as she screamed out, he kicked the front door closed. As he walked her through the white door, she began kicking wildly at his legs. She felt her heels connect several times and he swore at her, but his grip stayed strong. He set her on her feet, and as she yanked at her arms, he pushed her forward into the center of the room.

With her heart racing and her fingers tingling with adrenaline, she looked around the back room and stopped fighting, amazed at what she saw. When she had known Rafi, this space had been a store room with metal shelving and a ratty, corduroy couch. Now she found herself in what looked like a high-end gallery. She stood on thick carpeting the color of paprika. Small, ceiling-mounted halogen spot lamps, their glass bezels glowing with rainbows, illuminated stone sculptures and wall-mounted carvings. The steep angle of the light threw lengthened shadows down smooth, stone faces with broad eyes and symmetrically curling beards. The light glowing off the pieces left the room's dark-painted walls subdued. A vase to her right held two sticks of incense. Smoke curled from their glowing tips and floated in thin ribbons up around the jaw and eye sockets of a stone skull.

On a plush, leather couch in the back of the room sat Rafi Fraser. He wore a simple, white polo, gray slacks and black canvas shoes, the seams fashionably frayed.

"Know her, do ya?" the Irishman man asked.

"Erica," Rafi said with a hint of his peregrine Scottish-Iraqi accent, "how long has it been?" Rising from the couch, he walked up to her. He stood barely half an inch taller than

Erica, but strong, with square shoulders and a rakishly unkempt shag of brown hair. As he looked at her, a slight smile in his eyes, she found herself—as she had so many times before—trapped in those eyes. She looked across the long, curved lashes and then into the green of his irises, which had a mother-of-pearl radiance. The silence between them made her embarrassed, and she lowered her gaze.

Eyes still down, Erica smiled and said, "Four years Rafi." She expected the Irishman to let her go, but he didn't.

"Four years and you just walk into my store front again?"

Erica looked up.

The smile in Rafi's eyes narrowed, shifting to something unfriendly. "Why?"

Erica weighed how to approach the situation. She wished that the Irishman had just let her leave. She could have been back in the quiet safety of her car, heading back down Broadway toward the marina, just going back to her stupid life. She could still meet with Sarah for coffee… where she'd have to insist on sitting on the bar's patio so she could keep her sunglasses on to avoid questions about her eyes. The sunglasses that now sat in two pieces on the counter in the front room…

"You remember my husband, Brandon?"

He nodded and gave her a polite façade of a smile, the kind reserved for new acquaintances at dinner parties. "Yes."

"So you know he's a prick then?"

At this Rafi's authentic smile flourished broadly, and he laughed. "I knew it then, and I know it now." He lifted his hand, as if to touch her, but hesitated. "Did he do that to your eyes?"

With sudden insecurity, Erica tried to lift her hands to her face, but could not with the Irishman holding her arms. Rafi reached out to her face and she flinched away from him. His hand, warm with a dry softness, touched the side of her neck, and he stroked her cheek with the back of his fingers.

"You do not need to hide the truth from me, Erica. You are among friends here."

"If I'm among friends, why is my 'friend' still pinning my arms to my sides?"

"Yes, of course," Rafi said. "Please, Brogan, if you don't mind."

The Irishman, Brogan, let go of her arms and mumbled something. Erica couldn't understand what he had said through his accent. She assumed it had been some kind of apology and gave a polite smile in response. At that the man's tough face flushed red, and a slight smile lightened his features, making him less threatening, almost boyish with a rough innocence.

She looked back at Rafi. "My husband's a bastard."

"I told you as much when you met him."

She remembered Rafi's warning, remembered blowing it off thinking he made the comment in jealousy. That warning was part of the reason she had not come around again.

"I'm sorry, Rafi." She felt tears welling in her eyes and she drew a deep breath to settle them down. "I haven't been a very good friend have I?"

Rafi held his hand up, dismissing the comment. "None of that. You have come back, and you are always welcome here."

At that, one tear slipped past her defense and made a warm trail down her cheek. She drew another deep breath.

"My dear, Erica. You were so innocent." Rafi reached out and brushed the wetness from her face. "I am sorry to see that innocence mistreated. But," he said, his voice losing its

27

tenderness, going businesslike, "you did not come to me just to connect with old friends, did you?"

Erica felt her stomach knot up.

"What is it you want from me?"

Once you say it, you can't take it back.

"Erica?"

"I want you to kill him…" She shook her head, "…want *someone* to kill him." She went still, afraid how she would feel having said it. Something deeper inside of her, something darker, more driven, made the thought of Brandon's death glow with warmth. "I can pay. I've got a good amount of money. I can get more."

Rafi turned his head away and held out his hand in a dismissive gesture. "I have a successful art business here. People come to me in search of rare items, and I procure those items. I don't deal in death. Why would you act as though I am a criminal?"

Erica thought that was strange. Rafi was a criminal. None of the art in the room was legal. It had been stolen from villages and temples. But she knew that Rafi was not a violent man, and she understood that she had offended him.

"I'm sorry, Rafi. I should go."

"You're not goin' anywhere," Brogan said and looked at Rafi. "We should check for a wire."

Erica turned to Brogan. "What?"

The innocence in the Irishman's face had been replaced with concrete determination, his clear-blue eyes glaring at her. She turned to Rafi who stared past her at the open, white door. He stayed that way in silence for some time before walking over to the doorway and leaning through it, she assumed looking out the glazed windows to the street. Shoving the door closed, he took a keychain from his pocket and locked the dead-bolt. He pocketed the keys and stared at Erica, his eyes hard with anger.

"You come into my shop and ask me to kill someone like Brandon Calzavara? What kind of scheme this?" He walked up to her. "I don't understand it though. I have no direct involvement with the cartels, but..." He looked around at the statues, "...if the DEA thought I was moving drugs instead of art, and you," he pointed at Erica, "had somehow gotten into trouble with Brandon and needed to make a deal." He touched the knuckles of his fist to his mouth, deep in thought, and asked of himself, "But why a hired killing?" He shook his head. "I cannot make sense of it."

"What are you talking about, Rafi?"

Rafi's eyes scanned her face; he said nothing.

She reached out and touched Rafi's forearm. "I shouldn't have come." Rafi pushed her hand away as she said, "I don't have any purpose aside from what I just said. I'm sorry. It was stupid." She stepped around Rafi. "I should just go."

Walking up to the door, she pulled on it, but it wouldn't move. She knew it wouldn't but had no idea what else to do.

"For now, Erica, you may not leave."

She turned on Rafi and, attempting to cover her fear with anger, said, "Let me out of here... *now.*"

"Erica," Rafi said with a sigh, "you cannot simply walk into the back room of someone like me, say what you just said, and expect me to let you turn and walk out again."

"I didn't walk in," Erica said, her tone now pleading. "Your goon dragged me in."

"He is not a goon, Erica. He is my business partner."

Erica looked at the door and then back at Rafi. "I'm sorry. Can I just go?"

"No."

"What do you want from me?"

"Prove to me you're clean, that no one is hearing this conversation but us."

Erica met Rafi's eyes and found sincere distrust in them. That distrust made her feel alone and terribly out of place. She stared at Rafi not knowing what to do.

"Take off your clothes, down to your underwear," Rafi said.

"What?" Erica tried to sound indignant and angry but heard only weakness in her voice and hated it.

"If you don't have a wire or a recorder, you'll be fine."

"I'm not taking my clothes off, Rafi."

Now Rafi's voice became angry as he said, "Here are your options Mrs. Put-a-hit-on-my-husband: You either take off your own clothes, or we do it for you. You're an old friend Erica... *old.* I'm not in a position to trust you right now. You need to earn some of that trust."

Erica looked into Rafi's eyes. She saw anger, but not lust. Her chest rose with a deep breath, which she let out in resignation.

How the hell do I get myself into situations like this?

Rafi rolled his hand in a circle at her, 'get on with it.'

"Okay," she said with a nod. As she unbuttoned her pants and unzipped them, she had expected both men's eyes to drop. The Irishman's eyes followed her fingers, but as her panties became visible, Rafi did not look down. He kept his somewhat apologetic eyes on her face. She stepped out of her sandals, feeling the thickness of the carpet on the soles of her feet, warm and rich. Pushing her jeans off her butt, she shoved them down around her knees and pulled the snug legs off one at a time. Setting the jeans down beside her, she pulled her shirt over her head exposing her simple, white bra.

Rafi held out his hand, motioning for her to hand him the clothes. She gathered them up and handed the bundle to him. He looked over the clothes, running them through his fingers, searching. Taking her keys out of the pants pocket, he inspected each key and then the remote. He pushed on the remote until the Mercedes outside chirped. Sliding one of the keys off the ring, he used it to pry open the remote, and inspected the interior. He snapped the remote closed and slid the key back onto the ring.

He returned the keys to their pocket, set the bundle on the floor, and motioned with his hand, saying, "Shoes."

She picked up the sandals and handed them to Rafi. He bent them, twisted each strap, and turned them over, running his fingers over the soles. Motioning with his hand, he said, "Show me the bottoms of your feet." She did, and he motioned again saying, "Your bra."

"Rafi, I—"

"You come in here, ask me to put a hit on a cartel drug runner, this is what you get. Understand?"

"Cartel drug runner? Brandon's an idiot who sells boats."

"You really believe that?"

"He does sell boats. I've been to the marina, been there when he's doing the paperwork on a sale."

"Tell me something, Erica. Could you imagine that having someone in a drug cartel work at a place where new yachts from foreign ship builders come into the country would be convenient?"

"No. He's a frat boy who never grew up. Drug runners are—"

"What, dirty? Use run down boats and 1953 Cessnas? Or maybe they wear an expensive suit and slide a few bills over the counter when the customs agent comes to the marina. Or maybe they don't even need the bills. Do you know how many hiding places there are on a multi-million dollar yacht? One can't tear the whole ship apart."

Rafi's eyes lowered to her chest and then back up to her eyes. He held out his hand. "Give me the bra."

"Really?"

He said nothing, only stared at her.

She sighed again and unhooked the bra. As she slipped it off, she kept one forearm over her breasts. She held the bra out to him. Only then, her breasts curving up above her forearm, did Rafi's eyes drop down and rest on her chest too long, his irises relaxing wider. He took the bra and ran his fingertips over the straps and each cup.

He looked at Erica, a sincere and sad expression coming to his face. "I'm sorry I distrusted you, Erica. I can't be too careful." He picked up the other clothes, folded the bra on top of the bundle, and walked to the dark hallway entrance at the back of the room. He flicked on a light, illuminating the hallway.

He held the bundle of clothes out to her and, with his free hand, pointed to the first door on the left. "The bathroom is there. You can put your clothes on privately. Then we will talk. I cannot help you, but we can still talk."

Erica felt exposed standing in the center of the room wearing only her panties, her belly and back cold, and gooseflesh standing out on her forearms and thighs. She stood unmoving for a moment before walking over to Rafi, aware of every shift of her legs and butt; she could feel Brogan staring at her. Taking the bundle with her free hand, she went into the bathroom and pushed the door closed.

When the latch clicked, she felt relief at being alone, but still cold. Setting the bundle beside the sink, she dressed and then stared at the door wondering if the building had a rear exit. She didn't want to go back out among the two men, but unable to think of a way to quietly escape the situation, she gripped the door handle, opened the door, and walked into the main room. There the statuary stared at her with their corpse eyes.

From her right, Rafi said, "I apologize for my paranoia, Erica."

She turned and found him sitting, leaned back, on the brown leather couch, one foot up on a leather ottoman. He motioned for her to sit.

"Where did your friend go?" She said, motioning with her thumb toward the center of the room.

"Brogan? He had to make a delivery."

Erica nodded, glad he had gone. Walking around the ottoman, she sat down on the other end of the couch, sinking into the soft leather. She felt better there in the corner of the room, a wall at her back.

Rafi smiled and said, "Where should we begin?"

Erica paused for a moment before asking, "Are you sure about what you said about Brandon?"

"That he is an asshole or a drug runner?"

She wanted to laugh at Rafi's attempt at levity but couldn't find it in her heart to do so. Sitting forward, she put her elbows on her knees and forehead in her hands. "About being a drug runner."

She heard Rafi shifting on the couch and flinched when his hand touch her shoulder-blade.

Rafi said, "You really didn't know."

She looked up and shook her head.

Rafi smiled. "I am sorry to have mentioned it. I spoke too soon."

"Rafi, look at my face. I need to know what's going on."

"Are you going to leave him?"

Erica wanted to say yes, wanted to leave, but before she set claim on it, she needed to have a plan in mind. It would have been so much simpler if Brandon had just been an idiot who sold boats.

Erica leaned back into the couch again and said, "I wanted him dead."

"You're no killer Erica. Don't drop down to their level."

Erica laughed at that. "I just wish people like him weren't allowed to stay in the world."

Rafi took her hand and held it in both of his. "You could go back to how it was before. A simple life."

Erica sat in silence, not responding.

Rafi asked, "What was so wrong with your life before you married him?"

She looked up at him as a quick scoff slipped out. "Are you kidding me? Do you know how many days I had to skip food to make rent?"

"Is it so much better now?"

"It is on the good days."

"On the bad days?"

"On the bad days I feel like a dark age concubine. It's pointless anyway. He won't let me leave. Last night, after he did this," she said, pointing to her face, "he told me he'd cut my face off so no man would ever want me. I really think he'd do it."

"Erica, I'm so—"

"I don't need pity Rafi. I need an escape route."

Rafi crossed his arms on his knees and stared at the floor.

"Tell me what you know, Rafi. Please."

Rafi looked sideways at her. After a moment, he said, "You will make me a promise then. If I tell you what I know, you will never come back here. Never park his Mercedes in front of my shop again. I do not need attention from men like him."

At this Erica felt sorrow swamping her heart. In the last few moments she had felt a connection to her previous life, not the monetary poorness, but the richness of the true friends she had then, people with nothing more to do than walk on the beach or sit around a living room, drinking cheap beer and talking late into the night. She had rejected them for Italian crystal and German cars, and now he was rejecting her.

She looked down at her empty hands and said, "Okay. I promise."

"And," Rafi said reaching over and taking her hand again, "You must promise to see me again next week, have a walk with me, or coffee."

Erica felt her face flush as she looked into Rafi's luminous, green eyes. He gave her his broad smile.

"I've missed your friendship, Erica. I felt a great loss when he took you away from here, and yet I always knew you'd come back..." He paused for a moment and looked away toward the largest statue in the corner, his confidence seeming to flutter.

Erica watched him carefully. She was used to men coming on to her, but not Rafi. He had always been only a friend, which they both seemed to have been content with. However, now—as she looked at his face, his strong jaw, the symmetry of his nose, and the thick disorder of his hair—a glow in her chest pressed her nipples into her bra and burned down her belly toward her groin. She took her hand from him.

You're just frustrated, Erica. He's not suggesting that, and you don't want it.

She wasn't Rafi's kind of woman anyway. He went for the modern, punk Betty Page type. She had always been somewhat intimidated by those new-world bomber girls and their strength. They would have told Brandon off at the first slight, clawed his eyes out and walked away. Rafi's women glowed with ultraviolet light, and Erica had always been fascinated and slightly jealous of that xenon intensity.

"Erica?"

"I'm sorry, Rafi," she said. "I don't mean to be rude. I'd really like that. Thank you." The last words came in a whisper as sorrow welled up in her chest. "I'm sorry."

"You don't have to be sorry."

Erica smiled and, wanting to shove her emotions aside, said, "Now tell me about Brandon."

"He works for a cartel based in Venezuela. He's ideal for them; he has a look that people trust and a reputation for being ruthless."

Erica felt the truth of both of those statements.

"The yacht dealership is owned by a man called Antonio Camejo, a second in the cartel hierarchy."

"Antonio's a cartel boss? I know him. He's really... nice." She leaned forward, setting her forehead in the heels of her palms, and said, "I suppose I have a lot to learn about reading people."

"Don't feel bad, Camejo fools many people, including experienced DEA officials. He runs a successful business, is connected to wealthy and powerful people, and supports many charities. He is loved by many, particularly those in Venezuela whom he has brought wealth. In Caracas he has overseen the building of low income housing, schools, and clinics."

"That seems strange. I wouldn't figure a cartel man to do kind things like that."

Rafi shrugged at the comment. "I do not believe in altruism. He's a hero to those in his home town. That must bring him a sense of great importance, but it is business as well.

The cartel lets the politicians take significant credit for the improvements, and in return the cartel warehouses, trucks, and boats are ignored. Venezuela is better off, and very few there care if drug users in America suffer."

"How do you know all this?"

"From Camejo himself." Rafi pointed at the statue nearest them. "He is an art lover. I have acquired several pieces for him. He is also a braggart. He likes men like me to know my place, so he talks freely of his position and success."

"Hubris has a way of biting people in the ass."

Rafi laughed and said, "Erica, I know very few people who will discuss hubris. You are far too intelligent to be held down for long."

Erica ignored the compliment. "So how does Brandon fit in?"

"Brandon is a transfer agent for Camejo. The yachts he sells come from shipyards in Asia and Europe. When they are far out in the open ocean, cartel airplanes fly near them, dropping flotation cargo bins. The crew retrieves them, stows the cocaine, and scuttles the containers. It is the perfect method. The U.S. Coastguard polices aircraft coming into Texas and Florida. No one polices aircraft flying into the heart of the Atlantic Ocean. When the yachts come into the shipyard, Brandon and his crew remove the cocaine and deliver it to the Florida arm of the cartel for distribution."

"But Brandon is not just a mule. Brandon is known to be a dangerous man. He has personally helped clear the area of competition. Those who know him have described him as a very successful wartime cartel man."

At that Erica remembered the many fishing trips Brandon had taken and now imagined him, not setting tackle on a rod and reel, but lifting chunks of concrete over the side of the boat and dropping them with a heavy splash into the ocean. The concrete, she imagined, would be filled with sections of bodies. That's how she'd make a body disappear if she needed to. Bodies would float up, but if you cut them up into smaller segments and encased those segments in concrete, you could drop them in the ocean and they would sink to the bottom, never to be seen again. No body, no crime. She drifted for a moment into a daydream—Brandon lay on the carpet of his office, his arms and legs askew. Erica held a gun, the barrel still smoking. Could she cut it up? Hack through the ankles and thighs? Saw the skull off the neck? She smiled at the thought even as it gave her a chill.

Rafi put the palm of his hand between her shoulder blades, drawing her out of the daydream. She looked at his concerned face and then to the surrounding room. The reality of the trap she had become caught up in closed back around her.

"I can't kill him can I?"

"The entire cartel would come down on you."

"I have to run then."

"I do not want to lose you again, but yes, you really only have two choices, stay where you are or run."

"I have to have money, enough to disappear for good."

"I have some savings that—"

"I'm not asking that Rafi. I would never ask that... There's a safe in the house, a huge safe."

Rafi's eyes widened a bit. "How big?"

"The door is taller than me."

"That is promising."

"I suppose stealing a cartel man's money is almost as bad as killing him."

Rafi shrugged. "A body cannot help you disappear, the money will."

CHAPTER 4

Erica drove back south along the tar sealed concrete of Broadway, and as she passed over the shipping yards on the SkyBridge, she began to add to her plans. She'd get money, as much as she could, enough to start a new life. She'd disappear and go as far from Florida as she could—California or maybe even Hawaii. Then she thought about Sweden; her grandmother had been from Sweden.

Maybe there. Sure.

Perhaps Rafi could connect her to someone who could put together an alias and papers for her.

She curved right onto Flagler drive and drove down the wide, four-lane road. Seeing a silver SL65 AMG Mercedes approaching—Brandon's car—she felt herself tense; she didn't want him to see her even on the open road. As the car passed, she saw him inside, talking to someone on his cell phone.

Smug prick.

She turned on her turn signal, slowed—waiting for a truck to pass—and pulled into her... rather, his house. Driving up the brick driveway, she parked between the fountain and the stairs leading to the double front doors with their leaded-crystal windows. She got out of her car and looked at the fountain in the center of the driveway's turnaround. She stared at the carved-stone mermaid, water pouring from a jug she held over her shoulder. The cascading water created a mask of calm splashing that covered the rush of traffic from beyond the wall. She turned and looked at the house with its broad stairs and white columns. It seemed so obvious now. How could she have been so gullible? This wasn't the house of a salesman. She looked back at the mermaid, her empty, stone eyes staring south.

"I'm done," she said to the statue.

Walking around to the passenger side of the car, she opened the glove box and took out the car's manuals. She drew a scrap of paper from the lemon-law flier. The paper, which she had found in the hallway after one of Brandon's parties, read '47-13-193-62'.

Slipping the scrap into her back pocket, she put the manuals away and walked up to the front door. As she reached for the door, it opened; she found herself facing their maid, Estelle.

"Ma'am." Estelle said with a slight bow of her head.

Erica hoped she had kept the flushing shock she felt in her torso from showing on her face. She gave Estelle as much of a smile as she could muster. "Estelle... I didn't think you'd be here. It's not Wednesday."

"Forgive me ma'am," Estelle said in her Cuban accent, "I am early. Tomorrow we celebrate my son's birthday."

"Oh, yes. That's fine. Wish him a happy birthday for me."

Estelle gave her a professional smile and walked back into the living room. The vacuum clicked on.

Erica looked up the large, curved staircase.

It might as well be now.

The thought caused her heart to accelerate, and before she lost her nerve, she forced herself to go up the staircase. Arriving at his office door, she stood before it.

Don't chicken out, Erica. You have to do this.

She looked down the hallway. Estelle had shut the vacuum off, and clinking sounds came from the living room. As she pushed open the door, the scent of cigar smoke and lemon furniture-wax surrounded her. Brandon's broad desk sat centered in front of the windows. The wood-slat blinds had been turned shut against the sunlight. She walked into the room and, listening one last time down the hallway, pushed the door closed.

Once, while walking past the office, she had seen Brandon pull open a section of wood paneling; she had come back while he was away and found the safe.

Walking over to the panel, she gripped its edge and pulled. The panel swung open on smooth hinges exposing the safe's polished, ebony door, which was large enough to walk through.

She pressed her hand against the dark, cool metal of the door. The wall of metal should have made her feel hopeless, but it didn't. Instead she felt as though the door was a gateway to the rest of her life. Nothing and no one could prevent her from getting through it.

Centered in the door was a tri-spoked, rotatable handle. She gripped one of its bars, which felt fixed in place, immovable. Above the handle, a metal disk the size of a dinner plate encircled a hinged panel. She pulled on the panel's grip. Nothing. Mounted just above the panel was a small, coppery rectangle. She brushed her finger across it, and its border flickered with red light as a loud beep startled her.

Snatching her hand away, she looked at the office door, remaining still for a moment. She turned back to the safe and stared at the fingerprint scanner. Cursing under her breath, she stepped back and shoved the wall panel closed. She had no intention of giving up, but there was nothing for it, not right now.

Walking across the thick carpeting to the door, she looked down at the shoe prints she had pressed into the thick carpeting. They lay everywhere and would surely be noticed. She went back to the safe and, kneeling down, smoothed her hands over the footprints to match the vacuum marks.

Backing up, she did this again and again. When she had backed all the way across the room, she pulled open the door and smoothed the last few foot prints out of the carpeting.

Still on her hands and knees, she looked at her work. It looked like crap.

"Ma'am, what are you doing?"

The unexpected voice shocked Erica, and she looked up to find Estelle with an expression of horror on her face.

Estelle crouched down and took hold of Erica's wrist. "You should not be bothering Mr. Calzavara's office, ma'am."

Erica opened her mouth to speak, but could not think of what to say. She stared at Estelle, searching for some hint as to what the maid intended to do. Estelle pulled at Erica's wrist with a mother's grip.

"Stand up, ma'am, please."

"I was just—"

Estelle held up her free hand, cutting off Erica's words. "I do not want to know, ma'am." She pulled Erica to her feet. Now the formality left her voice, "Bonita, you should not do such things. He is a dangerous man…"

She fell silent, and in her eyes, Erica saw that she knew.

Erica felt even more the fool as she stood in silence beside Estelle. All she could think to say was, "How is it that it has taken me this long?"

Estelle took Erica by the shoulders, and her forehead wrinkled as she said, "You have faith in people, mija. That is no such a bad thing… but you have to learn to look through people. Faith alone without wisdom will damn you."

Erica looked away from Estelle.

Estelle said, "This room is not vacuumed yet. I will get it done right away."

Erica looked back at the freshly vacuumed carpeting. "Thank you, Estelle."

"Please do not enter the office again."

"I won't," Erica lied.

CHAPTER 5

Standing in the dark kitchen, Erica ran her fingertips along the cold granite of the island countertop. The glow from the light above the stove left the far walls in dim suggestion. Looking out the windows, she should have seen the lights of the city glowing beyond the stone wall, but not even the garden lights came through the glass. It seemed as though darkness had become solid and pushed itself up against the windows, sealing them. Hearing the quiet creaking of wood behind her, she turned to the pantry door. The dim light in the kitchen cast the room in shades of blues, but the edges of the pantry door glowed in a deeper-blue, almost violet light.

She looked back at the stove. The digital clock there showed 1:34 AM. She closed her eyes before looking back at the clock. 2:05 AM.

I'm dreaming.

The pantry door clicked in its frame as if a breeze pushed on it from the other side. She walked across the tile and touched one of the door's wooden panels. The door bumped against her fingertips as it shifted, clunking at the latch.

It's just a dream.

The curved door handle felt warm as she gripped it. She pressed the handle down and drew the door open a few inches. Peering into the pantry she saw, not white-wire shelves lined with pasta and Brandon's weight gainer, but black, rough-hewn rock. She fully opened the door and found herself looking down the gullet of a cave entrance. The cave travelled straight back, perhaps twenty feet, where it opened into a grotto, which glowed with the blue-violet light.

Stepping off the cool tile and into the humid air in the cave, her foot splashed into a bathtub-warm puddle of water. She stepped out of the water and made her way down to the grotto, sharp edges of hard stone digging into her feet. As she walked, the heat increased until she felt sweat prickling across her brow. The cave smelled of minerals and rot, which soured the pit of her stomach.

A broad, shallow pool of dark water, perhaps a foot deep, lay in the center of the grotto. She looked around the domed cavern, trying to make out the source of the deep light. It seemed to have no origin, to only reflect off the rocks and the dark surface of the water. Looking into the pool she saw a body beneath the surface of the water, its feet toward her. She felt the hair on the back of her neck and arms rise.

She crouched down. The surface of the water lay still, almost not perceivable aside from a faint glinting. There, his eyes closed and his hands folded across his chest, she saw Rafi. The fabric of his pants and shirt hung suspended in the pool. His expression struck her as peaceful, as if he were dreaming of something beautiful. That expression prevented her from feeling sorrow over his body. He seemed to have found an untroubled end.

As she looked back at his serene face, his eyelids shifted apart, exposing Rafi's green irises. They did not move but remained directed at the ceiling of the grotto, and Erica wondered what he might see, looking up out of the still water to the grotto's roof.

She sat down, folding her legs in front of her and stared at Rafi's eyes.

"What has become of you?" She said, her words staying close in the confined, stone space.

With her words, the eyes tilted down and locked on her. They were Rafi's eyes, but something evil lay in them, something she could feel pulling at her, making her want to slide into the pool beside him. She felt her weight shifting forward. Fear crystallized her heart and adrenaline flushed through her. She wanted to lean away from those eyes, but found no connection to her body, which without her will, continued to lean ever so subtly toward the pool.

Rafi moved. He had seemed perfectly preserved in the pool, but as he sat up, shifting his body through the clear water, the skin across his face cleaved down the middle and sloughed off to each side. As he came to full sitting, his hair and scalp shedded away, leaving only the sheets of muscle structure strapped across his skull. The water ran off of him, and like a pit cooked pig, the underlying facial tissues across the forehead, eyes, and mouth began sheeting away, falling down the front of his shirt. His jaw and temple muscles fell away, slapping down on his shoulders. She now stared at a skull, white tendons hanging from their mounts with scraps of red at their tips. His eyes, wide spheres, glared at her.

She wanted to shove away, to get up and run, but she could not so much as move her hands. She sat staring at the corpse, her body hypnotized but her mind fully aware and panicking. Rafi's hand rose up out of the water, the skin separating at the wrist as the fingers and palm degloved; the skin of his hand plunked into the water. As he reached out to her, the larger arm muscles disconnected from their tendons and hung from the sleeve of his shirt like red eels, water dripping from their ends. At the tips of his fingers, bits of skin remained trapped under askew fingernails. His hand turned, and the index finger-bone curled, beckoning her. Beyond the finger she saw the muscles under his shirt falling away, the strength of his shoulders sliding away to bone under the fabric as the belly of the shirt distended with his flesh. The water around the corpse had gone cloudy brown with disintegrated skin and blood.

Erica no longer understood that she was dreaming, and in her desperation to get away, she cried out. But her mouth would not open, and her cry muffled between her lips. The corpse leaned toward her. One of the eyes rolled forward, drawing out the attached muscles and optic nerve as it dropped into the water.

Erica's arms and legs began to tremor. She growled like a trapped animal desperate to escape. She wanted to stand up, to push away, to run, but she remained frozen in place staring at the bones of the corpse's hand coming closer.

Something gripped her shoulder with a cruel force. She felt herself wrapped up, suffocating. Descending into darkness and unable to move, she began to panic. The grip on her shoulder shook her, and in her fear she clawed at the mess around her, shoving at the grip.

Sitting up screaming, she found herself in her bed with her fingers digging into Brandon's forearm.

He pushed her hands off his arm and glared out of the darkness. "What the hell is wrong with you?"

Without answering, she looked at the windows. The electric glow of street lamps filtered through the closed slats of the blinds. He reached for the nightstand, and with a click, the lamp blared to life, casting the room in eye-watering, electric light.

It was a dream. Only a dream.

She looked at Brandon, so glad to see him next to her and not Rafi's corpse—

"How old are you?" Brandon asked, furious. "I mean, for the love of God, I've got a big sale to close tomorrow morning. If you're gonna freak out, go sleep in the guest room."

Still coming away from the terror of the dream, she felt no anger for Brandon. He shut off the light and rolled over, dragging the majority of the duvet off of her with his shoulder. She stared at him as his breath slowed and drew out. Looking into the darkness of the room, the memory of the dream came back to her, and she felt the echo of genuine fear only a truly visceral nightmare can bring. Her mind walked her unwillingly back through the small details, the bone-pores in the fingers, all the precisely strung muscles. She lay back down, but the moment she closed her eyes, the visage of the skull returned to her.

Rolling out of bed, she went to the guest room, flicked the light on, lay down, and stared at the bright ceiling.

•••

At some time in the night she had drifted off to sleep, and when she woke at dawn, she sat up, alarmed at the unexpected sight of the guest room. She looked around the smaller room, at the light coming in the window, mixing with the electric ceiling light. She remembered the dream. Swinging her legs off the side of the bed, she put her elbows on her knees and her face in her hands.

As she sat there, Brandon's words to her when she woke from the dream played through her mind. His heartlessness now infuriated her. But why should it? She had to get beyond reacting to him; she had to get one step ahead. The softball bat he kept in the corner of the office came into her mind's eye unbidden, and she found herself wandering down a daydream. She'd go into the office, get the bat, and steal into their bedroom where Brandon still slept. Standing over the disheveled head of black hair, she'd grip the white taped handle of the bat and whip it over her shoulder straight down on his temple. Then she'd cut his finger off for the safe.

"It'd be so easy," she said in a quiet voice and then heard Brandon open their bedroom door and walk down the hallway.

•••

Just after noon that day, Erica parked her car and walked into the plaza of West Palm Beach's CityPlace. High above the sun baked into the red, mission-tile roofs. Walking past the Harriet Himmel Theater, she looked up at its large clock with its white outer circle of Roman numerals and blue inner-circle detailed with zodiac signs. She had no use for the signs, but the clock told her she was running late. Quickening her pace, she crossed the pale brick courtyard, passing the columned shop-entrances. The breeze pushed at the broad-leafed palms, and their bladed shadows shifted over the benches, fountain pools, and walkways. Rich green awnings shaded the glass doorways to shops. People walked by her with bags, squared with shoe boxes and plump with new clothes. As shop doors opened and closed, the cool hint of air conditioning brushed at her, carrying with it the scent of new leather and dyed fabric.

As she walked, she felt a muted thrill of excitement at the expectation of seeing Rafi again. She hadn't felt that way about seeing a man in a long time, and it made her embarrassed at herself.

This isn't a date, just friends getting together for coffee.

Still, she sincerely liked Rafi… always had. His charming manners blended with unique handsomeness disarmed her and made her feel good about herself. His face had the strong angles of his Scottish father, who had travelled to northern Iraq as a geologist. His mother, a Kurdish villager Rafi had described as the most beautiful woman in the Middle East, had given him the mysterious depth of his eyes. Erica had once seen a photograph of her, and Rafi's description was not far off. She had dark, laughing eyes, smooth cheeks, and a delicately pointed chin, all framed by flowing, blue-black hair.

That one photograph and his father's stories were all Rafi had to know her by. She had died giving birth to him. In that seemed to be the core of Rafi's troubled heart. He had told Erica once that he felt a great deal of guilt at having stolen his mother from his father. His father had often told Rafi of her beauty and kindness, of her quick laughter. "They would have grown old together if it hadn't been for me," he had said to Erica. "I had intended to ask my father's forgiveness for her death, but could never build up the courage."

When Rafi was a teenager, his father had died unexpectedly, and Rafi lost the chance at resolution forever. Erica knew Rafi to be a moral man at his core, but the haunt of his mother's death had put him at odds with himself, and so, the world. Now only a smuggler, he should have been so much more.

As she approached Cassie's Brewery, she scanned the patio and found Rafi in the far corner sitting in the shadow of a palm tree. He wore sunglasses. She held up her hand, but he did not respond as his attention was on a book in his hands. She walked up and stood before him, but still he did not look up.

"You're late," he said.

"I'm sorry," Erica said, "I couldn't find a place to park." She felt instant guilt at the lie and wondered why she had said it.

"You come when you like," Rafi said as he closed the book and gave her a broad smile, "You are worth the wait."

Erica did not know how to respond to him. Life with Brandon had made her suspicious of everything, and she searched through his words for some hint of sarcasm.

Rafi took off his sunglasses and, after a moment of silence, held out his hand to the chair across the table. "Please sit."

She did so, and he stood.

"Where are you going?" she asked.

"I am going to buy you coffee. The server is busy, and I don't want you to have to wait."

She motioned for him to sit back down. "Please, I'm fine. Just sit."

Rafi did as she asked. Reaching across the table, he took her hand in the warmth of his. "It is good to see you."

Erica sat in silence for a moment, not knowing where to begin again. She said, "I dreamt of you last night."

"Really?" Rafi asked with a suggestive tone.

"Not like that." She let a small laugh out, and an unexpected, light-hearted feeling came to her. She told Rafi the details of the dream, and as she did so, a slight smile grew in Rafi's eyes.

"What?" she asked at the smile.

"There is a statue of Enlil, the Sumerian god of storms, in my gallery. Do you remember it? The largest statue in the corner."

"Large beard, symmetrical curls?"

"The very one. I bought that from a woman in Afak, which is built on the site of Nippur, one of the most ancient of Sumerian city states. This city held Enlil as their patron God. The statue was a rare find. There is not much left of that size still not locked away, stolen, or destroyed by war. The woman's husband, a priest whose family had continued to follow the old ways, had kept the statue secure in their home. Upon his death, the woman wanted it gone. She told me it had held an evil sway over her husband's heart."

"It is a bit... creepy."

Rafi nodded at this. "As I loaded the statue in my vehicle, I was struck on the back. I turned and found an old man with a stick who, if he hadn't been so frail, might have seriously injured me. I took the stick from him, threw it aside, and asked him what he thought he was doing. He pointed at me with a hooked finger," at this Rafi pointed at Erica, "and told me that I would be cursed if I took the statue. He said that Enlil would keep me from Anu."

"Anu?"

"Anu is the highest god in the Sumerian pantheon and Enlil was a proto-Christ-like figure who served as the conduit between the ultimate divine and the human race."

"So you're cursed."

"Apparently I am," he said laughing. "In truth, the curse was only the ranting of an old desert rat, meaningless, as was your dream."

"I don't like messing with anything like that. You shouldn't be taking cultural artifacts. That statue had probably been in that area since it was carved."

"The woman was selling, Erica, if not to me, then to someone else. It was inevitable, so why should I not be the one to make the profit?"

"That brings me to what I need to talk to you about."

"I thought we were meeting as friends, but you have brought business with you."

Erica brushed aside the comment with a wave of her hand and said, "You're a criminal right?"

A scowl closed off Rafi's expression. "I'll try not to take that as an insult. I compensate those I obtain my wares from. I pay agreed prices. Only at the borders do I..." He looked away before continuing with an insincere smile, "...bend laws."

"I fulfill the desires of those who do not have what they want, and in so doing, I profit." He held his hand six inches off the table. "Those who possess these items value them here, while others," he lifted his hand a few inches, "value it here, and I," he turned his hands palm up in supplication to a truth, "am the facilitator of a rebalancing of value."

Erica laughed and said, "So you're a thief with better justification."

Rafi shook his head in resignation and said, "I am a good man, Erica. I do not take. I pay." His eyes narrowed as he said, "Again, you come to me with questions I do not care for. Why are you pressing me so hard on this?"

The waitress walked up to their table. She wore her black hair short, cute bangs and a curl just behind her ear. She had beautiful eyes accentuated with dark liner that carried off slightly at the corners, hinting at an Egyptian style. She smiled at Rafi, who smiled back. Her arms showed some muscle tone, and one sharp arc of a black tattoo extended out from the right sleeve of her white Cassie's Brewery shirt. Erica felt sudden intimidation. The girl was very pretty, and when Erica looked back to Rafi, his eyes remained on the waitress.

"Ma'am," the girl said, "What can I get for you?" She gave Erica a charming smile, and Erica felt useless. These rocker girls with dark eye-makeup, black hair, and tattoos were the ones who were supposed to have the abusive, drugged out boyfriends. Not her.

The waitress' smile faded a bit as she asked, "Ma'am?"

"I'm sorry," Erica said, "Just an iced tea for me."

"We have a really nice mint and pomegranate iced tea today."

Erica hated her for being so freely pretty.

"That'll be fine. Thank you." Erica said.

The girl smiled and turned to Rafi, touching his shoulder. "Do you have everything you need?"

Rafi nodded at the girl, who turned and walked away. He watched her go.

"You want me to find out if she's single?"

Rafi looked at Erica and smiled, "My apologies. That is terribly rude of me. But," and a broad grin came across his face, "I do not think she is single."

"And you don't think that would stand in your way."

Rafi smiled and put a feigned look of shock on his face, "What do you think of me, Erica? I'm a good man."

"You keep saying."

Erica tried to smile, but the weight of her own love life in light of Rafi's casual freedom and lightheartedness pushed the smile away from her just as it was born. She picked the napkin-wrapped knife and fork up from the table and turned it in her hands.

"You have far too many troubles, Erica."

"What do you know about fingerprint scanners on safes?"

Again, the smile left Rafi's face.

"You must know something about them, right? Being a liberator of value?"

He waved away the comment. "What did you find?"

"I think I have the combination, but there's what looks like some kind of scanner. There's a panel on the front. I think it has the combination dial underneath, and I think that the thumbprint reader opens the panel. Is there way to get past it?"

Rafi stared at her for a moment before saying, "Are you still convinced this is the path you want to take? I have thought of this a great deal since we last spoke. To cross these men is terribly dangerous. Might it be better to leave well enough alone?"

"There is no *well enough* Rafi. I need to get the hell out of my life. I've been abused for four years by—I find out only yesterday—a cartel trafficker. I'm surprised I'm still alive. I need to leave, but I know he won't let me. We've been through this. I need help, Rafi, not a lot, but some. I can't do it otherwise."

"I'm so sorry, Erica," Rafi said and reached out for her hand.

Erica took her hands away before he could reach them and said, "Enough empathy Rafi; I need solutions not pity."

"Are you sure the safe is the right answer? You told me you had money, enough to..." He glanced over his shoulder at the couple sitting at the next table before saying, "Why don't you simply leave him?"

Erica leaned toward Rafi. "I need enough to disappear on. I have to be completely gone. If I stay in Florida, or even the U.S., he'll find me—at least I think he will. He doesn't take rejection." She fell silent and, feeling herself choking up, took the menu from its wire rack and opened it.

A hand set a glass down in front of her, full of light-brown tea. A mint leaf and a lemon wedge floated among the ice. She looked up to find the waitress smiling at her.

"Did you want something to eat?"

Erica felt tears rise in her eyes, and she looked down again and shook her head 'no'.

The waitress said with some hesitation, "All right, well... if there's anything I can do for you, just let me know."

"Thank you," Rafi said. Out of the corner of her eye Erica saw the waitress turn and walk away. Only then did she unwrap the napkin from the silverware and press it to her eyes. Feeling sorrow rising again, she pushed down on it, not wanting to break down in public. She knew she had to be stronger than this.

I've gotta get control of myself if I want to survive.

Drawing a deep breath, she willed herself to calm down and said, "I need money Rafi, real money, not just ten thousand. I need more, and I'm hoping there's enough in the safe."

"Do you think you can disappear, live as a fugitive?"

"I'm not sure, but at this point, I'd rather get the crap kicked out of me fighting. I'm done putting up with this."

"All right," Rafi said holding his hands up, "I'll help you at least with the scanner. If you have the combination you are as good as in. Get a glass that he has held and call me. We'll see what we can do."

Erica felt a rush of relief as she stood.

Rafi asked, "What are you doing?"

"Oh, I'm sorry." She opened her pocket book, took out a five-dollar bill, and set it down next to her untouched iced tea, beads of condensation now running down the sides of the glass.

"No," Rafi said pushing the bill back toward her, "I don't want your money, I want your time. Where are you going?"

"To get you that finger print."

CHAPTER 6

That night she sat in the kitchen, now more than ever feeling out of place in the house. A glass on the counter bent light to rainbows in the curved cuts of the leaded crystal. She listened for the garage door to rumble to life. The kitchen windows had gone dark with night, and she watched her reflection hovering in the dark pane over the sink. Her eyes looked suspicious. She smiled at her reflection and felt even more so. With a sigh, she tried to relax but felt the silent, yawning expanse of the house at her back, dark shadows hanging in among the furniture in room after empty room.

She looked over her shoulder, through the doorway, to the dining room beyond. A tingle ran up her spine, and she turned back to the glass.

Stay on track.

The green numbers of the clock over the stove showed 1:04 AM. Feeling exhaustion drawing her eyes down, she put her head in her hands. She'd have to wait another day. As she stood and made her way through the house, she felt exhausted. Walking up the staircase seemed to take an inordinate amount of effort. When she lay down in the soft bed, the clock read 1:18 AM. She stared at the ceiling.

Where the hell is he?

She hadn't worried about that in a long time. Recently, the longer he stayed away, the happier she had been. Imagining life without him, life on the run, she pictured herself somewhere in Northern Europe, in a small apartment, sitting on a couch reading a book—safe. A faint smile drew across her lips as she drifted off to sleep.

• • •

A thump woke her. She looked at the clock. 3:47 AM. Sitting up, she saw light under the bathroom door and heard the liquid roil of Brandon pissing in the toilet. The toilet flushed, and Brandon pushed open the door, light spilling into the bedroom.

She squinted into the bright light and heard him ask in a slurred voice, "You awake?"

At first she felt the impulse to ask him if he had driven home in that state, to ask him where the hell he had been, but the desire to challenge him had long been pushed down by the need to not be hit. Yet, something in her yearned to rebel this once. She was on the road out of here. She could feel her freedom as a faint, future glow, and she craved it. But she had something more important to do, and getting the crapped kicked out of herself would only make that more difficult.

"Yes," she said in an even tone she hoped would not provoke him.

He walked across the room, and as he sat on the bed, she saw the glass in his hand. Dark liquid tilted in it.

He set the glass on the night stand and asked, "Did I wake you?"

She knew the danger of a question like this. "Yes, but it doesn't matter. I'll be able to fall asleep again."

"Not just yet you won't," he said and gave her a lascivious smile. He reached for her, and she didn't flinch as he grabbed her by the back of the neck. Pulling her to him, he forced a kiss into her mouth, his tongue searching. She kissed back.

Just stay calm and let him have what he wants.

She felt his stubble digging into her face and wanted to push away, but instead she reached up and held the back of his neck.

One last time, no more.

He pushed her away. She did flinch somewhat at this, but he hadn't noticed. He was too busy fumbling with his belt. She knew the drill, get her own clothes off or have them torn off. That would ruin them and leave her with marks where the fabric had dug in before giving way. Pulling her pajama top over her head, she slid her thumbs under the sides of her panties and pulled them and the fleece pajama bottoms off her butt and down her legs. As she set them aside, he pulled his pants off and threw them, his belt clacking against the wall. Smiling at him, she felt sick at herself for how readily she could fall into the role.

She thought back to how many times she had played this game before, how many times she had almost convinced herself to buy into it. Now she could not, not when she was on the way out. The prospect of what was about to happen disgusted her. He grabbed her by the wrists and, shoving her onto her back, pressed them into to the mattress above her head. Shifting his weight, he pinned both arms down with one forearm and, with his free hand, pushed her legs apart. He shifted his hips between her thighs. She wanted to look at the drink on the nightstand, to stare at the thing that would help set her free, but she'd put her face into his armpit if she turned to that side. He kissed at her neck with a hunger, his stubble grating her skin. The sweet scent of alcohol surrounded her, mixed with spent deodorant and traces of floral perfume.

She felt him fumbling at her groin, felt his hardness there. Not being able to perform sometimes led to anger as well, so this was for the best. She looked above the headboard, through the window slats, to the night sky and hoped, as she had so many times before, that he didn't give her any diseases.

...

She lay next to him until his breathing began to rasp in a light snore. When she looked out the window she saw dawn fading into the sky. Sitting up, she looked over his shoulder at the clock. 5:45 AM. She lifted the covers, and when she slid off the bed, Brandon grunted and rolled to his back. He drew a ragged breath and wheezed it back out. On the balls of her feet, she walked around the bed. When she reached his nightstand, she stared at his eyes, waiting for them to crack open. He lay on his back, rasping away. Putting both her index fingers inside the glass, she pressed out with them and lifted the glass off the nightstand.

She turned with the glass suspended by the friction of her index fingers and walked across the room. When she was about halfway across the room Brandon snorted, and her arm jerked in reflex. The glass dropped to the floor, spilling rum and cola. She cursed under her breath as Brandon shuffled the comforter. She looked over her shoulder at him. He rolled over, and his breathing quieted.

She crouched down, and Brandon said from behind her, his voice thick with sleep, "What's going on?"

She looked over her shoulder again and found Brandon sitting up, staring at her. Her body tingled with the panicked impulse to run, but she couldn't lose this moment. She looked back to the glass, lying on its side with a delta of rum and Coke extending from it. She heard a ruffle of blankets and turned, expecting him to be coming at her, but he had laid back down and pulled the comforter over his shoulder. The bastard did that from time to time, woke up talking, sometimes screaming or hitting the headboard.

Lifting the now-empty glass with a single index finger, she carried it upside-down into the closet. She pushed her large handbag open with her free hand and set the glass in it. She pulled the zipper closed slow and quiet, allowing each tooth to catch and join. She did her best to clean the spill with a damp towel before sliding back into bed beside Brandon.

He huffed a bit, rolled onto his side facing away from her and slept. She stared at his side rising and falling for some time. Looking at the ceiling as light increased in the room, she wanted to fall asleep, but knew the electric nerves running through her wouldn't allow it.

...

She lay there drifting in thought until the rising sun hit the tops of the windows. The bar of light widened, filtering through the blinds, glowing into the room. She glanced at the clock over Brandon's shoulder. 6:55 AM. She wanted to get up now, but it was too early and if Brandon woke, she couldn't risk the suspicion. Brandon coughed, snorted, and violently threw the covers off of himself, wafting her with the stale scent of hangover sweat. He sat up, ran his hand through his disheveled hair, and shuffled into the bathroom. She looked at the carpeting. The faint trace of the rum and Coke still showed there between the bed and the closet.

The bathroom door opened again and Brandon stumbled out, walked right over the top of the stain, and fell back into bed. Erica sat in the bed for a moment, waiting for Brandon to fall asleep again, then went to the bathroom and showered. She kept catching herself rushing.

Take it easy. You have time.

When she was almost done, Brandon came into the bathroom. He stared at her in the shower, his eyes tracking up and down.

"Get done," he said. "I've got to get to work."

She nodded, rinsed the soap from her hair, and stepped out of the shower, leaving it running. She began to dry her hair, and a hard smack hit her bare ass. As he moved past her, she felt the urge to shove him through the shower's glass door.

After drying herself, she left the room and went to the closet. The handbag with the glass looked too exposed. With her foot, she shoved it back in between some shoes. She dressed and went back to the bathroom where she dried her hair with the blow dryer, draping its calming heat across her scalp and neck. She pulled her hair into a pony tail.

"You going to wear your hair like that today?" Brandon said from the shower.

She looked up to find him glaring at her in the foggy mirror. She looked at herself and back at him.

Kiss my ass.

"I know it's not that great," she said giving him her best smile, "but I have an errand to run this morning. I'll have my hair done while I'm out."

Brandon stared at her for a moment through the shower glass before saying, "That's good. You look like a dipshit with a pony tail."

She left the room with her fists clenched.

"I wasn't done talking to you," Brandon yelled from the shower. She felt her heart begin to race as she took the handbag from the closet.

Brandon shouted from the shower stall, "Erica!"

She stood in the bedroom, staring at the open bathroom door, sick to death of this dance.

"Erica!"

She would have to acknowledge him or face him later. With a sigh, she walked to the bathroom door and stuck her head in, saying, "Yes, Brandon? Sorry I couldn't hear you. I was in the closet."

"I wasn't done talking to you."

"I'm sorry, Brandon." She chose each word with as much practice and care as a bullfighter chooses a stance behind a cape. "I didn't realize. What do you need?"

"What do I need? I don't need anything from you." He pulled the shower door open and stared at her, water dripping off his hair and chest. "Where are you going this early in the morning?"

She hadn't thought of a reason to leave, should have had a story ready.

Make a joke out of it. Tell him you're having an affair. No. That could make him fly off the handle. The car. He likes it when you take care of the car, when it's clean.

61

"I want to get the car detailed first thing this morning. I don't want people to see it dirty. I have to take some friends to lunch."

"What friends?"

Jesus Christ, who the hell does he think he is?

Her anger began to push fear aside. In that she could misstep. Drawing a deep breath, she said, "Just some of the girls: Janice and Brandi, maybe Ashley."

"Boring," he said and slid the glass door closed. With that one word, she was free.

...

"Rafi?" Erica said into her phone. She sat parked on a worn-down side-street, several blocks inland. A trash truck rolled up on the opposite side of the street. Its hydraulic arm gripped a trash bin, lifted it, and shook the contents into the back. When Erica saw the truck's hydraulic ram shoving the trash into the body of the truck, she imagined Brandon's arm, sticking out of the mass of compressing plastic bags, being snipped off as he was crushed into the compactor's cavity.

"Yes," Rafi said, pulling her back to the phone call. His tone suggested that he did not recognize her voice.

"This is Erica."

"Yes." His voice still maintained a tone of separation, unfamiliarity. This threw her off for a moment.

After a pause she asked, "I have it. Can we meet?"

"Yes."

"Do you want me to come to the shop?"

"No. Go to where we had coffee. I'll be in the street to pick you up."

"Okay, when?" she asked just as the line went dead. She looked at the phone. "I guess that means now."

Driving to CityPlace, she parked her car and walked to the fountain in the plaza. Two people sat on the concrete curb in front of the pool, water burbling from the low fountains in the early-morning quiet. She looked up at the sky. Sunlight cut in at an angle along the tops of the second story shops. A woman walked past the store fronts on the second story behind the stucco arches, her shoes clacking and echoing through the Plaza.

A horn sounded in two beeps. She turned and saw Rafi waving from an older BMW 3 series with a dent on the driver-side front quarter-panel. She walked over to him, and as she approached, he pointed to the passenger side door. Going around behind, she saw the emblem on the trunk was missing. She pulled open the door with a creak of metal and got in. The interior of the car was clean and smelled of the same sandalwood of Rafi's shop.

Pointing at the dashboard, she said, "I thought you said you had money."

"I do," Rafi said as he pulled away from the curb. "I prefer to not waste it on automobiles."

Erica stared at Rafi and doubted him. Rafi had always talked about cars. He was a motor head on the highest order, and if he was doing well, he'd show it in what he drove.

Rafi glanced at her.

She continued to stare at him.

He looked at her again and asked, "What?"

"The car Rafi."

"I make a decent living."

"Having a lot of money and making a decent living are two different things."

"You know, all you seem to do is judge me. My occupation is not to your liking, my means not good enough for you. Not all of us are beautiful enough to sleep our way into wealth."

"How dare you—" she began, but Rafi held up his hand.

"I am sorry," he said. "Truly. I spoke out of emotion. That was rude and unfair..." He fell silent for a moment before saying, "It is true I do not have an expensive car, but someday I will."

"I'm sorry I snapped at you—"

"No, Erica, what I said just now was terrible."

Erica put her hand on his shoulder. "I forgive you, Rafi."

Rafi looked over at her, uncharacteristic doubt in his eyes, and she smiled at him.

As Rafi turned the car up an on-ramp and merged onto the divided Australian Avenue, he said, "Thank you."

In Rafi's humble acceptance of her forgiveness she felt bonded to him, safer for the easy resolution. As they drove she looked out the side window, but could not help stealing quick glances at Rafi. His good looks were outpaced by his intelligence and fire for life, and she felt that spirit pulling her in. Glancing at her arm, she wondered if she could handle the pain of a tattoo. She imagined herself with short black hair and then stopped herself. No more making herself what men wanted. She was going to be herself from here on out. Yet in that conviction she felt lost. As they drove by the mirrored windows of a business complex she saw the car's reflection, saw herself in the passenger seat. She had no idea who that woman really was.

"What is it?" Rafi asked.

"What?"

"You just shook your head, what is wrong?"

"Nothing, just nervous."

"There is nothing to worry about; all that is at risk is our lives." At this Rafi laughed out, rich and full, but Erica felt the words make her stomach flip, and she could only so much as smile.

"Your hair is nice that way," Rafi said. "You have a beautiful neck and shoulder, and to show it off is a grace."

Erica felt her face flush, and an impulse to lean over and kiss his cheek took her over.

Where the hell did that come from?

She was only weakened by Brandon's cruelty, and Rafi had stumbled on something. He was merely being charming to help her calm down, just being Rafi. She looked over at him and he smiled and looked back at the road. She realized with a blend of thrill and faint sadness that she wished he wasn't just being Rafi.

CHAPTER 7

Rafi drove back to his shop, pulling in behind the building. He turned and looked at Erica. "Shall we get this done?"

He got out of the car, and Erica pushed open her door. The heat and humidity had come on early this morning, magnifying behind the building where the cinderblock wall met the weedy gravel.

Rafi walked to the back door of his shop, rattled a key into the lock and let himself in. Erica followed him through the door and pulled it shut. The shift from light to dark completely blinded her for a moment. She stood still in the cool darkness listening to Rafi's footsteps moving away from her. A light came on down the hallway, and she found herself standing in the small backroom among wooden crates and statues, stacked neatly, tags hanging from each.

Rafi motioned for her to follow him into the only lit room, a cluttered office with metal wall-brackets supporting pine-board shelves. On the shelves sat all manner of things: papers, stone heads, a jade turtle, a large femur.

Rafi took a folding metal chair from the wall, pulled it open, and offered it to Erica.

As she sat, he asked, "You have the glass?"

"Yes, right here." She propped the bag in her lap, opened it and, putting her index fingers inside the edges of the glass, lifted it out and set it on the counter.

Rafi took blue gloves from a drawer, pulled them on, and—opening a second drawer—took out a bottle of superglue. He opened a third drawer and looked inside it.

"Not here," he said. He left the room and wood clattered to the ground in the back store room. Returning he carried a bottle of wood glue and a box of transparencies.

"I had hoped you would find another, safer path," Rafi said as he set down the supplies, "but I have to admit this is very exciting."

Erica felt a kindling in Rafi's playful happiness, and she smiled, now feeling some of the same excitement.

Rafi took out a plastic cap and emptied superglue into it. Picking up the glass, he looked it over and held it sideways over the cap.

After a moment, he held the glass up and inspected the side. "This is very good luck. We seem to have all five prints."

He held up the glass, and she saw the smoky, pale swirl of a finger print. "There you have your loving husband's thumbprint."

He held the glass back over the cap of superglue.

"You know," Rafi said his attention on his work, "when I met you, you fairly amazed me. Surely you were stunning in your beauty, but I could almost not see that for the vibrant energy of your spirit."

"Rafi, I don't—"

"Hear me out. Please. The past four years have changed you, caused you to doubt yourself, to hold back, and I am glad to see you willing to fight. The damage he has done will heal."

"I'd like to believe that."

"You know I grew up in northern Iraq."

"I remember."

"If you only understood what those people have been through in the decade of war with Iran, the oppression of Hussein. If they can heal, and they are, then you will heal."

"Thank you Rafi, but I don't feel strong."

"You should. Consider what we are doing here."

Erica looked at Rafi, felt herself considering the room and its contents objectively. "You're lifting fingerprints from a glass to help me get past a fingerprint scanner so I can…"

"So you can attempt to rob a dangerous cartel man."

Erica felt a lift in her confidence. "It is pretty dangerous isn't it?"

Rafi set the glass down and said in a definitive tone, "Yes."

"If it's so dangerous, why are you helping me?"

"Because," he said, looking back to his work, "I've always had a weakness for strong women."

Erica felt a rush from her neck to her toes, and her heart accelerated at the sudden realization that, despite her designer clothes and bare, pale skin, she was Rafi's kind of girl, and in the rush of the moment, she leaned forward and took the sides of his head in her hands lifting his eyes from his work and kissed him. The scent of clean soap surrounded her, and she was surprised by the softness of his lips, which was contrasted by the roughness of his face on the palms of her hands and on her chin. At first he did not kiss her, but went still. She felt suddenly foolish and began to pull away from him. As her lips left his, one of his gloved hands came up behind her neck and pulled her to him. She felt the thrill of his kiss run down from the back of her neck to her tailbone. Then she remembered Brandon's weight pressing her down last night. She remembered how his drunken breath and body odor had made it difficult to find fresh air while he pinned her arms above her head.

She pushed gently on Rafi's chest, separating. "I'm sorry, Rafi." In embarrassment, she looked down. "I just don't know what I'm doing right now."

His look of confusion shifted to frustration, but she saw him collect himself, and he said, "It's all right, Erica."

"No, it's not all right. I'm screwed up right now."

"I'm sorry Erica, I didn't intend for it..." and he trailed off. He sat staring at the glass on the desk. His despondent look, so unlike his usual confident and jovial self, made Erica feel even worse.

She touched his arm, saying, "I'm sorry, Rafi. Can we go back about two minutes?"

"I will pretend we can if you will."

"Let's at least forget about it... for now."

He smiled and said, "I pray for guidance and believe that all happens for a reason, and then you walk back through my door and stop my heart..." He fell silent and Erica did not know what to do. She wanted to put her arms around him. She wanted to kiss him again but would not allow herself to move.

She whispered, "I'm so sorry, Rafi."

He reached out and touched her chin. "No more regrets out of you," and the old, confident Rafi boiled up. "We have far more pressing matters. I for one, would like to know what is hidden in the safe."

He abruptly returned to his task, picking up his camera and taking close photos of the exposed fingerprints. He connected the camera to the computer, downloaded the photos, and began modifying them, cropping them down and altering them to bring more detail to the swirling lines. He arranged the images in rows. Putting a transparency in the laser printer, he clicked a button, and the laser printer hummed, sucked the transparency in, and rolled it back out on top. He held the transparency up to her, and she saw the fingerprints imprinted on it. Laying it down, he dabbed a pearl of wood glue on a swab and painted the glue over a print.

He did this for each print. When he had finished, he said, "There we are. Now all there is to do is wait."

"How long?"

"A few hours."

"I can stay, if I'm not in your way. Brandon will be at work the rest of the day and will probably go out to the clubs afterwards." After she had suggested she stay, the image of her sitting next to Rafi on the couch in the gallery came to her. She had her head on his shoulder and his fingertips trailed along the back of her neck. She pushed the image out of her mind.

Rafi stood breaking her out of the daydream.

"Where are you going?"

"We should get out of this dark pit. Let's get something to eat." He side-stepped past her, leaving the room. She heard him say from the back room. "Come on now. I'll leave you here if you don't keep up."

...

They had eaten and returned to Rafi's shop and now sat in the cluttered office under the fluorescent lights looking over the sheet of glue-coated fingerprints. Rafi brushed his fingertip along the surface of one and then peeled it away from the transparency. Placing the pale oval on his index-finger, he held it out for Erica.

"Done," he said.

Erica looked at the pad, seeing the ridges of fingerprint the toner had left in the transparency now imbedded in the wood glue.

She lifted the oval from his finger and ran her finger over the flexible ridges. "Will it work?"

Rafi shrugged his shoulders and said, "If it does not you will need someone with greater skills than mine." He looked at the patch of glue perched on Erica's finger. "We need to attach them to your fingers. If the scanner reads body heat and pulse, it will then have both. Then the only trouble would come if I have the size wrong, which," he took the print from Erica and held it up to the original on the glass, "I do not think I do."

"Okay," Erica said as she stood, "it's time to crack a safe."

CHAPTER 8

Erica walked down the hallway toward Brandon's office feeling her heart hammering in her neck. Her arms tingled, and she began to feel light headed. She realized she was hyperventilating and forced herself to take slow, deliberate breaths. Afternoon sunlight came through the high hallway windows at an angle, landing in bright squares at the base of the opposite wall.

Brandon should be at the marina for another two hours at least. Hopefully, he'll be out all evening, coked up and out of my hair.

She stepped through the beams of sunlight, scattering rainbows off the diamond in her wedding ring. At his office door, she stepped out of her shoes, pushed the door open, and paused, listening. Muffled through the windows, a dog barked, and the air conditioner hushed on. It sounded almost like the vibration of the garage door. Her heart stuttered in her chest and pulsed heavy and strong, flushing blood through her. Feeling light headed again, she drew a slow breath.

She stepped into the office. Across the room, sunlight came through the wood-slat blinds, landing in long blades across the brandy-colored wood of the desk. Bare feet sinking into the plush carpeting, she walked over to the panel and pulled it open. The machined hulk of the safe stared back at her.

She looked at the fingerprint replicas glued to her finger tips, one set on each hand, both right-handed, just in case one set didn't work. Rafi had told her that Brandon would have been smart to use his left hand, as people are less likely to leave fingerprints with their non-dominant hand. She had to bank on Brandon not being that smart.

Pressing her thumb on the fingerprint scanner, she felt its cold surface through the wood glue. Nothing happened—no red light, no beep. She pressed her left thumb to the pad, trying the second version of his fingerprint. Nothing. She pressed harder and worried that she might smash the ridges in the wood glue. As she looked at her thumb, she had the sinking feeling that she had no idea what she was doing but then remembered what Rafi had said about a temperature sensor. She held her right thumb in the palm of her left hand. Both hands felt the same temperature. Lifting her shirt, she held her cold hand to her belly until it felt warm. She pressed her thumb on the scanner again. The light flickered red, and the loud beep sounded out. She looked back over her shoulder at the door.

At least that's some progress.

Her right thumb still on the scanner, she pulled at the handle of the door. Nothing.

She pressed the index finger of her right hand on the scanner. The light flickered red and the beep sounded. She warmed her left hand on her belly and tried the copies of the thumb and index finger. Red lights and beeps. Rafi had told her that most people use the thumb or index finger to program a scanner.

Maybe Brandon was bright enough to use his left hand after all.

She looked at her middle finger, her other fingers curled down and realized she was flipping the safe off. Now that was something Brandon would do, in a lot of ways he was still thirteen years old. She warmed her fingertips on her belly and pressed her middle finger to the scanner. The circle surrounding the scanner flashed green, and she heard a sliding of smooth steel, which thumped to a rubberized stop.

Keeping her finger on the scanner, she pulled at the handle with her left hand, and the circular door opened without resistance.

She stared at the exposed keypad.

I did it.

Thoughts of failure had been trying to sneak into her mind over the last few days, trying to break her down, to make her feel like a damn fool, and yet with Rafi's help, she had just cracked a fingerprint scanner on a high-end safe. A smile tremored at the corners of her mouth as she felt the sudden possibility that she wasn't kidding herself. She might actually pull this off. A small laugh escaped as she said to herself, "I can't believe that actually worked."

Remembering herself, she took out the scrap of paper with the numbers on it: '47-13-193-62' and looked to the black keypad with a pale-green, digital display above it. Below the keypad, the symbol of a hand, the index finger extended, pointed at a button which read 'START'. She pressed the button, and a beep sounded out. She entered '4-7-1' and each number came up on the screen, but when she touched the '3' nothing happened. She jammed her fingertip into the button, the nail going white—still nothing. On either side of the '0' were up and down arrow keys; she pressed the downward arrow, and the '471' moved up on the display. When she entered '1-3' and the numbers appeared on the screen.

Got it.

She pressed the 'START' button, and the display cleared. She entered '4-7' and touched the down-arrow key. The '47' moved up. Now '1-3' and the down-arrow. The '13' moved up, forcing the '47' off the screen. She entered the third and fourth numbers in the same manner and stared at the pad. Nothing. She pressed the pound sign, and the rim of the keypad flashed red. The display went blank.

That seems like the right way to enter the combination.

She looked at the scrap again.

It's not the right numbers.

Letting out a breath, she ran her fingers through her hair over the crown of her head as she growled in frustration. Staring at the worn surface of the paper, she slid her thumb over it.

Maybe it's written in the wrong order, some way of letting him remember it, but not giving it all away.

She entered the numbers in backwards, '62'-'193'-'13'-'47'. The rim of the keypad flashed red. She stared at the scrap of paper, thinking. She tried again, leaving the numbers in reverse order, but turning them around. '26'-'391'-'31'-'74'. The safe flashed red.

"Dammit." The safe might lock her out if she got the combination wrong too many times.

She walked over to the desk, tossed the scrap of paper on it, and sat in the leather chair, legs out, leaning back in defeat. Looking across the surface of the desk, she felt a rising sense of dread at where she now sat. She wondered what kind of deals had been made from there. What exactly had he done while

she lived in the house? Had he ever killed someone here?
Looking at the white carpeting, she considered anything
possible at this point.

She stared at the scrap of paper sitting half folded in a beam
of sunlight. A dust mote, floating just above the note, glowed
in the light.

"I know you're the combination, you son-of-a-bitch," she
said to the scrap, "but what the hell did he do to you?" She ran
the numbers through her mind again as if they might reorder
themselves. On the other side of the house, the garage door
opener thumped and ground to life.

"No," she said, leaning forward and listening to the sound.
Definitely the garage door.

She jumped up, ran to the safe, closed the small, circular
door to the combination pad and felt defeated as she heard the
lock thump to. Pushing the wooden panel closed, she hurried
to the office door and listened.

Down below, the door to the garage slammed shut and
Brandon's heavy footfalls moved across the kitchen tile. She
felt her neck cool with the tingle of sweat as she turned and
looked at the carpeting. Despite her bare feet, she had left
trails of impressions up to the safe and around the desk.

No time to do anything about it.

She pulled the door closed.

Stepping into her shoes, she walked down the hallway to the
balcony above the foyer and leaned over the railing, looking at
the entryway to the dining room. Beyond, she heard the
refrigerator door open, the bottles in the door clinking.

Should I go down and talk, or stay upstairs?

Her mind raced for what she would normally do. Would
she go down? She thought she might, but she would have to
be careful. She made her way to the kitchen where she found

Brandon standing with refrigerator door open. Another man, Antonio Camejo, sat at the kitchen table, his back to Erica. He wore a white suit coat, and as he lifted a glass to his lips, the fabric bent with silken luminosity. His flawlessly black hair should have had at least some gray. Its thickly combed waves lay in the style of a man who considers himself debonair, but had held on to fashions as passed by as his youth now was.

What the hell is he doing here?

Antonio looked over his shoulder at her and stood with a formal smoothness. "Erica, my dear, you are so beautiful, how wonderful it is to see you."

Just do what you normally would.

She smiled. "Mr. Camejo, how are you today?"

"So formal," Camejo said taking both of her hands in his. As he took hold of them, Erica remembered with horror she still had the prints glued to the tips of her fingers. "Please, how many times must I ask? Call me Antonio. Being on a first name basis with such a beautiful creature is good for a man's heart."

Erica tried to extend her fingertips away from his encircling hands, as she gave him a warm smile and said, "Of course, Antonio. Thank you."

He smiled back and reached up with one hand, still holding the other, and brushed at the side of her face. "You certainly are a fortunate man Brandon. You should make sure to treat this one right."

Brandon looked at them. His eyes skipped across Erica's and landed on the back of Antonio's head. At first he held a look of irritation, but as Antonio turned to Brandon, Brandon's eyes softened to submission.

"Yes, of course, sir."

It was only then that Erica remembered her eyes. The left still had a fairly horrific undercarriage of black-purple, and the right had gone faintly green. He was telling Brandon to lay off of her. It was the message, not of a businessman who should have been shocked by her eyes, not knowing what had happened, but of someone well-versed in dealing with rough underlings. She looked into the cartel boss' dark eyes and became ever more aware of the woodglue fingerprints touching the sides of his hand—fingerprints designed to rob him.

She drew a breath, which stuttered a bit in her chest, and fought the urge to pull her hand from his. She gave him her best smile and said, "Please sit. Don't let me interrupt your drink."

Antonio nodded, released her hand, and sat, "Only if you join me my dear."

She sat down just as Brandon walked out of the room.

She called after him, "Where are you going?"

He looked at her from the dining room, anger flashing in his eyes, but as his gaze shifted from her to Antonio, he masked his anger, his eyes going dead. "I have to get something. That's why we came from the marina. I'll be right back."

She assumed he would go to the office and, thinking of the footprints in the carpeting, fought the urge to shout after him.

"Erica," Antonio said as he took her hand again, but he stopped short and turned her hand over and scowled at it. Her shoulder twitched, but she was able to hold the impulse to yank her arm back. Antonio gently tilted her finger one way and then the other.

He looked up at her. "What is this, Erica?"

"That, oh it's nothing. It's embarrassing really." Now she did try to pull her hand away, but Antonio did not release it, his grip tightening on her wrist.

"Please," was all Erica could think to say as she pulled again.

Antonio looked up at her. "Where have I seen this kind of thing before? What are you up to?"

"I'd really rather not say," she said, doing her best to hide the fear in her voice.

"I would prefer you did. It almost looks as though you are—"

"I hurt my hands, burned the fingertips." She touched her face with her free hand just where the bruising was the worst. "I'm sorry; I shouldn't trouble you with my problems."

Antonio's eyes came up to meet hers and rested there for a moment. His bronze skin went a shade darker, and he let her hand go.

"I'm sorry," Erica said, "I should…" and she let her voice trail off as she leaned forward, staring at the floor, doing her best to look pitiful, but in her heart she felt hope burning.

"It is all right my dear." Antonio's hand touched her face and she gave a slight, intended flinch.

"It's been horrible, Antonio." She took hold of Antonio's wrist and kissed the inside of his hand, just touching the tip of her tongue to the flesh. She gave him an unsure smile. "You are so much more refined than Brandon—"

"What?" Antonio rose. "This is unacceptable. You are a married woman."

Erica looked into the dining room and then back to Antonio. She said in a desperate whisper, "But I thought you meant… oh God," she put her head in her hands and remembering the fingerprints, crossed her hands on her lap and looked out the window. "I misunderstood."

She glanced at him and he slid his hands into his pants pockets, a rare submissive gesture for the powerful man. He seemed to realize it was out of character because he drew them out again, leaving them hanging at his sides and looked around the room and then at his watch.

She lowered her eyes to show deference and to cover her thrill at having conned him.

Antonio moved over to the island and sat on a bar stool. "Erica, I hope you are not being unfaithful to Brandon. I understand that it is difficult. He is not an easy man, but he does love you very much. He tells me this."

At this a tear fell from her eye, surprising her as much as it seemed to shock him. He looked out the window, and she brushed it away.

"I should go," she said as she rose. Antonio made no effort to stop her, and she left the room with a slight smile on her lips. She passed through the dining room, and as she entered the foyer, she heard Brandon coming down the upper hallway. She continued across the foyer, past the tall windows framing the front door, and into the living room. As he came down the stairs and walked through the foyer, she put her hand in her pocket. The scrap of paper wasn't there. Fear flushed icy down her back and into her guts as she realized that, in her haste to leave the office, she had left it sitting on the center of his desk.

"Erica," Brandon said in a cool tone. She looked up and found him standing in the entry to the living room, glaring at her. He curled his finger. "Come with me."

As he walked up the stairs, she glanced at the front door and considered running.

Not yet. Stay calm.

She reached for the banister to follow Brandon up the stairs and noticed her hand trembling. As she made her way up the staircase, her legs felt weak. He stalked down the hallway and she followed, wondering if she could get to the softball bat in his office before he got his hands on her. He wouldn't do it with Antonio here, or would he? Was this it? Time for her to be encased in concrete and sunk in the Atlantic? Brandon walked past the office door and continued on to the bedroom, and relief overwhelmed her. She followed him into the bedroom, and he walked into the closet. She leaned her head in.

Pointing at a solitary, brown shoe, he said, "One of my Ferragamos is gone. Did you do something with it?"

Her relief that this was not about the scrap of paper had left her unprepared to deal with this lesser problem. The urge to tell him off flashed through her mind.

What the hell would I do with one of your overpriced shoes? Pinhead.

"I don't know, but let me help you," she said with a smile. Entering the closet, she walked around him, feeling him next to her, boiling. She studied the shoe rack and leaned over, peering behind it. The second shoe lay there, jammed sideways between the rack and the wall. She pulled it out and held it out to him. He snatched it from her.

Stay calm, be brave.

"It was sideways in the back of the rack. I would have missed it too, at first glance."

He stared at her. She could see him measuring her words, looking for an excuse to lash out. She dropped her gaze to the shoe and considered what to do next. Any choice could be wrong. Pleasantness might trigger him, brashness might diffuse him. She remained silent, staring at the shoe.

"We made a big sales goal, and Antonio is taking us all out. We won't be back until late, and I don't want any shit out of you for it."

She looked up at him and said, "Okay."

She sensed he wasn't going to back down. When it came on like this, when she had done nothing, said nothing, it was always worse. He curled one of his hands into a fist. She saw the door in her peripheral vision. A direct look at it would have lit him up, the predator seeing weakness in his prey. Trying to walk past him would surely set him off as well.

She had to take a risk and decided to appeal to his ego. She moved close to him, close enough that her breasts touched his hand which held the shoe.

"Will you be in good enough condition to do what you did last night?" She pushed the shoe aside and put her hands on his waist, feeling the burgeoning fat there. She arched her back so her hips pushed into his groin and rolled into him, letting her breasts swell as they connected with his chest. His eyes remained cold and angry. She was losing the bet. He grabbed her by the throat and shoved her; the room flipped, the carpet smacked her butt, and the wall cracked her in the back of the skull.

"Fucking slut. Is that all you think about?"

The back of her head throbbing with pain, she sat against the closet wall and didn't move. Acknowledging the pain could make him want more. She stared at his socks and waited. He didn't move. She could hear him breathing in short huffs.

"Stupid cunt," he said and finally walked out of the closet, clicking off the light as he left.

His voice trailed off as he walked down the hallway. "Another thing, get your car into the damn garage. I told you not to leave it out in the sun."

One day someone might put Brandon Calzavara in his place, but today she only needed to survive him. She stayed there in the darkness of the closet listening to Brandon and Antonio's muffled voices.

"I've got to figure out other ways to win," she said and laughed at herself, feeling strangely free from care in light of what had just happened, as if she had already escaped. She'd get into the safe one way or another.

She stood and left the closet thinking about Brandon and his damn shoe; he could never keep anything straight. Then it came to her; Brandon couldn't keep anything straight. That's why he wrote the combination down, but if he mixed up the numbers, he wouldn't be able to keep that straight either...

She jogged with bare feet along the hallway, down the staircase, through the foyer, and into the kitchen. Pulling open the door to the garage, she found the scent of gas and noon-heat baking into the dark space. There the gray, sealed-epoxy concrete where his car belonged sat empty. Running back up into the office, she shut the door behind her and stepped out of her sandals.

She took the scrap of paper from the center of the desk, shoved it in her pocket, sat in the chair, and pulled open one of the large, lower drawers releasing the scent of cedar and wood stain. A half-empty bottle of Dalmore 18 year old scotch rolled away, clunking into the side of the drawer. Searching the remaining side drawers, she found nothing but disorganized papers and supplies. She opened the center drawer and shoved pens and notepads aside.

So much clutter, just like his drugged up brain.

As she closed the drawer, the worn corner of a photograph caught her eye. She pulled it out from the mass of papers, a photo of her and Brandon on their wedding day. She hadn't seen it in years. Her long, white dress ran down her body like a field of snow, ending in red velvet at the hem. She held Brandon's arm. He looked a decade younger, handsome and lean with a serious expression. The edges of the photograph were folded and separating. Where her thumb held it, Brandon's left leg had been worn down to the backing. She looked closely at herself and realized the surface of her face in the photo had also been worn with touch. She imagined Brandon looking at the photo, caressing her face with a fingertip. Antonio had spoken truthfully. Somewhere, deep down in his screwed-up mind, Brandon really had loved her.

She tore the photo in half, then into quarters, and tucked the pieces back into the pile of papers. She'd have burned it if she'd had a match.

Closing the three top drawers, she exposed the final side drawer, still open. She drew a file folder out and opened it. Empty. Sliding the file back home, she drew out the second. Again, nothing. She returned the file to the rack and shoved them all to the back. Nothing. Frustrated and feeling her newfound hope ebbing away, she sat back in the chair and looked up at the ceiling. The sunlight coming through the slatted widows cut across her arms. If she concentrated, she could hear cars going by on the street and the breeze bustling through the palm trees. The sounds came so faintly, they created a dreamlike state.

If I can't get into the safe, I'll have to run broke, which will be so much harder.

While thinking, she had been digging her toes into the carpeting. She looked down and saw that she had made a mess of the carpet under the desk. At first, she felt concern for leaving the evidence of her having been there, but as she leaned under the desk, she sensed it was the right direction. She got down on her hands and knees, looked up, and saw something black on the bottom of the desk drawer. She peered at it in the dim light and saw '3142' written in small letters with a black sharpie.

Her heartbeat quickened.

Could it be that easy?

Taking the scrap of paper from her pocket, she wrote '3142' on it and went to the wall panel and pulled it open. Pressing her middle finger against the scanner, she got nothing. She warmed her hand on her belly and tried again. The light flashed green followed by the internal thump of the lock releasing. She opened the panel and looked at the two sets of numbers on the scrap of paper, '47-13-193-62' and '3142'.

She pressed the 'Start' button and entered '193', pressed the down arrow key, then '47', and '62', and then '13'. After entering the last number, she stared at the keypad. She wanted this to work, wanted the safe to open and deliver something wonderful. Once she pressed the down arrow key, what happened next, would change the course of her entire life. She imagined the door pulling open, exposing stacks of white powder in plastic bags and brand new $100 bills bound with strips of paper.

It couldn't be that good could it? If there is enough to disappear on, that's all I need.

She pressed the down arrow. The bar of light surrounding the keypad glowed green and she heard a thump deep inside the door. Her heart felt as though it might have stopped beating, and in that stillness, she only stared, not able to fully comprehend that she had succeeded. She reached out and pushed on one of the tri-spoke handles. Instead of immovable resistance, the bar turned with hydraulic smoothness. She spun it until it came to its stop and pulled. The foot-thick door came open, resisting only with its mass.

High mounted LED lights clicked on and sent their white brilliance straight down, leaving hard shadows along stainless steel panels. She stood awestruck. Instead of the small space she had expected, she stood before a safe the size of a walk in closet. At the far end racks of drawers sat under a bank of circular watch mounts, rotating slowly. She stepped inside, and the concrete floor soaked coldness into her bare feet.

She pushed on one of the stainless steel panels, and it lifted open with hydraulic slowness, rocking back into the wall like a tiny one-piece garage door.

Her eyes dropped from the raised panel to the revealed space, and she couldn't immediately make sense of what she saw. She thought she understood what it was, but couldn't quite believe it. Reaching out, she touched one of the glowing-yellow stacks of metal plates. Her finger tips ran down the sides of the plates, and she picked up the top plate. She felt a rush of fear as she did it. What if the drawer was somehow alarmed? The thought had caused her to freeze, holding the plate hovering over the rest of the stack. But nothing happened. She took the plate out and turned it over in her hand.

The thin plate, as long as her hand and almost as wide, felt bizarrely heavy. Across the face, something had been stamped out with an 'X' shaped tool. Below that, stamped into the soft metal, was "1 Kilo", "Fine Gold", and "99.99." She dug her fingernail in under the "99.99," leaving a gouge.

The halogen lights coming down from the ceiling of the safe caught in the bar and she stared for some time at the shelving reflected in the brightness. She pressed her other hand on top of the bar and felt dizzy.

How much was an ounce of gold going for now? How many ounces in a Kilo?

Her mind raced.

This is worth a lot by itself.

She looked at the open compartment, back at the three stacks of gold. 15 bars. Fifteen kilograms of gold. She began pressing panels, each lifting with a hydraulic slowness, exposing similar stacks of gold. Some of the panels had stacks of paperwork, others had clear plastic bricks with duct-taped straps around them. Erica assumed they must be cocaine or heroin. When she had all 20 panels open, ten to each side, she counted. 14 compartments... 15 bars in each... 210 kilograms.

She should have been worried about how to transport so much weight, but with what she had overcome, it meant nothing to her. This was her way out, and she would make it work. Taking her cell phone from her back pocket, she saw it had no signal and stepped out of the safe, giving one more look to the stainless steel shelves, tinted with the rich yellowed reflection coming off the gold.

Checking her phone for signal again, she dialed Rafi. In her rushed excitement, she had trouble controlling her fingers and had to re-dial twice. She had been committed to running but felt fearful at the prospect of heading into the world alone. Without worldly experience, she could only tell herself she'd be fine, but now she had enough to do what she had not yet allowed herself to admit she wanted to do.

"Hello," Rafi said, "What have you got?"

"How much is a kilo of gold worth?"

"You have a kilo of gold? That's good. It would be..." She heard the clicking of keys. "...worth nearly fifty five thousand dollars at current prices. You would of course need to take a lower price than that if you wanted to liquidate it quickly and quietly."

"Will you run away with me, Rafi?"

Silence.

"Will you?"

"I… we cannot go on only fifty thousand dollars."

Erica felt electrified as she turned back to the safe. "I don't have fifty thousand dollars in gold, Rafi." She paused and thought through the multiplication for a moment. "I have a lot more."

Silence. She imagined Rafi looking around his office, taking stock of his life's work.

"I need help carrying this stuff, Rafi; I need help selling it. Run away with me. Let's go have the adventure of a lifetime."

"How much do you have?"

"I'm looking at 210 kilos."

Silence, and then, "Two hundred… I… that's nearly five hundred pounds…"

Her voice came out in a whisper, "I know."

But Rafi had not answered her question.

"Will you come with me?"

There was silence on the other end again, and then without ceremony, Rafi said, "Yes."

She felt nothing short of ecstatic at his answer.

"Can you be here in thirty minutes?"

"I have a boat at the harbor. It is small and a risk, but I'll check the weather. We should be able to slip away tonight. My car will handle the weight, barely."

Erica felt fearless now. "We need guns."

"Guns might be a problem. I have only one."

Erica looked at the back end of the safe, to the drawers under the rotating watches.

"I might find some here. If we have to go without them, then we go without them. Just get over here."

CHAPTER 9

After Rafi had disconnected, Erica walked back into the safe, picked up one of the stacks of gold plates, brought it out, and set it on the desk.

I've got to package this stuff somehow. Moving it out in the open will attract way too much attention.

She looked at the clock. 4PM. Brandon would be gone the rest of the evening.

Take your time.

But she didn't feel safe. She left the stack of gold on the desk and walked out of the office and down the hallway. Leaning over the banister to the foyer, she listened to the silence of the house, thinking. She could only hear yard equipment off in the distance through the broad windows. Her mind tracked through the house, imagining the boxes in closets and the contents of the shelves in the garage

What can I put gold in?

She remembered the duct taped bags of drugs in the safe.

That would do it.

She ran down the stairs and into the garage. Pulling open cabinets, she found what she was looking for—ten rolls of duct tape in a stack. She put the stack under her arm and went back into the house. In the kitchen her feet padded along the cool tile. She took a thin box of plastic wrap from a drawer and ran out of the room. Back in the office, she wrapped plastic wrap around one of the stacks of gold plates and wrapped tape around the plastic. She added more wraps of tape until she had completely covered the plates. Pulling a long strip of tape from the roll, she lay it on the desk, set the wrapped stack on it, and pulled the strap up, fashioning a crude handle. When she had finished, she looked over her handiwork, a nondescript silver bundle. She sighed.

The damn thing looks more suspicious than ever.

She gripped the handle, hefting it off the desk. The weight of the small object amazed her, but the handle held well and made the bundle easy to lift and move. It would have to work. She brought out all forty-six stacks of gold, setting them across the surface of the desk, and wrapped each with plastic and tape.

When she had finished, she took two of the bundles down to the kitchen. As she set them on the kitchen table, she realized she would need clothes and other essentials. She ran upstairs to her room, into the closet, took down two duffel bags, and shoved the bags full of various clothes, shoes, and a light windbreaker. Looking at the bag, she felt totally unprepared. She pulled up the floor vent in the closet and reached in, drawing out the manila envelope she had stored there, filled with just over ten thousand dollars in cash she had effectively embezzled from her marriage. She tipped the contents of her jewelry box in—diamonds, gold and pearls ingloriously jammed into the bag.

Running into the bathroom, she filled her ditty bag with essentials. She looked at herself in the mirror and, for the first time in several years, loved what she saw. Her face was flushed, and her eyes had the intensity of the young girl she had been, full of pith and life. That intensity made the bruising around her left eye look, not like the wounds of abuse, but the price a prizefighter had paid on the road to victory. She felt young and strong again and smiled as an old memory came back to her, something she hadn't recalled in a long time. She saw herself on the porch, sixteen years old, still a child at heart but already a woman in form. The salesman stood before her, a hint of sweat staining the armpits of his shirt. When she said she wasn't interested in the cleaning supplies, he had smiled and told her how dangerous it could be for a young woman like her to be, "all alone out here in the middle of nowhere."

She went inside, and he followed her, his eyes haunted, knowing he wasn't invited. She met him in the entryway with a baseball bat. When he laughed at her, she whipped it past his nose. His expression turned deadly. She swung the bat again and blew the case he held into a mess of splinters and crushed bottles. He ran. Holding the bat cocked over her shoulder, she roared as if to war and chased him off the porch and across the yard. The salesman had tripped, and she stood over him as he crawled away from her, cowering. She had felt power then and later guilt, had felt so awkward to have reduced a grown man to that sniveling mess. Now she felt that beast awakening in her heart again, and it pulsed through her, brutal and welcome.

She smiled at the woman in the mirror and slammed the drawer closed. Taking the bag she went to the closet and stuffed it into one of the duffels. Her head came up. She looked toward the hallway. Had that been the garage door?

...

Brandon drove toward home along Royal Palm Way cursing his secretary. He hadn't been back at the dealership thirty minutes before the ditz plopped her ass down in his lap. He didn't mind the attention, but she had ignored the cup of coffee in his hand.

Maybe she fell head-first off the pole at her previous job.

He had thrown her off his lap and told her she was fired and to get out, but she knew how to keep her job. When she had finished, he told her to go home early. He was done looking at her for the day. A perfect body could only go so far against stupid.

He had to get changed and get back to the marina. Antonio and the boys were going out, and that meant a good night. He couldn't help but think of the new girl at the club, fresh from the Midwest. Tonight he was going to welcome that rookie piece of ass to the big city. She had no idea, but she was going to walk out with a lot more money than she came in with. What a lucrative change of job title from dancer to whore.

He pulled into his driveway and saw Erica's car still parked in the driveway.

God dammit. She doesn't listen... doesn't give two shits about anything I've given her. How hard do I have to hit her to make her learn?

He'd just about had it with that little swamp rat, but he had to keep her around. None of the other women looked like her, and the fact that she was smart was even better. Fooling around on her had become a kind of sport, and keeping an intelligent woman under his thumb, her knowing he was doing it, felt even better.

He parked in the garage and went into the kitchen, had intended to walk to the fridge and have a beer, but two duct-taped bundles on the breakfast table caught his eye. He walked over to the table and picked one up by its tape handle.

That's fucking heavy.

Setting it down, he took a folding knife from his pocket and cut across the tape, exposing the gold.

He heard the thump of a door upstairs and crouched down, pulling his Sig Sauer P290 from its ankle holster. The fat chunk of a gun was small enough that his pinkie didn't fit on the grip. As he walked into the dining room, he thought better of having the gun out and put it in his pocket, keeping his hand on the grip.

He walked with slow steps into the foyer, his dress shoes clicking more than he'd like on the marble floor. He stopped in the center of the room and listened again. Nothing. He walked up the stairs. As his eyes crested the upper floor level, he saw Erica turn the corner of the hallway at a sprint.

"Erica?" he shouted at her. "What the hell are you up to?"

He listened again. Nothing.

"Erica, get your ass out here."

If it's just her, then no problem.

He let go of the gun and walked down the hallway, his hands balling up in fists. He felt his groin going tight.

I'm going to beat that girl half to death if she's up to what I think she's up to.

He reached the end of the hallway just as his office door clicked shut.

"Bitch," he yelled out, "You're done."

Four years of bullshit... She's going down hard. No more smart girls.

When he reached the office door, he found the door locked.

She thinks she can lock me out of my own office?

He kicked the door. The latch broke away with a crack, and the door slapped open. Erica, who had been hiding beside the door, backed away from him, his softball bat cocked over her shoulder. The safe stood open, and duct-taped bundles had been stacked across the desk. It looked like everything from inside the safe.

He laughed at her. "What? Did you think you were gonna ambush me?"

She continued backing away, her hands trembling. "Get the fuck away from me Brandon." Her voice came thin and scared from her pretty mouth. "I've had it with your shit. No more."

His anger boiled over, and he screamed at her, "You thought this was going to work? You thought that I would so much as let you live?" He laughed again and pointed to his shirt, "You might have gotten away with it if my secretary hadn't spilled coffee on my shirt." He smiled at her, glad to no longer have to mince words with this speed bump. "You should have seen what I made her do to make up for it."

"I couldn't care less," Erica said, her voice quailing.

"Oh, Erica," Brandon said, "How I'm going to enjoy this last dance. I'm gonna make you ugly and let you heal before I kill you."

Erica brought the bat around, holding it between them, fear cresting in her eyes. The end of the bat trembled. He walked forward smiling, and she shrank back. Her hands were spread apart on the bat's handle.

This stupid bitch is useless. She can't even hold a bat right.

He wouldn't need the gun for this so left it in his pocket as he walked toward her. "I'm gonna rip that bat out of your hands and shove it up your ass." This was going to be more fun than he'd had in a long time. It was always better when you knew you didn't have to keep them alive, no boundaries, nothing forbidden. "You'll beg to die."

He reached for the bat, but just as his hand would have gripped it, Erica whipped it back, her hands sliding together. She brought her foot back into a batting stance and her hip twisted.

Brandon held his hand up, and the bat slammed into his forearm with a resonating clank. His arm folded in half around the bat and pulled his torso forward. His arm dropped and pendulumed in the middle as if rubber. He felt a coldness run down his back and his mind screamed at him, *pull the trigger, pull the trigger*, but he felt confused and nauseated.

I don't have the gun in my hand.

She fixed him with hard eyes and drew the bat back. All Brandon could think to say was, "I loved you." She whipped the bat at his head, and a hollow ring of aluminum joined with a sound like a coconut cracking under a truck tire. The world went brilliant white and burned with brutal pain.

He thought he felt himself fall to the floor, but before he could make sense of it, the pain vanished, and he seemed to float. The white light now had a warmth to it, and he felt... loved. He had the sensation of being young, very young, sitting in his grandmother's rocking chair, the soft fabric of her blue dress beside him. He caught the detergent and flour scent of her hands as she turned the page of a book with a flip. Br'er Rabbit. It had been his favorite. The white light no longer surrounded him; it shined down, separating. The sensation of love became infected with stains of disappointment and sorrow. Those imperfections grew, and he became aware that the grief was for him. Something terrible was about to happen. He looked up as the light lofted away... rather as he sank down from it.

He descended into blackness, not so much the lack of light, but a soulless void, into which his self seemed to distend, stretching at the seams of his being. He sensed hate below him, reaching up with smoking tendrils, lusting to rend him. Below him, down in the pit, he felt profound suffering and knew he was going to join it. His body, his essence, began to burn, the muscles and joints smoldering under the skin. He pulled at nothing, trying to claw his way back toward the light, now only a dim fog high above. He had nothing to grasp hold of and screamed. The covetousness below sipped at his screams as the burning grew. Its intensity scorched his lungs, incinerated his eyes, and caused his bones to glow like coals, and he descended into a suffocating fume of brimstone.

CHAPTER 10

Erica, sucking air through her clenched teeth, stood over Brandon. She kept her grip tight on the bat, waiting for him to move, but there was nothing, not even death tremors.

As she leaned over him, her arms trembled with spent adrenaline. She had smashed his eye socket and temple. Ocular jelly drained down his nose. His other eye stared into his precious, white carpeting. Dizziness overwhelmed her, and she sat straight down on her butt with a thump and stared at Brandon's corpse. She saw a dark swath grow at his groin and spread down his hip toward the carpet. She pushed at his shoulder with the tip of the bat and his body shifted easily, relaxed.

He'll never raise a hand against me again.

In that thought, she felt a flush of joy, but the joy was short-lived because her restless mind turned immediately to the cartel. Now they had two reasons to come after her. At this moment she could go straight—go to the police, tell them what she knew. She had this one chance. She'd probably get off due to the abuse, but that would pin her down and make a nice, stationary target for the cartel. They'd never let her live. She saw herself walking through the hallway of the courthouse, her public defender next to her, congratulating her on her freedom. She'd see the chrome spike of the ice pick too late, just as an anonymous hand rammed it expertly between two ribs, just below the heart.

No way. If I'm going to live or die, I'm going to do it on my terms.

But now the stakes were raised for Rafi as well.

He's a grown man. If he wants to come, he knows the risk. I'll give him one more chance to back out.

She stood and considered some kind of ceremony before she walked away from the body, perhaps spitting on it… but she had nothing left for him. Dropping the dented bat, she walked over to the desk. As she gripped two of the gold bundles, she heard a buzzing sound behind her. She turned around. It had come from the body. She walked over to it and pulled Brandon's cell phone from his pocket. The phone showed a photo of Antonio Camejo standing on a beach, a wide smile on his face and a young, dark-haired girl in his embrace.

The reality of her situation compressed down on her. She no longer had all night to disappear, and if Brandon didn't answer his phone…

The phone continued to buzz in her hand.

If she answered the phone, she might be able to buy some time, but would fully incriminate herself in Brandon's death.

The phone buzzed again.

You have to decide. Time… Time is more important.

She flicked the green icon and said into the phone, "Hello Mr. Camejo, this is Erica." Before he could speak she continued, "Brandon's in the shower and asked me to answer his phone. Is everything okay? He doesn't usually ask me to cover calls."

That was terrible.

A half-heartbeat of silence followed before Camejo said with a gentleman's smoothness, "Why Erica, so nice to hear your angelic voice."

"Thank you, Antonio." Erica looked down at Camejo's employee lying dead beside her. "Should I give Brandon a message for you?"

"Yes, thank you. Please have him call me the moment he is available. Our customer has arrived earlier than we expected."

She sensed the faintest irritation in his voice.

"I'll tell him right now."

"Good. Thank you." The phone went dead, and Erica tossed it on Brandon's body. It bounced off his hip and landed beside him.

Erica went to the desk, hefted three stacks in each hand, and ignored the body as she left the room and again when she returned for more.

When she had finished moving all the gold to the kitchen table, she heard a car in the driveway and looked out the window. Rafi. She went into the garage, opened the door, and ran up to Rafi's driver side window.

She pointed at the center garage bay and said, "Back in there."

Rafi turned the car, and as he began backing into the garage, Erica felt as though everything was moving in slow motion. She looked up at the second story windows.

I wonder if I should try and hide the body. There's no blood. Maybe Brandon should just disappear in the ocean.

She imagined herself and Rafi, each with a leg, dragging the hulk of the body—its arms up over its head—down the staircase, Rafi sliding it through the dining room, through the kitchen. She imagined the car, loaded down with gold and the body, dragging the rear bumper.

Rafi now stood beside his car in the garage, waiting for her. "What do you need me to do?"

Erica motioned for him to follow her into the kitchen and pointed at the bundles. "I need you to start loading these into the trunk."

Rafi stopped, his eyes going wide. "Is this all gold?"

"Yes."

"It's amazing the table can even hold it up."

"I didn't even consider that."

Should I tell him about Brandon? Or should I just load the gold and go?

Rafi gave her his confident smile as he gripped six bundles of gold, three to each hand. She felt so good to have someone she could trust, but as he left the kitchen with more than a million and a half in gold she wondered if she really could trust him. How well did she really know him? When she was poor and had nothing for him to take, he had been a good friend. Would that change with so much on the line? She remembered a black and white movie set in remote, Mexican mountains; the characters' paranoia and greed over gold caused them to turn on each other. She sighed as she looked at the bundles covering the table.

I have no choice but to trust him. It's a gamble, and with any gamble, some insurance might be a good idea. Perhaps seeing Brandon is a good way for him to know not to cross me.

Rafi came back into the kitchen, and she motioned with her hand. "Follow me. There's something I need you to see."

She walked out of the kitchen, through the foyer, and up the staircase. At the top of the stairs, she turned and looked back down. The large windows surrounding the rainbow-glassed front doors let in streams of afternoon sunlight. Now the room with its white marble floor should have seemed peaceful. No one was going to come storming out of the living room. But she still felt the echoes of the past four years in the room, felt exposed there at the top of the stairs.

She heard a car pull into the driveway and saw its green shape park beside the fountain. A blurred man got out of the car and walked up the steps. His shadow fell across the rainbow of the door. The door handle dipped down, and the door rattled against the deadbolt.

"Brandon?" a voice said from the other side. The shadow of an arm lifted over the window and a loud knock resounded in the foyer. "Brandon!"

Rafi leaned close and whispered, "Who the hell is that?"

She recognized the voice. Camejo had seen right through her and had sent one of his men to check on Brandon. She had failed to buy more time.

She whispered to Rafi, "It's Alex Maietta, Brandon's partner in crime. They've known each other since high school."

"You think he's dangerous?"

"Definitely."

Alex pounded on the door.

Erica squared on Rafi. "Are you ready if this goes south?"

Rafi smiled and said in a quiet voice, "I grew up in Northern Iraq."

Erica looked Rafi over. He was strong and fit. While Alex was a big guy, he had gone soft in the four years she had known him. Rafi didn't look Iraqi, he had his father's Scottish jaw and eyes, and simply seemed a northern Britain with a suntan, but he had grown up in a war zone. He had the genetic strength of two hardened people in him.

"Go answer the door, Rafi."

"What? Why me?"

"Because I have to go and get the guns."

"I have a gun in the car."

"Not enough time. Go get the door. Tell him you're the neighbor or something. Just stall him long enough for me to get back."

"Okay."

Rafi went down the stairs as Erica ran down the hallway. She heard the door click open.

"Who the hell are you?" she heard Alex ask. Rafi's response faded away as she entered the office. She went to the safe. The interior had gone dark, and as she stepped in the muted space, the LED lamps clicked on. At the back of the safe by the rotating watches, she pulled open a drawer and found stacks of white powder. She pulled open the next drawer and found the same. The third held densely packed bags of marijuana. She pulled open the last drawer and found more weed.

No guns.

She crouched down beside the drawer and, as she considered where guns might be, looked up at the watches: Omegas, Rolexes, Hublots. One of the Hublots had a black band and a gold face. She pulled it from its place, pushed the felt holder out of the middle, and pocketed the watch—a gift for Rafi. He deserved as much.

Leaving the safe, she looked at the desk. She had been through it all, had been through the whole office. Going to Brandon's body, she patted at the pockets. The body had already begun to cool. She felt a metal lump under the urine soaked fabric and pushed the body to its back. Sliding her hand into the pocket's wet fabric, she drew out a small, brick-like gun.

A Sig… my dad's favorite.

She ran out of the office tucking the gun in the small of her back.

As she came down the hallway, she heard Alex talking to Rafi, his irritation clear. "Why do you think I care, man? Where the hell's Brandon?"

She came up to the banister. "Alex," she said, doing her best to not be too bright in her tone. She hated Alex, and he damn well knew it.

His pale eyes targeted her. While he might have been handsome once, drinking and drug use had already taken their toll. Deep lines had begun to furrow out bags under his eyes, and the sides of his neck, just under his jaw, pudged outward. He was a big enough guy, but without Brandon as backup, he was only one big guy. That thought drew Erica's lips into an ever-so-slight smile.

"Erica, I want to talk to Brandon, *right now.*"

As she came down the stairs, he said, "No, don't come down here; get your hot ass up the stairs. Go get him."

She continued down the stairs. "You want to visit him in the bathroom? Be my guest."

Alex glared at her as she came to stand in front of him. He stepped in on her, his nose just a few inches from hers. "Erica, what the fuck is your problem?"

"I don't—"

"Stuff it Erica. Go get Brandon, *now.*"

Rafi stepped closer.

Alex turned on him, putting his hand in his pants pocket. "You really think that's a good idea?"

Rafi looked to Erica.

"Don't look at her for your balls," Alex said. "You either have 'em, or you don't."

As Alex waited for Rafi's reaction, Erica took the gun from the behind her and leveled it at Alex.

"Alex," Erica said.

Alex continued to stare at Rafi.

In a sharp tone, Erica said, "Hey, dumbass."

Alex kept his eyes on Rafi as he said, "Erica, I swear to God your husband should have sorted you out a long—" He looked at her and fell silent.

"I'm not married anymore, Alex."

His expression remained calm, and his hand was still in his pocket.

He doesn't think I know how to fire a double action pistol? Fair enough.

She pulled the slide back—cocking the hammer—shifted the muzzle just to the side of his head and pulled the trigger. The gunshot hammered the room, its loudness in the enclosed space shocking Erica, who had only fired guns in the open marshes.

Alex recoiled from the flame of the muzzle blast, covering his head with his arms. As he looked between his forearms, Erica saw fear in his eyes and, in that weakness, the four years of dealing with Brandon's buddy rushed up on her in a black fury.

As he lowered his arms, her finger pressed on the trigger, the blocky hammer lifting back. She felt strangely outside of herself, an observer.

Alex stared at the gun, his eyes wide. He held up his hands and, in a pleading tone she never thought she would hear from him, said, "Don't Erica. I— I know we haven't been on the best terms, but no matter what kind of trouble you're in, I can help. I know people."

"You know people who are too high a risk to your life, Alex."

Genuine confusion came to his face, and he asked, "Who?"

"Me."

The hammer came back further. She felt the autopilot still on and considered that Alex's death wouldn't be self defense.

I don't care.

The thought came through her mind, machine oiled and heartless as her finger kept gripping. But she saw the tips of his fingers trembling, and that subtle fragility disconnected her from her anger. He could act afraid, hold his hands up and beg. In those things he could actively deceive, but that trembling was real.

Her finger released its pressure on the trigger.

He said, "Just stay calm Erica."

"Are you telling me what to do, Alex?"

"I—"

"Who's in charge here, Alex?"

"You are," he said, nodding his assent, "you are."

"You're not as stupid as I thought."

He nodded again.

Erica said to Rafi, "Go get some rope from the garage, center cabinet."

Rafi walked out of the foyer.

"So Brandon...?" Alex asked.

"Is dead. Turns out I had a limit on how many times I'd let him kick the crap out of me."

After a moment in which Alex avoided Erica's stare, Rafi came back into the foyer and, with quick motions, pulled Alex's arms behind his back and tied them. With a series of complex knots, he used the rope to hobble Alex's ankles. When he had finished, he patted Alex down, removing a pistol from his front pocket, a smaller gun from his ankle, and a folding box-cutter from his back pocket. He ran his fingers around the inside of Alex's belt and pulled out a one-inch blade with a two-knuckle grip. Alex looked at the blade with a flicker of disappointment.

Erica took pride in how efficiently Rafi had processed Alex. *He's done a lot more than he lets on.*

With Alex restrained, she walked up close to him and said, "I suppose Brandon just thought he could do whatever the hell he wanted to anyone he wanted."

Alex still wouldn't make eye contact with her.

"I know someone else like that, don't I?" She smiled at him, pulling her shoulders back. "What? Not going to stare now?"

His eyes flicked down instinctively and came back up, locking on her face. A bead of sweat, born in his hairline, ran down to his eyebrow.

She put the squared muzzle of the Sig Sauer under his chin and pushed, lifting his head.

"He came at me in his office," she said, as the muzzle dug into the soft skin under his jaw. "He told me he was going to make me ugly, that he'd let me heal before he killed me."

She leaned close to him now, into the leather scent of his aftershave. "Do I look ugly to you, Alex?"

He shook his head.

"He is though. Big dent in his temple the shape of a softball bat. His skin color is all wrong too, a bit blue."

Alex said in a whisper, "I'm sorry, Erica. I never meant—"

She lowered the gun and, with her free hand, slapped him as hard as she could. A hand shaped welt bloomed on his face.

"Don't be like that, Alex, backpedaling. You meant every word. If you could have, if he had let you, you would have.

What have you done to the girls at the clubs, Alex?" She placed the muzzle of the gun between his eyes. "How many times? Go on, now's the time for honesty. The truth, Alex."

Alex shook his head.

"How many?" Erica asked.

"Please, Erica."

She growled the words at him, "Tell me how many."

Tears brimmed in his eyes as he swallowed and whispered, "I... don't know. A lot."

Erica smiled at him, motioned toward the door with the gun, and said, "Go in the kitchen."

Alex shuffled his feet, moving ahead of her and Rafi. When they reached the kitchen, Alex looked at the bundles on the table.

Erica asked him, "Whose gold is this?"

He looked from the gold to Erica, and understanding grew in his eyes. "You can't take this gold, Erica. It's the cartel's. You think Brandon and I were bad? You don't want to cross these guys. I've seen what they do; it's brutal."

"What's it for?"

"It's untraceable money, Erica. It can be melted down any way they need. We make brass fittings on the boats out of it. If it's boarded, it seems there's nothing on it. Last year we had a shipment inspected by the Coast Guard. With seven million dollars in gold right in front of them, they couldn't find a damn thing."

He looked back over the stacks of gold. "If you take that gold, they won't stop until you're dead... Let me help you. They won't care if you killed Brandon. We're all expendable to them, and he was dipping into product a *lot* lately. Let me talk to Antonio, explain what happened. If you can take down Brandon, they'll probably want to put you to work."

"Oh, good idea," Erica said, "I could end up with another Brandon, just a little higher up the food chain."

Alex had what seemed to be genuine concern in his voice when he said, "They won't kill you, Erica, not at first. I've seen girls raped by guard dogs."

"I bet you've held the leash, haven't you?" She didn't let her shock at what he'd said show. "But they won't just be looking for me. They're going to be looking for you too."

"What?" Both Rafi and Alex asked at the same time.

Erica turned to Rafi and said, "Just trust me. Get the car loaded with the gold."

Rafi nodded, picked up several bundles of gold, and walked out.

Alex continued to stare at Erica in disbelief.

"Don't look at me like that, Alex. I can't leave you here; you'd run straight to Camejo and destroy my lead. I don't have a lot of space for dead weight, and that's exactly what you'll be if you cross me. So keep yourself useful."

Rafi came back in, grabbed more bricks of gold, and went back out.

Alex looked at Erica in a strange way.

"What?"

"I never knew you had it in you."

Erica looked away from him.

Neither did I.

She wondered if what she was doing now was some kind of adrenalized version of herself, wondered how long it would last.

Until my last breath if I can help it.

Rafi picked up the last few bundles and said as he walked out, "Okay, We're ready to go."

"Get him in the car. I'll be right down." Erica returned the gun to the small of her back, ran to the bedroom, and grabbed the two duffel bags from the closet.

When she came back to the garage, she saw the BMW's rear fenders hiding the tops of the tires from the weight of the gold. Alex sat in the back seat, hands and feet still tied.

Erica got into the passenger seat. "Should we do something with Alex's car?"

"Like what?" Alex asked from the back.

Rafi told Alex to be quiet as he looked at the green Jaguar parked beside the fountain. "No. Camejo knows he came here. Moving the car offers us no benefit."

He pulled out of the garage, around the fountain, and away from the house.

CHAPTER 11

Moving the gold in the daylight would be far too risky. They waited in the Marina parking lot with the windows open; the evening breeze cut coolly through the heat radiating from the car's black interior. Erica tracked every car that came into the lot to its parking spot, watching the people as they made their way to the docks. By now, Camejo knew. He had to know. She imagined cartel men standing over Brandon's body. If they had known where Rafi kept his boat, she'd already be dead. She kept waiting for a black sedan to come rolling into the parking lot, drifting down each row of cars until it came to a stop behind the BMW, the smoked windows lowering.

"Erica," Alex said.

"Shut up, Alex."

"Hear me out."

Erica twisted the rear view mirror so she could see him sitting in the back seat; his gelled hair had collapsed, falling over his forehead.

"I don't want to hear anything right now but silence."

"I get that, I do, but I've been thinking okay? What I know can help you."

Erica stared at him in the mirror.

"I've got a contact in the Bahamas who can move the gold. Bertram Webber. He's a Swiss guy living on Abaco. He handles large black market transactions. Ten million would be nothing to him."

"I can't trust you at all Alex. Why do you think I'd listen to your advice?"

"You don't really have a choice do you? Who do you know who can move that much gold? You're not even off to a good start. I'm mean, if we're in this marina, we're going out on a small boat. That means we're going to the Bahamas right? You're sure as hell not going to Cuba."

Erica glanced at Rafi, who kept his gaze on the boats in the marina.

"Those Islands are a drug highway; they're crusted with cartel guys. Camejo himself has a villa there. You see? Your first plan is to go right into the lion's den. You have no idea what you're doing. If you go to the Bahamas and start trying to find buyers for your gold, you're going to run headlong into a nightmare. Webber's the only one there you can trust."

Erica looked at Rafi again, trying to judge her experienced smuggler's reactions to Alex's words. Rafi seemed off in another world, as if he hadn't heard Alex speak.

He knows better.

She looked into the mirror. "Or he's the one guy I can't trust. Your help is just a name? That's it?"

"He won't talk to you without me there. You can't just walk up on him. He owes me."

She sat in silence for a moment before saying, "A high-end launderer owes *you*? You expect me to believe that?"

Alex laughed. The tone of it brought her back to her living room, to Brandon slapping her as Alex stood behind him. Brandon had ripped her shirt exposing her chest, and Alex had stared at her, saying with slurred words, "Oh god, Brandon, what a rack you get to play with!"

From the back seat, Alex said, "Antonio will come after you, him and his men. It won't take him long to figure out where you went. He's connected. He'll know you didn't fly. He knows you won't go to Cuba, and you can't reach the Caymans in a small boat. He'll know you went to the Bahamas."

"I could be on the road, past Orlando by now, on my way to Georgia."

Alex had no quick answer for that, so he dodged the comment. "Look, you're playing right into his hands. You need to hit Nassau and be gone, or he'll have you."

"And what do you get out of it, aside from staying alive?"

"You're gonna cut me in for a third is why. Look, you know I'm a greedy bastard, and I know a good opportunity when I see it. I assume you and Ewan McGregor there want to split even. So that'd be something like three million for me. I'm okay with that. I could live really nicely with that."

"We'll see."

"We'll see?"

"Yes, we'll see. Now shut up."

Alex did as he was told.

...

Thirty minutes after the sun had disappeared over the rooftops on the far side of Lake Worth Lagoon, Erica got out of the car and walked around to the trunk. Rafi released the trunk and came around to meet her.

Alex stuck his head out the rear-side window and said, "Now's the time to trust me. We have to make quick trips, be gone fast. This is your chance to see that I'm on the up and up."

Rafi shrugged and said, "We do need to be quick. We both have guns." He opened the rear door and said, "If I cut you free and you cross us, I will shoot you and go. I can be gone long before the authorities arrive."

Alex nodded. "Gotcha, I'm good. You'll see. I'm already figuring out how to spend my share, dude. You good with that deal?"

"Fine with it." Rafi said, and in his eyes, Erica could see that he was not.

Erica nodded her assent.

Rafi opened the door. Alex shifted out of his seat, and Rafi untied him. Without a word, Alex gripped six bundles of gold, three duct taped handles in each hand, and lifted them out of the trunk. "Lead the way."

Rafi closed the car's windows, shut the doors, and took six more bundles from the trunk. Erica also picked up six, her shoulders immediately burning with the weight, and followed them through the parking lot with stiff steps. They clanged down the metal grating of the ramp and walked along the dock. On several boats, people sat in the warm night talking and laughing. The smell of grilling chicken drifted among the piers, making Erica's stomach grumble. A group of young men drinking beer in a larger boat turned and watched her walk by. She gave them a brief smile, hoping they would ignore her. Ahead, the dock branched off.

"Left," Rafi said to Alex.

They turned and walked past several slips.

Rafi stopped at a small boat, perhaps just over 20 feet long, which had "Storm Lord" painted in script on its transom. The boat seemed, to Erica, too tall and thin for the open ocean. It was just wide enough for a split bench at the rear, one on either side of a large outboard motor, and two swiveling seats up front. Between the seats a walkway led to a door, which Erica presumed opened into a small berth. A set of metal-rod towers held up a flat, fiberglass roof over the windshield and helm, and several antennas stuck up above the roof. The wooden fantail and fiberglass decking had some worn areas, but overall the boat seemed to be in good shape. She stepped aboard, and the boat rocked underfoot. Setting the bundles of gold on the rear deck, she flexed her fingers.

"Only two more trips," Rafi said, motioning for Alex to step off the boat ahead of him. Erica followed them, wishing they would walk faster and took measured breaths to calm herself.

At the car, Rafi and Alex took more bundles out of the trunk and walked away. She gripped three more duct tape handles in each hand and looked over the interior of Rafi's trunk. Behind the stacks of gold, she saw evidence of Rafi's life. A box with shipping information written in black Sharpie had been jammed back, out of the way. Beside it lay a gym membership card on a lanyard, a flashlight, and dress shoes.

She looked out to the marina, at all the boats sitting under the electric lamps along the docks.

If he'd give up everything so readily, he must not be that happy here.

She hefted the gold out of the trunk and, stepping around the side of the car, saw her reflection in the side-window. The weight of the gold caused her to stand with her shoulders back and braced. This pressed her breasts out, and she followed the curve down to her flat belly. Looking back up, she met her own eyes in the reflection. Her hair, tousled during the last few hours, now hung in waves over her shoulders. Maybe Rafi wasn't so unhappy here. She began to walk toward the dock with the stacks of gold, worrying what kind of expectations he might have of her. No matter how good a man he was, she couldn't fall for anyone right now, not if she tried.

As her weighted footfalls thumped along, the dock moved in subtle shifts. Her back began to complain from the weight of the gold, but she put the burn out of her mind. She walked past the berths with their perfect coils of rope, orange and yellow power chords draped over gunwales, and the boat with the young men on it. One raised his hand and waved at her, smiling. She smiled back trying to find that treacherous balance of being polite and giving off a strong leave-me-alone air.

She dropped off the gold and jogged to catch up with Rafi and Alex. When they reached the car, Rafi and Alex hefted the remaining bundles of gold and walked away. Erica pulled her bags from the trunk and set them on the asphalt. As she grabbed Rafi's bag from the back seat, she heard an engine racing along the road. She looked up to see a pale-blue Chrysler 300 squeal its tires as it pulled into the lot. The car slowed and began trolling through the parked cars. She picked up the bags and began walking as quickly as she could toward the docks. When her feet hit the ramp to the dock she heard a shout and looked over her shoulder to see two men out of the car, eyes on her.

She ran as best she could with the weight of the bag. The young men stared at her with curiosity as she ran by. When she reached Rafi's boat, she tossed the bags over the transom and jumped onboard. "We need to go *now*."

Rafi looked at her, alarmed.

"Don't ask," she said, "just go." She heard the metal ramp clang with running feet and thudding coming down the dock.

Rafi hopped off the boat, uncoiled the lines, and threw them in. As he jumped back aboard, Alex took a step forward. She drew her gun from the small of her back and leveled it on him.

"Sit."

Sitting on the bench beside the outboard, he opened his mouth to speak, but Erica held her finger over her own lips, and he remained silent.

Rafi slammed the throttles back, yanking the boat out of the slip. As the boat pulled away, the two men came around the corner, guns out but too exposed. Gripping one of the aluminum roof supports for balance against the pitching of the boat, she aimed the Sig at them and fired. One of the men took a hasty side step and fell off the side of the dock. She hadn't hit him; he had simply overreacted. The other man ducked back behind the nearest boat.

"Hold on," Rafi said and slammed the throttle forward. As the boat reared up and tore through the marina, rocking the other boats in its wake, several people peered over pitching cabins and gunwales.

Erica kept her eyes on the spot where the man had taken cover. He gave a quick look around the side of the boat, and she fired again, forcing him back. She kept the gun aimed, but knew she'd never hit him at this distance from a pitching deck.

The boat leaned as it turned out of the marina, and Rafi shoved the throttle on full-bore. The bow reared up so high Erica thought they might tip over backwards, but it settled down onto its plane as it moved out onto Lake Worth Lagoon. She saw the man, now exposed, his pistol aimed at them. If she fired on him from this angle, it would be directly into the people in the marina. Dropping her aim a few inches, she fired into the water. The man jumped into the boat and ducked away. A flash bloomed out above the gunwale, and a bullet zipped past followed by the crack of the gunshot. Another flash and the bullet whizzed past even further off target.

"This is not ideal," Rafi shouted over to Erica. "We have drawn far too much attention and have only a few minutes before county authorities and possibly the Coast Guard are on us."

Behind them, the boat's three-tailed wake streamed away into the dark lagoon where the lights from moored boats reflected out across the water in long, warping ribbons. To their left, the low mass of Peanut Island slid by, and when it blocked their view of the marina, Rafi slowed the boat to a less suspicious pace, and they made their way across the lagoon with the engine burbling.

"How do you think they found us?" She asked Rafi.

"I would guess they had been searching all marinas. It is unfortunate that we were not away before they arrived."

She nodded and looked to the east where the tall silhouettes of palm trees stood against the night sky. In among their bases, the flat lines of roofs framed lighted windows. A break in the long horizon of trees and houses left a sheet of water out to the open ocean, dark and unknown. Two jagged rock jetties stood on either side like doors to a cage, standing open but able to snap shut at any moment. She felt herself leaning forward, her stomach fluttering and electricity tingling at her shoulders and neck. She had no idea what came next: where they would sleep tonight, what she could possibly do with five hundred pounds of gold, or how to safely separate herself from Alex.

As they passed another boat coming in from the ocean, Erica looked behind her. Off in the distance she saw the rising girders of cranes, their spotlights bright against the dark sky.

One crane held a rust-red shipping container suspended from its cables. To the north, she saw strobing blue lights, a Sheriff's boat racing down the lagoon toward them. If the boat turned toward them, it was over. She wasn't going to get in a shootout with the police. As the lights came down the bay, she thought over the charges: murder, kidnapping, grand theft. The lights approached the point in the bay where they would either turn to the marina or follow their small boat. The lights turned toward the marina.

As the flashing lights disappeared behind Peanut Island, she felt tremendous relief and turned to find that they had entered the inlet, the stacked-boulder jetties on either side. She looked again at the open ocean out ahead and felt in its breadth the great possibility of freedom and the trepidation of the unknown. It felt wonderful.

The oval monolith of the Singer Island pump house passed by, and surf broke in pale ribbons at the end of the jetty. Then the jetties no longer penned them in. As the boat broke out onto the open ocean, the warm night air went cooler, and the bow began to loft and sink with the swell. The darkness of the wide-open world surrounded Erica, and gooseflesh rose across her arms.

"Excellent," Rafi said, breaking her out of her thoughts. "Now we are away. The weather report is good; I have spent many days out in heavier seas than we will see tonight."

"Do we have enough gas?" Erica asked. She felt so much relief at being away, she almost didn't care about the answer.

"I always keep full tanks. In my line of work, you never know when you might have to make a quick pickup or delivery."

Erica turned her seat and looked over Alex's head to the diminishing glow of Palm Beach. Its blade of light lay framed between the dark sky and the ocean streaming away behind them. Her eyes dropped to Alex, who looked off to the south.

Now what am I supposed to do with you?

CHAPTER 12

The muted glow from the instruments illuminated Rafi's face and shoulders in a ghostly pallor as the wind tussled his hair. Beyond him the ocean extended in a great darkness. Here and there the glow of ships hung in the blackness. Suspended above those distant ships, the light of the half-waxed moon filtered in a broad incandescence through a veil of thin clouds.

Alex sat in the back looking out on the ocean as if he were on a cruise. Looking at him made her think through how many rounds she had left in the gun. She had fired once past Alex's head and three times at the men. There should be two left.

...but only if Brandon had a full magazine.

Reaching behind herself, she released the magazine, and—keeping it behind her back—drew it out. She felt a spring-loaded round at the end of the magazine and slid the magazine back into the gun.

One there and the other chambered. Two rounds.

Alex had claimed he would help her, but she knew better. If she kept him, he'd burn her down at the first opportunity. If she let him go, he'd have the cartel on them. Having no idea what to do with him, she felt like a kid playing behind the shed, making up silly plans. She'd have to figure out a way to control him or cut him loose but didn't believe for a moment that there was a way to control him.

"Alex," she yelled over the motor.

He turned to look at her, his eyes narrowing for just a moment before he smiled.

If I shoot him in the chest from here, will the bullet knock him into the ocean? If not, I could kick him overboard.

Alex shouted over the motor, "You and I are going to be good friends, Erica. You'll see."

Erica shouted back, "You might profit from this, Alex, but you and I will never be friends. Got it?"

She felt the gun pressing into the small of her back. Live or die. Her heart accelerated, and she shifted in her seat. Killing him would be cold-blooded murder. Brandon had been attacking her. His death was self-defense.

"I'm in it for the money then," Alex said, the smile she hated so much broadening on his smug face.

That smile made her remember him again, standing close behind Brandon as Brandon held her up against the wall. His eyes had been vague with the cocaine and his smile arrogant, so full of himself, a god among mortals.

"Let me have a piece of that," he had said.

Brandon had turned on him then, shifting lightning quick from the abuser to the defender. But she knew even then that he wasn't defending her, not the person up against the wall with her eye swelling and ribs hurting. He was protecting his possession. She was no better than a bowl of food with two dogs snapping over it.

Maybe Alex thinks that it's his turn now...

With that thought she had a revelation into Alex's mind.

When he sells us out, he's going to kill Rafi and ask for me as his reward.

She saw herself tied to Alex's pool table and shook the image out of her head.

"What's going on Erica?" Alex asked.

"I'm sorry, I was just remembering you asking Brandon if you could rape me."

Alex gave her a salesman's smile and said, "Erica, why dig into the past? That was then. We're partners now, not—"

"I'm not just a toy anymore?"

Alex fell silent.

"Well? Admit it; you'd have done some pretty horrible things if he had let you."

"Erica, let's not get into it. I—"

Erica pulled the gun from behind her and held it in her lap.

"Admit it."

"Erica, what're you doing?"

"I just want you to admit that you would have beaten me and raped me in one of your coke binges if Brandon had let you."

He held up his hands as if he had some control of the situation and said in a relaxed tone, "Erica, we need to be friends. We have to put these things behind us."

"I will, just as soon as you admit it."

"Fine," he said, anger now shading his words. "I would have, okay? I mean look at you. Brandon couldn't handle a woman as willful as you. You drove him crazy. That's why he did what he did. When you pulled back from him, he had to go out to the clubs to get it out of his system."

"I pulled back from him because he hit me."

"You just didn't understand him. Where he and I come from, women defer to the men. You didn't. You gave him lip and he had to..." He fell silent again, perhaps realizing that he was about to kill himself with his own words.

"He had to do what, Alex?"

"I- I don't want to talk about it, Erica. I—"

"I want to talk about it."

"Erica, you need me. We have to work together. You killed my partner, and I'm here working with you aren't I? You have to meet me halfway."

"So you'd just forgive your friend's killer that easily? Just switch sides?" She turned to Rafi. "What do you think? Should we trust him?"

Rafi gave her a measured look before saying, "We do not need him. He is too big a risk, and we cannot have that. We had two choices on the mainland, take him with us or kill him. Now," he shut off the throttle and, as the boat slowed, faced Alex, "we have only one choice."

Alex gave him a nervous laugh, "What? You can't just kill me. I haven't done anything."

In a matter of fact tone, Rafi said, "I have learned to judge people on two things, what they have done and what I suspect they will do. What they have done almost always tells me accurately what they will do."

"I've told you man, I'm on your side now. I want the money too."

"My friend, people are terribly consistent," Rafi said as he drew a Berretta from the cargo pocket on his thigh, "and from what I am hearing, you have led a consistently untrustworthy life."

"No dude," Alex held up his hands in supplication, "I'm a loyal guy. Maybe not the way society has always wanted me to be, but I'm loyal all the way."

"You were loyal to the man we killed, yes?"

Alex's eyes went hard, and he leaned forward. "So?"

"Yet you so easily side with his killer… I find that no better than a dog."

Alex's face grew dark. With a glance at the gun in Erica's lap, he launched at her, slapping the Sig from her hand. The gun flipped out into the night with a splash as Alex turned and crashed into Rafi. Rafi had his gun up, but Alex bear-hugged him. The gun, now extending under Alex's arm, fired just a few degrees away from Erica's head. The two men fell to the deck; Alex gripped Rafi's wrist, forcing Rafi's arm to bend. As the barrel of the gun came to bear on Rafi's chin, Erica grabbed it, threading her index finger behind the trigger. Alex gripped the trigger, crushing the second joint of her finger. Pain overwhelmed her, but the gun did not fire. As Erica's mind raced for what to do next, Alex continued crushing down on the trigger. Rafi, growling like a bear, tugged at his own wrist. Erica punched Alex in the side of the face, and Alex turned and looked at her, his eyes glittering in the darkness.

"Erica, I'm gonna enjoy the next few minutes more than I can tell you."

She dug her thumbnail into the soft, wet mass of his left eye.

Alex screamed and shoved away from Rafi, standing half-crouched as a guttural sound, a choked mixture of anger and pain, came up from his chest. He held one hand over his left eye; the other eye glared at her. Realizing she had come up with the Berretta, she leveled the gun at him.

"Erica, I'm gonna tear—"

She fired into his chest.

The recoil of the gun shocked into her hand as the muzzle flash lit Alex's torso and face. Spent gunpowder swirled around Alex as he looked down at the small, black hole that had appeared just under his right shoulder.

He touched the hole. "You fucking shot me."

Reaching for the gun, he caught her wrist and pulled. She didn't fight him, but shoved the gun forward into his chest and pulled the trigger again. The sound of the shot came muffled by fabric and skin, and the muzzle flash illuminated the space between them, its heat flaring around her hand and forearm. Over his shoulder she saw a wet darkness spray away. He bear-hugged her, and she felt him lifting her, shoving her back toward the gunwale.

He said into her ear, "I'm going to take you with me, bitch."

She pulled the trigger again, and the gunshot seemed louder, more decisive, and the anger in Alex's face melted away as he fell forward. Erica's legs hit the gunwale, and she tipped backwards, Alex's weight shoving her out over the open water. She braced for the crash of water around her, but a crushing grip caught her by the upper arm. Spinning sideways, her right arm dunked in the water, pistol and all.

That's the only gun we have.

She focused on holding the gun as Rafi yanked her back. He set her on her feet and, with his foot, shoved Alex onto his back and crouched over him.

Alex's eyes roamed the stars for a moment before settling on Erica. Blood pooled in a dark swath on the deck beneath him.

He opened his mouth for a moment, closed it, and said, his voice ragged and deep, "I'm dead aren't I?"

"Yes," Rafi said.

Alex kept his eyes on Erica. "Guess I was wrong about you."

Erica remained standing over him. "How?"

Alex coughed with a wet sound and smiled. "I thought you were just one of them—not smart enough to make it on your own and greedy enough to let guys like me, guys like Brandon, do whatever we wanted to you. You're like dogs, willing to take a beating as long as you get a bone now and again."

"Not me."

"You were." A faint smile drew across his lips. "Your daddy probably raped you too, so it was just about the same with Brandon except at least it wasn't your own daddy, and at least you were in a nice bed, not the floor of a swamp shack."

"My dad was a drunk, but he never touched me, never so much as raised a hand against me. Now shut up."

"Or what," Alex asked, "you'll kill me sooner? I'm dying sweetness, and you can take full credit for it."

"What do you want to do with him?" Rafi asked.

"Get him off the boat."

"I'm not dead yet," Alex said, reaching out and gripping Erica's pant leg. "Just let me die. I don't want to drown." His eyes had sincere fear in them. "Not that way Erica, please."

She kicked his hand aside.

"Don't put me overboard, Erica. Please."

Erica looked up to Rafi. "How long until he dies?"

"Only a moment or two," Rafi said with a tone of separation, as if he were looking at a flattened carcass on the side of the road.

Erica said to Alex, "Get to dying then, if you don't want to have your last memory be drowning."

"Thanks Erica, I was scared as hell just then. Thank you." His face had lost its arrogance, becoming almost boy-like. In that moment she understood Alex had no capacity to be anything other than what he had been. He had either been raised by someone like himself, or his brain was broken. He'd had neither the strength nor the intelligence to be anything more than a druggie and an abuser.

"I'm still scared, though," Alex said, his eyes staring up at the stars as the boat rocked with the swell of the ocean.

"Of what?"

"Hell."

"I cannot believe," Rafi said, "that someone like you believes in Hell."

"No...," Alex said, his voice growing quieter with each word, "it's there... Oh God..." His eyes went wider as tears welled in them and spilled down his temples. "It's there." His chest began to tremble, and he kicked one heel against the decking. "Oh shit, it's right there." He took one last heaving breath, the holes in his chest sucking with air, and his jaw went slack. His eyes, still aimed up at the stars, seeing nothing for him.

Erica stared at the body.

Two men dead by my hand in one day—

Rafi interrupted her thoughts, saying, "Let's get him off the boat and get going. We need to flush this blood off the deck as well." Rafi walked around Alex's head and squatted, lifting the body by the armpits. He rested its shoulders on the bench. Straddling the transom with his butt against the outboard, he hauled the body up onto the ledge. Holding it there, he motioned for Erica to bring the legs up. She lifted on the legs, but only succeeded in getting the legs themselves off the ground. The body, still warm with life, had gone completely slack and folded like a wet sack. She got the legs up on the gunwale and Rafi bent over, gripped Alex's belt, and pulled back. The body rolled up and balanced on the rear corner of the boat. Erica shoved at the torso, and the body splashed into the water, settling face-down, arms and legs spread out.

"Dammit," Rafi said as he reached out for the body, just managing to catch the shirt.

"What?" Erica asked as Rafi stood up holding Alex's wallet.

"If he's found, there is no reason to make identifying the body that easy." Pocketing the wallet, he opened a storage compartment, took out a bucket, and dipped it over the side. Drawing it up out of the ocean, he poured the water over the gunwale, washing away the dark swath of blood. He did this a few more times until the blood had swirled away in the scupper drains.

Setting the bucket aside, Rafi sat at the helm and began shuffling through the contents of Alex's wallet. The bank of clouds had broken up, and the moon hung in the breadth of the Milky Way. Erica watched the long, dark shape of Alex's body floating away from them as the breeze coming in across the deck flowed over her shoulders and the back of her neck, pulling her hair to the side. In that moment, she felt something let go. For the next few hours no one would be able to find her, nothing was at risk. It was just her and Rafi. She sat down in the seat beside him, already feeling the moment passing too quickly.

Rafi held something up from the wallet. "This will come in handy."

He handed her a stack of bills. She counted through twenty-seven new hundreds.

Rafi fanned out the cards from the wallet and handed something to Erica.

She took it and felt the rubbery, circular ridge of a condom in its package. Her hand reflexed, dropping it. "Gross, Rafi."

"Sorry," he said with a laugh, and she found herself laughing with him. After the intensity of the last few hours, the glow of humor felt terribly strange.

Rafi started the engine and slid the throttle forward. The boat's nose lifted up, and it planed over the swell.

Sitting beside Rafi, she looked out the back of the boat across the ocean and thought of Alex floating face-down, looking at the depths. She wished she had been able to weight the body down, make it disappear.

Rafi tossed one of the cards from Alex's wallet overboard. He did this at intervals until all the cards were gone. "We are officially done with him."

"Do you think there was any merit to Alex's contact?" she asked him.

"It does not matter. I have an old friend who now makes his home on New Providence, a Ukrainian smuggler named Abram Malevich. He will help us with the gold."

"You trust him?"

"Implicitly."

As Rafi fell into silence, Erica felt a doubt so subtle she wondered if Rafi knew it existed.

After a moment, he said, "My father's death left me without purpose. I became nothing better than a common thief. Abram found me, rather caught me stealing from him, and took me under his wing, taught me his trade. He is a second father to me."

Erica nodded in the darkness. "My troubles seem like nothing to the life you've led."

Rafi gave a small laugh and said, "I play it up well. It was nothing really—some scuffles in the street and a few hungry days. It has all turned out well enough."

Feeling Rafi's infectious resilience, she looked out over the moon's cross-hatched glitter on the water, out to where the horizon lay in darkness.

Rafi touched the GPS, changing the display, and pointed to a ragged set of three islands. "We're making good progress, those are the Bimini Islands."

They fell into silence for a moment.

Erica said, "Thank you, Rafi."

Rafi shrugged. "I was bored with antiquities anyway."

"It's half yours you know."

Rafi laughed and said, "Yes, thank you, but I don't want to split it. I want to keep it together as long as we can."

His calm eyes drew her away from the horrors of the last several hours, and she felt whole and safe. Taking hold of the sides of his face, she kissed him and then held him away from her. "I'm pretty damaged goods, Rafi. I'm probably some kind of psycho at this point."

Taking her hands from his face, he kissed the back of each, held them for a moment, and released them. He leaned back in his seat, propped his feet on the rail in front of him, and said, "At this point all I want is your trust and friendship. I know from experience what will grow from that."

"And what's that?" she said, feeling suddenly defensive.

"Whatever should grow from it; whatever is right between us."

She felt a thrilling heat in her chest and the desire to kiss him again, but she let it pass.

He's right... there's time.

She looked out toward the darkness ahead of them.

"I almost forgot," she said in a bright tone. Reaching into the front pocket of her jeans, she pulled out the Hublot watch and handed it to Rafi.

He took the watch and looked over its gold and matte black face.

"I found it in the safe. I brought it for you."

"This was Brandon's?"

"Yes, why?"

"I should throw it overboard. I don't want anything of his."

"The gold was his; we took that. I was his."

He looked away from her, and she felt as though she had touched too deeply on something. She wished she could take the last comment back.

Just loud enough for her to hear over the engines and the rush of the wind, he said, "You were never his."

CHAPTER 13

With the darkness and the drone of the wind and engines, Erica had drifted off into her life, thinking through her childhood in the Everglades, her time in Riviera Beach, and her marriage to Brandon. She looked down at her hands.

Two men dead...

Rafi pointed at the GPS screen and said, "We are between Joulters Cays north of Andros and the Berry Islands." He looked out into the darkness ahead and, pointing off to the left, said, "You see those lights?"

Erica looked into the night, across the moonlit glimmer rushing by, and saw a short, dark rise along the horizon speckled with bright lights.

"That's Chub Cay," Rafi said. "We're only about thirty or forty miles from Nassau now."

Erica nodded.

Thirty or forty miles...

A few hours ago, the Bahamas had felt infinitely far away. She looked behind them to the dark expanse of the Atlantic and wished they could go back there, exist in that midnight void and live in peace. But it couldn't be. Time had rushed away from her.

What the hell am I going to do with 500 pounds of gold and a drug cartel hunting me?

She felt the world pressing in on her, decisions to make, people to avoid. Sitting in the darkness, she thought of the gold—saw herself walking into a bank with the heavy bundles. It wouldn't do. Trying to imagine Rafi's Abram Malevich— what he looked like, where he lived—she pictured a great pillared estate with an ocean view. She saw a man, his body narrowed by Eastern Block cigarettes and his nose rosy with broken capillaries from years of vodka, sitting on the balcony of a colonial plantation. The vision unsettled her.

First, she had to store the gold, hide it away, but how to hide that much? She thought about a safe deposit box or an airport locker. How could she possibly get the gold to the lockers without being noticed? Neither would work. They couldn't go trucking the bundles around Nassau. She needed someplace remote and pictured herself digging in the sand of a deserted beach, throwing the bundles into the hole. That felt too risky. Someone could see them digging or stumble on it. She looked out across the darkness of the water again. Standing, she leaned over the gunwale, looking down at the blackness rushing beside the boat.

"Rafi," she said, "I have an idea where we can put the gold."

...

She told Rafi to go past Nassau, to find someplace shallow along a remote island. Worrying that she was about to make a terrible mistake, she reminded herself that she had to be brave, would have to take some calculated risks.

The lights of Nassau appeared, slid by starboard in the distance, and disappeared again. Rafi continued on for another twenty minutes as low, dark islands passed nearby. Finally, he pulled back on the throttle, and the boat settled down into the water. The drifting of the boat on the calm ocean and the sudden silence brought Erica into a strange state. The doubt folded away from her as she stood and looked up at the stars. She felt that sense of excitement and freedom again and decided to trust in it.

This must be right.

"What is your plan?" Rafi asked.

She looked down into the water, dark and unknown beneath the boat, and almost felt that she could see vague shapes. "How deep is the water here?"

"Less than forty feet."

"How many people come out here?"

"The commercial dive boats don't come this far from Nassau. Too much time and fuel. The area is not very interesting for more advanced divers, they go further south."

"We'll leave the gold here then, throw it over the side and note the GPS coordinates. We can come back for it when we know what we're going to do with it. Are there patches of plants?" She said, peering into the darkness.

"Yes. Coral outcroppings."

"That's where we'll drop it, someplace that will obscure it."

Rafi nodded at this. The boat had been drifting with the current, and Rafi fired the motor again, turning into the current. He pressed a switch marked "windlass" and Erica saw the anchor, mounted to the bow of the boat, tip away and disappear with a splash. Rafi held the switch, and the electric windlass hummed. He released the switch and backed off the throttle. The boat began to drift, and Erica felt the nose pull down as the anchor set into the sand.

Rafi shut the motor off and watched the shore for some time, finally saying, "There. We appear to be set. The current is not strong here and should hold the rest of the night. He flicked a switch, illuminating a white light mounted on a pole at the back of the boat.

"Won't that attract attention?"

Rafi smiled. "Attention is what we want. What we do not want is to be hit by another boat in the night."

Erica nodded and looked out at the trees on the low island beside them, the white line of the beach only a suggestion in the moonlight. The wind picked up, coursing over the boat from nose to tail.

Rafi turned off the key, and the instruments went black.

He touched the GPS. "I will set this to alarm if we move more than 200 feet. Then, if the anchor loses its footing, we will be warned before we drift too far."

Erica felt a paralyzing tiredness draw over her. She leaned forward, elbows on knees, and her eyes fluttered.

"You need rest," Rafi said, standing and pulling her to her feet. She leaned on him and felt his hands on her back, and she set her chin on his shoulder, the muscle there shifting as he supported her. She felt strangely dizzy, and darkness descended on her as she fell asleep.

•••

When she woke, the faint light of dawn glowed around the half-open hatch over the bed. Cool night air, purified by the open ocean, streamed through the hatch. Rafi had left the gangway to the helm partially open, letting the air flow through the berth. She felt a blanket over her and something warm in her hand. Rafi's hand. He lay on his side next to her, drawing deep breaths. The innocence of their position brought a smile to her face, and she drifted back to sleep.

...

In the darkness of sleep she found herself in a heated space. She could see nothing. Hollow drips of water echoed around her. The dank musk of the cave filled her nose and mouth. Warm water lapped around her ankles.

It's the cave from the pantry... another dream.

She heard, at a distance as if from down a passageway, a wet slap on rock. A dragging sound followed—cloth and skin on stone. A low, primal growl resounded through the cave followed by slap... drag.

She stepped backward, her foot sloshing in the water, and heard it again, dragging toward her.

A deep and rotten voice said, "Erica."

She continued backing away from the sound. The water swished around her ankles.

The growl came again and the now louder slap... drag. She felt her chest tightening, banding her breath into short gasps. Her heel cracked painfully into a stone and she fell backward, hitting a rock wall.

The dragging became louder still, as if what made it had come out of the passageway. The scent of rot filtered into her awareness. She turned and felt for an escape across the surface of the rough stone behind her. A splash echoed through the chamber as the thing entered the pool. She moved quickly in the darkness and caught her big toe on a rock; the nail tore away from the bed with searing pain.

Ignoring it, she moved a few more feet along the wall, which began to curve back toward the thing in the water. She crouched down, silent, listening. The splashing echoed through the cave and now closer... splash... drag. She heard a low grunting and the rasping of breath. Reaching into the pool, she felt along the bottom, searching for a loose rock, but found only solid stone. She could feel the will of the thing, its desire so strong it extended out into something palpable, horrendous and gluttonous—a soul eater. The splash and swirl of water ended just a few feet from her, followed by a low growl.

She remained perfectly still and listened into the void: the water dripping, the soft swish of wavelets cresting at the edges of the pool, the ragged breathing. The stench of rot had become so strong that it filled her mouth, making her stomach quaver, and she felt bile rising in her throat.

The water beside her exploded, and the thing hit her, gripping her knee and thigh with cold fingers, knocking her backwards. She shoved her hands into the darkness and connected with a head and shoulders. The hair across the head hung off in tendrils, long and sparse, and as she shoved on the crown of the skull, the skin shed away, scalping the beast. Her hand slipped and she fumbled to find the head again. Teeth clamped into the meat between her thumb and index finger. She screamed, and a brilliant light filled the cave, burning away the darkness, the beast, the water, the stone itself.

She sat up, her heart racing, not quite able to fix where she was. A hot breeze drifted across her and sunlight blazed off the edges of a hatch above. In front of her a partially open gangway. She remembered the boat... remembered Rafi, and she drew a deep breath and let it out in one gust. Pushing the blanket off of her, she wiped sweat from her forehead and shifted off of the berth. She shoved the gangway open and found Rafi sitting in the back of the boat, looking over the edge. He turned and motioned for her to come over. When she sat beside him, she wrapped her arms around his waist and held him.

"You're shaking," Rafi said. "Are you all right?"

"I will be," Erica said, her face turned into his neck. "I think my subconscious is trying to work out what I've been through."

Rafi held her for a moment, and when her heart rate had dropped somewhat, he drew her to the side of the boat and said, "Look at this."

She leaned over the gunwale and saw the clarity of the blue water over dark patches of coral below.

"Can you see it?" Rafi asked.

She saw only dark and light masses bending under the surface, the glitter of the sunlight half blinding her.

"No." She looked back to Rafi.

"I threw two of the bundles over."

Erica looked back over the side.

"I wanted to test to see how visible they were." He handed her a diving mask. "Put that on and look. They are very difficult to see, even with the mask. The gray of the duct tape camouflages perfectly in the coral. Unless someone dives right here and knows to look for it, we should have no problems."

Erica looked at the mask and asked, "Are you sure no one will dive here?"

"Very few do. We're over halfway to Eleuthera along a strip of unpopulated cays. We shouldn't wait too long though. We don't want to tempt fate."

"It's better than walking into Nassau with 500 pounds of gold."

"Far better."

Erica pulled her hair back and felt the last day's travel in the knots in it. She didn't want to think how long it would take to brush out. She pulled the mask over her head and leaned over the side. Her hair spilled forward, and she sat back up.

"Let me help you," Rafi said as he reached for her hair.

She flinched away from him, grabbing his wrist with both of her hands.

Rafi put his hand down and said, "I'm sorry Erica, I didn't mean to startle you."

"I'm sorry. I really want to trust you, Rafi. It's just going to take me time. Can you live with that?"

"I'm glad to live with that."

"Okay," she said holding her hair in a pony tail behind her head, "you were going to help me?"

Rafi reached more slowly this time and held her hair. Erica leaned over the side and submerged her face. Scanning the bottom, she saw a tangle of coral—soft, plate, and fan—mixed in with sea whips and anemones. Brilliant fish flitted in and around the coral. She became aware of her position with her head underwater and Rafi gripping her pony tail. He had the gold and could easily overpower her. All he had to do was keep her down. She pushed back, and he hugged her lower ribs, helping her up.

He said, "You see, the duct tape is invisible. We'll need to use metal detectors to find them all."

Erica opened the hatch beside her and pulled out a duct-taped stack of gold. She hefted the weight of it in her hand. "Before we chuck this over the side, are we going to be able to get it back?"

"We can rent dive equipment and get it easily."

Erica tossed the bundle over the side and felt good about it; it was the right thing to do.

"Spread it around," Rafi said. "Keep it in a loose circle so it doesn't pile up."

When they had thrown all but four of the bundles overboard, Erica asked, "How much should we keep?"

"Each stack is five kilos. We won't need more than two."

She nodded and tossed two more bundles over the side.

Rafi held out a scrap of paper, which read, 24-12-42.42/76-1-59.50.

"That's latitude and longitude for the gold."

"We should be careful no one finds this."

"It's okay. I subtracted one digit from the degrees, added one to the minutes, swapped the seconds, and transposed each. Someone finds this, I have no idea where they'll be, but it won't be this spot. Somewhere southeast of here."

"I'll need a guide just to figure that out."

"Make sure you have it down. If something happens to me, you'll need to know how to decode it." He moved to the helm and fired the engine. "Now we need to go to town and find Abram."

CHAPTER 14

After unseating the anchor and securing it, Rafi shoved the throttle forward. The boat leaned back and settled onto its plane; behind them, the engines chopped the jeweled water into a torrent. The cool morning air streamed around the windscreen, and coral rolled beneath them in the shallow, pale-green water, darkening it as if the shadows of clouds were passing by. Yet, the sky lay in a smooth sheet of blue with only a few, high wisps to the south.

The Atlantis Resort came into view in the distance with its bold, sandstone-tinted towers standing out against the horizon. Within the hour, Rafi turned the boat to the south and came around a long, low island. Behind the island lay the house-ridden coast of New Providence. The ocean swell had risen with the wind, but the boat cut through the low chop with ease as they entered the channel between New Providence and Paradise Islands. Boats motored through the channel, bobbing on the swells, their rigging and antennas leaning back and forth.

Slowing the boat, Rafi cut around a catamaran, heavy with tourists and blaring music. At the far end of the channel, three monstrous cruise ships lay docked. Erica could see people all along the docks surrounding the ships. The congestion of the area made her nervous.

Rafi had a look on his face as if he hadn't a care in the world and seemed to know exactly what he was doing. He steered the boat under a long, curve-backed bridge, and as they came under its shadow, Erica looked up at the rough, concrete underbelly, rumbling with traffic. They broke out into the sun again and passed under a second bridge. Rafi turned the boat into a marina and into a slip. A young African man with a stern face walked up on bare feet and gripped the side of the boat. He took lines from Rafi and secured them to the cleats.

Rafi handed him a tip, and the young man walked away.

Reaching under the gunwale, Rafi opened a compartment and took out a small nylon satchel. From it he secured his passport. Erica retrieved hers from one of her bags.

"I am hoping no one has reported Brandon as dead. These people will handle their business themselves. If so, the customs officials here will not be too strict with us," he said.

"Them handling business themselves doesn't quite feel like a benefit."

"For now, it might be," he said as he pulled out a bundle of gold. Cutting it open, he pocketed one plate and placed the half-open bundle back in storage. He hopped off the boat and held out his hand to Erica. Taking his hand, she stood on the gunwale, hopped down onto the dock, and poked him in the ribs as she walked past him, causing him to jump.

After several paces, she realized he was not following and turned to find him standing beside the boat staring at her. She held out her hand. "Are you going to walk with me?"

Rafi jogged to catch up with her, took hold of her hand, and they walked together down the dock.

...

They walked among the crowds from the cruise ships, the narrow sidewalk changing width at every building. Sand mixed with scraps of trash filled the gutter seams and drifted up against the buildings' footings. The buildings sat close together, squared structures painted in various shades of light pastels. Unlike the sidewalks, they had been well kept with fresh, white-painted shutters and clean windows.

Rafi turned down a side street and crossed two busy intersections, the heat of the day simmering off the asphalt. After a few more blocks, they had entered a quieter part of the city. The houses, still close, had more trees here, growing up to shade the second-story windows. The sidewalk led up a steep hill and ended at a broad, slab-stone staircase. They walked up the staircase and entered a peaceful block of houses. Halfway down, Rafi stopped at a dark-green, two-story house. Its upper decking sagged on old timbers. Tree branches grew into the second-story balcony, and a birdcage hung from one of those branches; finches twittered in the cooler air.

"This is Abram's house."

Erica nodded. "Okay... let's see if he can help us."

A low, stone wall bordered the property. Rafi pushed open the gate and walked the few paces to the porch. The paint on the house had become shredded from the elements, exposing white primer and gray wood; however, bright flowers and trimmed plants grew in the pots on the porch. Rafi walked up the wooden steps, the edges of which had splayed with rot. The boards creaked under Erica's feet as she followed him up.

There in the shade, Erica caught the mingled scent of brewed tea and baking bread. Rafi rapped his knuckles on the door.

Erica had just looked at the window beside the door, when the curtain there drew aside, and an old face appeared. The curtain dropped before she could fully register the face. After a moment the door opened exposing an old man, hunched over and thin. He had the remnants of curly gray hair on his head, and his pale face, mottled by many years in the sun, was framed by thick ears, blooming with tufts of white hair. His eyes, the last evidence of the handsome man he had been long ago, lay narrow and even across his face like a horizon, and his amber irises glowed like two setting suns.

The old man blinked into the sunlight, first looking at Rafi and then Erica. His eyes tracked down her body and back up, pausing on her hips, then up a bit, and finally back to her face. She felt as if she had just been graded by a butcher.

The sudden impulse to leave caused her to take hold of Rafi's arm, but Rafi said, "Abram, how are you?"

The old man's scowl stretched out into a grandfather's smile.

In a concrete, Eastern-Bloc accent, Abram said, "How can it be?" and reached out, taking both of Rafi's hands, "You live only across the water and you finally come to visit me after how long?"

"It has only been a year since we last saw each other."

Abram stepped back with stiff hips and waved them in through the doorway. "Get in, get in," he said. "Do you know how long a year is at my age? I could have been dead for all you knew."

Rafi smiled at this and placed his hand on the old man's back. "Abram, this is Erica."

Abram took her hand in his, light and bony like a bird's talon, and kissed the back of it with a dry peck. He let her hand go, timing the moment perfectly; the act of a gentleman.

"Come... sit." He motioned them toward a green velvet couch in his small living room. "Sit." He left the room through a small passageway and turned into the kitchen, its cupboard and counter bright with sunlight.

She couldn't quite place his broad, machined accent, so she leaned in on Rafi and whispered, "Where's he from?"

"The Ukraine originally, but learned English in Israel. You won't find another man like Abram."

"I've just finished brewing some tea," Abram said from the other room, "and how wonderful that you should come when I have made this kind."

He walked into the room carrying a tray with three small glasses filled with a dark, steaming tea.

Rafi laughed and said, "Wonderful," as he took a glass off the tray before Abram had set it down.

Abram lowered his old frame into a cushioned chair on the other side of the coffee table and smiled at Rafi.

"Drink my friend, drink. Guests bring good luck with them." He picked up the tea and held it up, looking at the light passing through the tea. "To home."

Rafi held up the glass between his index finger and thumb. "To home." Sipping at the tea, he closed his eyes and smiled.

"Good?" Abram asked.

"Like home, yes." Rafi said.

"Good... but enough of this," Abram said, clapping his hands on his knees. "Tell me, how you have come to be here with such a beautiful woman? An elopement perhaps? Running from a father?" He gave Erica a smile, which was so different from his first cold stare, that Erica felt guilty for having judged him badly.

"We are running," Rafi said, "but not away from a father. If only it were that simple. We need your help Abram, and as I know you are a business man first, I will tell you that there is a profit to be made."

Abram shook his head and held up a hand. "If you need my help, you have it." Then he laughed, saying, "If I can make a profit in the bargain, all the better." Looking to Erica, he said, "He knows me well, eh?" and then to Rafi, "It has been a long time since I found you on the streets of Arbil... lifetimes it seems. You've lived too much for a young man. God rest your parents."

At this Rafi went quiet for a moment, looking at the cup of tea in his hands. "Thank you for helping me, Abram... for everything." He looked up. "As my mother's people say, two thirds of a boy is his uncle. You have been like an uncle to me but had no obligation to do so."

"Put it aside. You were a good boy; I saw that in you right away." The old man's eyes reddened, and he shifted the conversation, "I knew that you'd be successful and you have been. You've made me a great deal of money. Now tell me... how is it that I can help?"

As Rafi related the story to Abram, the old man's face darkened. Something in that darkness made Erica uncomfortable. Even when Rafi took the gold from his pocket, Abram's expression did not lighten. He motioned for Rafi to put the gold away and sat with his head down, his fingers interlaced, and his thumbs tapping together.

After a moment, he nodded and said, "It is good you have come to me. I do not want to worry you, but I have already heard talk of this. This morning, down at the port, some friends told me that Camejo has asked his contacts to keep an eye out for a beautiful woman. But not you," he said to Rafi. He pointed at Erica. "She was to be travelling alone, or perhaps with an American, a cartel member who they thought might have gone against them. No one knew why she was sought. This man you left at sea must be the one they think might be with you."

She nodded, saying, "I would guess so."

Abram measured Erica for a moment before saying, "It is good he is gone, and the same for your husband. These are evil men. But to take the gold, that may have been a... mistake."

Erica asked, "Do you think they would have let me go if I only killed Brandon?"

"There is pride," Abram said, as he held up his narrow hands in supplication to the truth, "and then there is profit. Both can get you killed." He gave her a thoughtful look and levered himself forward, reached over the table, and patted her knee. "Do not worry, my beautiful girl, we will sort this out." He looked to Rafi. "The rest of the gold?"

"We have it in a safe place for now."

"Where is that?"

"Near the docks."

The slight deceit startled Erica. She wondered if Rafi did not fully trust the old man, or if he would have obscured the location of the gold to anyone, no matter how close.

Abram searched Rafi's face, then Erica's, and smiled. "You don't want to say?" He held up a finger. "Good... caution is the right thing."

"It's not that I don't trust you Abram—"

"Don't," Abram said with a somewhat harsh tone, "give it another thought." He leaned back into the chair. "I can help you, but we must look to Europe, to those who have no dealings with the South American cartels. I know a man who will serve well."

Rafi nodded. "I felt sure you would be able to help."

Abram pushed himself up out of the chair, saying, "I have work to do then."

Rafi stood as well, and Erica followed his lead.

Abram walked over to a side table and wrote something on a notepad. He tore off the square of paper and handed it to Rafi. "This is a name of a friend. He runs a motel down by the harbor. Go to him and tell him I sent you, tell him that you need a room. You will not need to pay."

"I can pay for the room, Abram. I have cash."

"Keep it," Abram said, dismissing Rafi's comment with a wave of his hand. "I pay with debts, and he owes me. It will cost me nothing. You may need your cash later."

"Thank you," Erica said, taking the old man's hand again.

He patted the back of her hand. "It is my pleasure. Now go and have a day. I will find you tomorrow morning with what news I can offer." He pointed at Rafi, "But stay on his arm and tell people nothing... No one is looking for a couple in love."

"We're not in love," she said.

Abram gave her a wise smile as he touched her shoulder. "You are an honest woman and so have had very little practice deceiving."

...

As they walked back down the staircase toward downtown Nassau, Erica said, "I don't want to stay in town. It's too exposed."

The air among the buildings and sun-heated streets had grown stagnant, and Rafi said, "It will be far too hot today to stay on the boat. We will eat and then find a quiet place to spend the day."

As they walked down the hill, the wind came in from the ocean, pushing between the buildings and rustling the palms against stone church walls. The breeze cooled Erica's neck and arms. They walked down the narrow, weedy sidewalks with traffic rumbling by, past the Parliament building with its statue of Christopher Columbus, his broad hat shading his stone eyes. Rafi seemed much more at ease knowing that Abram was helping them. In that contentment he walked at a casual pace, smiling and holding her hand. Erica could almost fool herself that she was simply another tourist from the cruise ships.

They found a small restaurant, and as they ate, Erica found herself stealing glances at Rafi. It wasn't that he was handsome, which he was. It wasn't that he had helped her in a time of need, which of course he had. It was his manner, his politeness, which drew her gaze. Everywhere they went, he allowed her to go first. He opened doors for her, and when they spoke to others to order food or to ask directions, he deferred to her, never speaking over her. But his courtesy wasn't just limited to her. She saw in him grace for others. When they left the restaurant, a man with coal-black skin and neck-length braided hair bumped into him.

"Sorry daddy," the man said, fixing Rafi with a blank stare.

Erica wondered if it was meant to be an insult, but Rafi— neither cowed nor angry—said, "Please do not give it a second thought my friend. I was as much to blame."

With that the man tilted his head in deference and walked on.

Rafi's reaction then, standing so starkly against the other men in her life, exposed his true self—calm and genuine. In that moment, she let her guarded heart open and fell in love with him. She stood staring at him, her pulse racing as the tourists bumped by, and a question began to form in his eyes. Before he could ask it, she pulled him close and held him, her lips on his collar bone. The warm scent of his neck and the bunched fabric of his shirt made her feel as though the world beyond them had diminished to nothing.

...

They made their way out of town down a long, winding road with sandy shoulders. Rafi's 'quiet place' had turned out be a lonely beach to the west. They spent the day there, and in the evening, when the sun touched the western horizon, the light, scattering across the surface of the water in a brilliant, blood-red dazzle, led from the disk on the horizon across the ocean to the wet sand at their feet. A gull floated by, its wings held in little arcs.

They sat in the warm sand and watched the sun sink into the ocean. When its crown dipped away, Erica leaned over and kissed Rafi. He slid his arms around her waist and kissed her again. The night had come on fully, and they found themselves in the darkness under a broad field of stars.

They made their way toward town, back to the motel.

Rafi unlocked the room door and pushed it open for her. He followed her in and said, "I'm sorry, I did not realize there was only one bed."

Erica laughed at this and shoved the door closed. She took him in her arms, feeling the strength of him and smelling the scent of soap and sweat on him. She pulled him backwards toward the bed just as a deep voice behind her said, "How very romantic."

CHAPTER 15

Erica looked around the room and, at first, saw nothing. Her eyes came to rest on a shape in the corner, on what appeared to be the shadow of a man. As she stared at the dark shape, white eyes opened wider, and she realized she was looking at a man with pure, African skin dressed all in black. The pink of his fingernails traced the motion of his hand as he reached out and drew the blinds aside. Reddish, electric light flooded the room. In that new light, she saw that his head had been shaved bare and his arms and chest stretched the fabric of his collared shirt.

"You will come wit me," the African said in a dulcet West-African accent. The deep resonance of his voice seemed inhumanly powerful.

"Who are you?" Rafi asked.

"You," he said, "ah in no position to ask questions."

Rafi leaned in on Erica, whispered in her ear, "Run," and lunged at the African.

Erica went for the door, but yanking it open, she found a second man with high cheekbones and dark, native eyes blocking the doorway. He shoved her back into the hotel room just as the African picked Rafi up and threw him into the painting above the bed. The wall caved in, and Rafi fell to the bed, leaving the canvas of the painting bunched into the mortar and lathe.

Rage pulsed through Erica as she screamed, "NO," and leapt at the African, her fists clenched. The African slapped at her with his broad palm. Ducking under it, she reached over his shoulder, grabbed his ear, and tried to rip it off. He shouted out and caught hold of her neck. She kicked into his groin, and his grip faltered as he bent forward. Shoving away from him, she turned and saw the native whip something at her. The room went flash-cube white and faded to black.

...

When Erica woke, darkness surrounded her. She sat with her legs and arms bound to a stiff-backed chair. A ball of rough fabric had been jammed in her mouth. The fabric was soaked through with her saliva. Tape covered her mouth and cheeks from ear to ear. As she lifted her head, the saliva went down her throat and she coughed, blowing air and spit through her nose. She swallowed hard and strained her eyes but could see nothing, only blackness.

Listening, she thought she could hear voices out to her left, somewhere in another room. As she turned her head, a pain spiked at the back of her skull and faded off into a dull burn behind her eyes.

A metal door slid open some distance away and clanged to its stop. She heard a light flick on but felt disoriented as, instead of seeing the space she was in, saw only a dim grid of heavy fabric close to her face.

She heard a familiar voice say in his smooth, South-American accent, "Take it off. Let's see what she has to say for herself."

The fabric pulled forward, yanking her head with it, and the light blinded her. She squinted into the brightness, her eyes watering as they adjusted. Three unfocused figures stood in front of her. She blinked and the moisture cleared her eyes, running down the sides of her face. The African stood on the right, a head taller than the other two men. On the left side, the native—who had blocked Erica from leaving the motel room—held a black, nylon club. In the center stood Antonio Camejo. He wore an old style fedora hat and a burgundy, button-up shirt. She looked to her left and right, nothing.

Where's Rafi?

Camejo gave her his polished smile and took his hat from his head, holding it at his side.

"You're quite a problem for me. I sit enjoying a beautiful afternoon while your friend kills one of my best men, and you and he steal my gold." As he spoke, he walked up to her and touched the side of her face with gentle fingers. "But you were so easy to catch. I put out my nets, listen for talk of gold," his fingers traced across her temple and along the side of her head, past her ear, "and you fall right into my hands." Interlacing his fingers into her hair, he gripped and pulled her head back. "You are such a disappointment for so many reasons, Erica." He stared at her upturned face for a moment, her neck crimped with the strength of his arm.

"It just goes to show, you cannot trust beautiful women. A man gives you everything, a beautiful home, cars, jewels, yet you want more, so you take everything—his money and his life." He pulled her head back farther. "You are a greedy one, aren't you? How could you turn on your husband that way? You swore before God that you would defer to his will, and then you had him killed."

He picked at the edge of the tape and ripped it off her face, the skin beneath flashing with pain. Pulling the rag from her mouth, he threw it aside.

"What do you have to say for yourself?"

She spit out the taste of the rag and said, "My friend didn't kill him. I did. He beat me, so I bashed in his head with a bat."

Camejo paused for a moment, watching her eyes, and she thought she saw the flicker of a smile. He said, "So? You think you are the only woman to ever be corrected? My women know to do as I say."

Fury rose up in her, pressurizing her face, and she clenched her jaw.

"But you," Camejo said, "You are too much to control." He looked back at the two men behind him. "Women this beautiful may seem like a fantasy come to life, but they think too much of themselves and so are the work of the devil himself."

The motor oil and dust taste of the rag still swilled in her mouth, and she spit again before asking, "What do you want from me?"

"Right to business then." He motioned to the African, who brought a steel chair in front of Erica. Camejo sat. "I want my gold, which brings me to my problem. You do not seem to have my gold. My men found only a sample of it on your boat." He leaned forward, elbows on knees, and slid the brim of his hat through his fingers as he asked, "Where is my gold?"

She remembered Rafi laying face down on the motel bed, coated with wall mortar. "Where's the man I was with?"

Camejo smiled, sitting upright again. "So inexperienced in these matters. You should never ask after your accomplices. If you want to play these games," he held out his hat and let it fall to the floor, "you have to be willing to let them go as if they meant nothing to you. By asking for this Rafi Frasier, you let me know the great deal of leverage I have with his life."

He smiled now and settled back in the chair, crossing his ankle over his knee. "So you bashed in Brandon's skull with a bat." He shrugged, "It is the way of things. We all die, and he lacked discretion." He gave Erica a sincerely warm smile. "He misread your strength... should have been more careful with you. I do not so much mind that he is dead. Recently he had become a bit... problematic. However, I cannot forgive the theft; those I work for will not forgive it."

Erica stared at him.

"You see that?" He said, with a laugh. "You have the strength of a lioness, beautiful and dangerous. I thought you were attractive before, but now I must admit, as a killer you truly bring heat to me." He looked back at the African. "Do you feel it?"

The African stared at him.

Camejo waved the man's stare away. "That one. His wife and children live in a shit-box in Senegal; he is so dedicated to them. I tell him he's a fool, but he will not hear it. I cannot understand it, loving just one woman. Tell me friend," he said, looking again at the African, "Is your wife so beautiful that you," he opened his hands toward Erica's torso, "cannot look at another?"

The African stared at him.

Camejo looked back at Erica with sincere frustration on his face. "I do not understand him." With the back of his hand, he stroked the side of Erica's face. "How a man can be exposed to such amazing creatures and not falter. I never have had that kind of strength." He stood up. "But then again, I never sought virtue." He laughed and turned to the African. "Bring in the lover." He looked back at Erica. "We can dispense with the usual tactics. I have a feeling these two will want to talk soon enough."

The African nodded and walked away, past aisles of metal shelves, turned between two, and went out of sight. Erica heard a door clang open, and the African said in his deep voice, "He want them togetha'." A mumbled acknowledgement came from further away and shuffling came into the room. The African came back out between the shelves just as the door clanked shut. Two more men came into view walking on either side of Rafi. Rafi had a black eye, but beyond that, he seemed fine. The native pulled up a chair, set it beside Erica, and the men pushed Rafi down onto it.

"Are you hurt?" Rafi asked, but Camejo held up his hand for silence.

"It is my time to speak, not yours. I will ask you to respect that, but you have been so disrespectful up to this point. You have disrespected our property, our men, and my time. It is the middle of the night, and I should be asleep, and with what we have planned for you, I will not sleep until well after dawn. I do not appreciate that."

He gave them both the warm smile of a gentle host. "Why don't we all get some sleep? Tell me where the gold is."

"What will you do with us?" Rafi asked.

At this the smile faded from Camejo's eyes. "I have not decided yet. If you give me the gold, I suppose I should let you go. You must have some incentive I would think. But to let those who have killed cartel men go… such is not our way. I think the incentive needs to come from the other direction, so I will tell you what will happen if you do not tell me. We will make you tell us. Then," he pointed at Rafi, "we will kill you because you have no value."

He stood and walked around behind Erica. "But you," he stroked the side of Erica's face and brought his hands around her sides and cupped her breasts, "you will have a great value to us. I think your friend, Abram Molovich, was at least right in that." Camejo's fingers stroked at Erica's breasts and her skin crawled. She tried to shift away from him, but he gripped her with strong fingers. Despite herself, she whimpered.

"So soft," he said as he released her breasts and wrenched her head backward by her hair. Her eyes locked onto a caged light. The pain from her scalp and the brightness of the light made her eyes water, and she willed herself to stay calm, to not show the fear she felt. Imagining Brandon lying on the carpet of his office, his temple smashed in, she remembered him with as much detail as she could: the broken blood vessels, the bit of blood in his nostril, the vacant eye.

Camejo's face came into view above her. He stared at her, his eyes not hard, but searching. He smiled and released her hair. Walking around in front of her, he adjusted a lump in his groin as he sat. Erica held herself still, keeping her disgust to herself.

"I have always liked you, Erica," he said. "You have a strong spirit, and I understand why Brandon failed to control you. I wonder if you can be controlled. What do you think?"

Erica gave him nothing.

He nodded and smiled, but sadly this time. "You are such a beautiful woman, it is entirely too bad, but there will be many happy men in your future."

Rafi said, "If you've hurt Abram—"

Camejo let out a barking laugh and slapped his knee. "Faithful to the end I see, pero no es muy intelligente." He looked at the two men who had brought Rafi in. "Go tell him his time to talk has come."

The men walked away, going in between the metal shelves. The door clanked, and footfalls came back toward them. Erica had expected something Hollywood, expected the old man to have his arms bound behind him, to have the marks of a beating on his face. What she saw, she had not expected; it broke her heart. Abram came around the corner wearing slacks and a white dress shirt. He walked with a cane, but moved along quickly enough. His weathered face had a grave expression, sad or stern, Erica could not quite discern.

He walked up beside Camejo. Camejo stood, put his hand gently on Abram's back, and motioned for him to sit.

"What have you done, Abram?" Rafi asked, his eyes darkening.

Abram lowered himself down onto the chair. "What I have done," he said, setting his cane across his thighs, "is protect myself from a damn fool." He stared at Rafi for a moment with hard amber eyes. "I gave you everything you needed. Without me you'd have been nothing more than a desert rat, who died young. I had no use for an orphan, but I saw potential in you. It has worked out for me, somewhat to my surprise. But in the end you proved to be too weak for your own good." He regarded his thin fingers a moment and said in an angry tone, "You dare try to bring this on me? You think that I will allow it? I am a business man, a smuggler, and a thief." He fell silent for a time before holding up a hand, indicating Erica, derision in his eyes.

"Then you bring me this... How could you Rafi?" Sorrow overrode his anger. "You let yourself be swayed by a beautiful woman..." He trailed off and a faint smile drew across his old face. "I suppose I understand it. I suppose it is this way for all of us. Look at her. They don't come much better than that. I can understand how you became weak, but weakness, no matter the cause, I cannot forgive. You brought these men down on my neck, or would have if I had not made the first move. Did you truly think I would stand against them to help a desert rat?"

He tapped his cane of the floor. "I suppose it is my fault. In dealing with you, I obscured too much of my true nature. You came to believe that I was a good man, but I am not a good man. I am a smuggler. Before I ran art, I moved women. I stopped only when I became too old to deal with angry fathers, brothers, and husbands." He laughed to himself. "The money was better and so easy to make. Odessa is filled with beautiful, young women, who are poor in cash and rich in body. All you have to do is tell them you can get them work in America and they are yours. You load them on a boat, and instead of New York, they get Turkey. Those girls have to serve several men a day, every day of the week, but," he shrugged at this, "who am I to care? I made my money, and they should have been more prudent in whom they trusted."

"So you see I am out for me," he touched his fingers to his chest, "for Abram, and Abram alone. I have a decent life here and would not risk it for you." Leaning back, he said, "I have asked them to let you live. Whether they will or not is beyond me. But if they do, I will take you back. I will—"

"If they let me live," Rafi said, his voice low, "I will come to your house in the night and see you dead."

Abram shook his head. "No Rafi, you will not. You are no killer. She," he pointed at Erica, "she is. That I can see in her eyes, and now that she has the taste of blood... well, she would have been very dangerous. But you... you are too bound up in your confused morals. If they let you live, you will be lost, and you will seek out what you know. You know me. You will come back."

He lifted his cane and pressed it into the floor, standing. "Well, we are done for now." He took Camejo's hand. "Please let me know when you are ready to move the woman. I have made calls and have decent bids already."

Without another word Abram walked away, turning and going out of view between the metal shelves. Erica heard the door pull open and clank shut.

"Well there you have it," Camejo said as he sat down. "So you face maybe a terrible death, and you," he looked at Erica, "will be used by several men a day for years, until your beauty has been... How do you say?" He looked over his shoulder at the native. "Estar rendido?"

The native shrugged.

"No matter," he said. "So here is my offer to you. If you give the gold now, I will let you live. I will let you both go free. You will not have the cartel after you, you can go and be poor and live together."

Erica looked at Rafi, who met her gaze. She wished she could read his mind. What would he have her do? She wanted to take the deal. She didn't care about the gold. She wanted to be free from these men, wanted to be done with it. Rafi nodded at her.

"Can we have time to think about it?" Erica asked.

161

Camejo smiled. "No."

Erica drew a breath and let it out to calm herself. "We have the coordinates written down. We dumped the gold in the ocean." But something caused her to hold back.

Don't tell them that the numbers were jumbled. Don't give it all away just yet.

"Ah," Camejo said, "You must be referring to this." He leaned to the side, took a scrap of paper from his pocket, and unfolded it. It was the scrap of paper Rafi had written the coordinates on.

Rafi said to Erica, "It is going to be fine. If they will let us go, that is all we need. I didn't come with you for the promise of gold—"

"This is too much to bear," Camejo said. "You pretend you do not want the money. You hint that it is for love that you helped her. But look at her. She doesn't inspire love. A woman who can cook inspires love."

"I can fucking cook," Erica said, surprising herself at the anger in her voice.

Camejo looked at her with sincere shock and laughed. He leaned forward and lifted her chin with his fingers. "Yes, I'm sure you can heat up a kitchen to Hell's own fires." He looked over at Rafi. "You see, I cannot stand those who are not honest with themselves. If you did not want the gold, you would not have taken it. If you did not take it, you would not be here."

Erica said, "You would have come looking for us even if we didn't take the gold. Brandon's dead..." When she had spoken of Brandon's death, something honest and horrible had come into the depth of Camejo's eyes, and she knew that if they gave up the gold, they'd die. The cartel wouldn't let those who kill their men live.

She looked at the scrap of paper in Camejo's hand. Would they take the time to check the location? If they took her at her word, they would die now. But only Rafi would die right away; she would go to Turkey.

CHAPTER 16

Standing between them, Camejo yawned and said, "I am tired and have had enough of you for the night." He walked out without another word.

His men untied Erica and Rafi from the chairs—leaving their hands restrained behind their backs—and led them to a car. The African pushed them into the back seat and sat beside Erica, his powerful arm pressing against her shoulder. The native got into the driver's seat and drove the car to a dark harbor, where the two men ushered them onto a small yacht and down into a stateroom.

When the door clicked shut, Rafi said, "Sit back to back."

Erica did as he said, and she felt his fingers digging painfully at the ropes that bound her wrists. The ropes loosened and fell away, and she turned and untied the ropes around Rafi's wrists. When she had freed him, he went to the door and listened for a long time.

He returned to the bed and whispered to her, "There is at least one man standing guard. I can hear him shifting his feet, and..." he stood on the bed and pushed on the ceiling, "there seems to be no other exit."

They sat on the bed and soon lay back. Erica rested her head on his shoulder and said, "If we tell them where the gold is they'll kill us."

"I agree. Keeping its location secret is our one chance."

He said nothing more.

Laying there feeling the warmth of his side against her, she wondered what would become of them. She felt that she loved Rafi, but she had felt love for other men, and it had gone badly. No relationship had ever gone this bad this fast, but for the first time, it wasn't the man's doing. She didn't want to lose this chance with Rafi, but to keep it, she'd have to outwit Camejo or kill him.

As she imagined Camejo on the white carpeting beside Brandon, she drifted off to sleep. In that sleep, she dreamt that she lay on a banistered bed in a dark room. To her left, the night air billowed gossamer drapes out from arched windows. The scent of the ocean had infused itself in the warm air, which rustled through dry palm fronds just outside the windows. The soft bed called her back to sleep, and she would have drifted off in her dream, down deeper, but the air in the room turned icy. A faint fog of breath rose from her mouth, and she smelled the thick rot from the cavern.

Something shifted in the corner, and that thing cleared its throat, not a dry cough but a splattering of water and saliva. She sat up and peered into the darkness. As she narrowed her eyes, a dark figure clarified, sitting with elbows on knees. She recognized Rafi's face under a mop of dripping hair. His skin had gone gray, and she could see rotten holes in his forearms, the flesh hanging open exposing muscle and bone.

Rafi's head began to lift, but as his eyes found hers, he faded into an insubstantial haze, becoming only a ghostly vapor, and vanished. The stench faded from the room, driven out by the warm air blowing in through the windows.

...

The stateroom door opened, waking her. She squinted into the glaring sunlight, disoriented, as the native and the African came into the room and pulled them up from the bed. The native let out a muttered curse and retied their hands behind their backs as the cabin rocked with a subtle instability under her feet. The men pushed Rafi and her out of the stateroom. She stole glances at Rafi, glad to see him as he was and not as the apparition from the dream.

The African and the native took them up on deck into a stiff breeze, and she found herself looking out on a jade cove formed by a horseshoe of white sand and low trees.

"Where are we?" she asked the African.

He did not look at her.

A dingy had been lowered into the strong chop, and the men gripped Rafi's shoulders and set him followed by Erica into the tipping boat. The men also came aboard, and the African motioned for them to sit and fired the outboard motor, steering the dingy around the yacht's anchor chains toward the beach. As he approached the beach, he gave the engine one last burst of speed and lifted the outboard. The boat coasted up, cresting on a wave, and collided into the sand. Erica tipped sideways and caught her shoe under the seat just in time to pull herself upright. The African stepped out into the shallow water and indicated they should follow him. When they had, he shoved the boat back off the beach. The native dropped the outboard into the water, backed the boat away, and throttled on, turning in a wide arc out across the green chop, back toward the yacht.

The African walked them up the beach toward a gray Land Rover Defender. A man of Caucasian descent stood expressionless beside the truck, his eyes hidden behind narrow sunglasses. The man opened the rear gate, and the African pointed into the truck. Erica looked into the forest for a moment and considered running. She knew she'd never outpace the two men and had no way to confidentially let Rafi know to run as well. She'd have to wait for her time. Hands still tied behind her back, she shimmied into the truck and sat in one of the side-facing jump seats. Rafi did the same. The African climbed into the back with them, sitting between their knees.

The Defender drove off the beach and down a sandy pair of ruts cut into the forest. Tree branches scraped the mirrors and side-windows, and bushes brushed along the truck's sides. After a short time, the truck slowed and crawled up the gravel shoulder of an asphalt road. They travelled along the smooth road, the off-road tires howling. The truck slowed again and turned down another rutted trail. A few moments later, the truck came to a stop next to two other Land Rovers. The African opened the rear gate, slid out, and motioned for them to follow. Out of the truck, he pushed them forward.

Rafi lifted his chin indicating a tree beside the Rover with a thin, gray trunk speckled with dark, oily patches. "Erica, that is black poisonwood and is best avoided. The sap has an effect like poison ivy."

She nodded and, looking through the thin spires of the open forest, realized over half the trees were this black poisonwood. Through those thin trunks she could see the flatness of the island. The African pushed her forward, and she walked around the Rover into a clearing of low plants and stony, packed earth. The humidity and heat of the sun pressed in on her, and she felt sweat dampening the fabric between her shoulder blades and at the small of her back.

Across the clearing Erica saw a low shelf of rock bright with sunlight. Bushes grew along the top of the limestone, which was the color and texture of old bones. At its base lay a wide pit about twenty feet across and some forty feet long in the forest floor. It seemed a great axe-cut in the island's skin. She walked up to the pit and looked down some fifteen feet to dark water, still and mirroring the sky. As she stared at the water, she caught sight of herself and Rafi peering over the edge.

Rafi turned to the African. "What are you going to do with us?"

The African stared at Rafi for a moment before looking back down into the water.

"I want to know what is going on," Rafi said, angry now. "Camejo said he would let us go if we gave up the gold."

"I do not have the gold in my hands though." Erica heard Camejo's voice behind her and turned to find him walking up from a side trail. "You see, I do not have our gold back until it is in my hand. But it is not, and when my associates reference your coordinates, they tell me that the ocean there is almost two kilometers deep."

Erica felt fear scatter down her back to her heels.

"You see," Camejo said, "now you have wasted my time, and I cannot abide thieves who also waste my time. But," he turned to Erica and said, "I don't want you to feel badly. I would not have let you go anyway. The moment I had the gold, your man here would have died and you would have been sold." He turned and nodded to the native who punched Rafi in the stomach. Rafi doubled over and let out a groan.

"Untie his hands," Camejo said. "We are not monsters."

The native gripped Rafi's arm, turning him, and untied the rope around his wrists. Rafi spun back and gripped the native by the neck. The native's eyes went wide just as the top of Rafi's head planted in his face. With a far-off look, the native fell to the ground as if dead. The African turned and gripped Rafi by the upper arm and threw him backwards toward the hole. Rafi tripped and fell off the ledge, and Erica heard a punching crash of water, the sound echoing up the limestone walls.

Leaning over the edge, she looked down into the now turbulent water. She saw that it was not black, but pure and clear, and she could see Rafi's entire body, hands and legs swimming. As the water settled, she saw the limestone walls of the hole extending straight down below the surface of the water, deep into the clearness. Rafi swam toward the side and gripped the rock.

A gunshot cracked out beside Erica causing her to jump as rock splintered off the limestone near Rafi. He pushed off the rock, covering his head from the shower of stone, and floated to the center of the pool treading water.

Camejo kept the gun on Rafi as he said, "Your purpose is to drown, and her," he pointed the pistol at Erica, "will be to talk after you are dead."

Erica said, "I'll talk now."

"Erica!" Rafi shouted up to her. "Don't tell them anything. The moment they have what they want, it'll be you down here."

"I can't let them do this," she said and turned to Camejo. "Let him climb up, and I'll tell you where the gold is."

Camejo smiled and shook his head in a slow 'no'. "You must pay a price first. I want you to learn humility." He put his arm around her. "You have pushed me too far, pushed our cartel too far. Now it is time for us to push you." He looked down at Rafi and then back at her. "You must pay a price, which is his life."

"Please don't," Erica said. Tears began to fill her vision, and she tried to force them down, but they spilled in hot streaks down her face. "Please—" a sob cut her off, "Please don't do this."

"You are such a beautiful woman," Camejo said, turning to her and taking her face in his hands. "You should not cry. It makes you look ugly." He released her and smiled. "What did you think would happen when you steal from a cartel? Did you think we would simply ask for what you have taken? Did you think we would not find you?"

He raised his hand and cracked it across her face, snapping her head to the side. The numbing shock of the slap came to Erica as an old, familiar sensation. Keeping her eyes down, tears flowed from them, down her face, to drip off of her chin. She had come right back to where she had been. Despite her best efforts, she had failed to escape men like this, and she doubted Camejo would be as careless as Brandon had been.

Still...

A bloom of hope warmed her chest and the tears slowed and stopped. She looked up at Camejo and gave nothing more, emptiness.

I'll wait... and I'll find my opening, just like I did with Brandon.

CHAPTER 17

Rafi looked up at the faces peering over the ledge of rock as he swept his arms and legs back and forth through the clear water.

Camejo shouted over the ledge. "Adiós mi amigo. You cost me one restless night and nothing more. May you die well." He disappeared and Rafi heard him say, "Stay here and make sure he does not climb out. If he touches the wall, shoot him, but only injure him. I want him to drown. Wait for him to tire, no matter how long it takes." Camejo's head came back over the ledge of stone. "Do you understand pendejo? You will have more than enough time to regret crossing me."

From beyond the ridge he had heard Erica crying, but she had gone quiet. He hoped she was all right. "Erica, don't tell them anything," he said again.

"Rafi," he heard Erica call out, but a slap followed. She said nothing more.

"Now is not the time for lover's talk," Camejo said from beyond the ledge. "Now is the time for him to die and for you to come with me."

Footsteps moved away, and he shouted out, "Erica, don't tell them anything." But he didn't want that to be the last thing he said to her. "I've loved you," he yelled out, "since the first day," but didn't know if she'd heard.

He swam over and hung off the stone wall resting his arms and legs. The water went still, and the native's head appeared over the ledge. He raised his gun and fired, hitting the stone a few feet to Rafi's right. The rock fractured, spraying Rafi with stabbing shards. Turning his head away, he dropped back into the water and went under for a moment before he recovered himself and floated back to the center of the pool. The native remained in view, gun ready.

"If you let me up, we can make a deal. I know where the gold is."

The native smiled and, in an unexpectedly high voice quick with a Nahuan accent, said, "Es too late for that. La chica will tell us."

Rafi scanned the walls of the pit. He couldn't just leave Erica to them. The limestone walls would be easy enough to climb without the native there ready to shoot him; treading water with a bullet wound wasn't an option. He looked into the water and traced the limestone walls down into the darkness. Sweeping his arms, he turned and scanned the other side of the submerged wall. About fifteen feet beneath the surface of the water, that side of the wall ended in a ledge.

He drew a deep breath and dove down. When he opened his eyes, he could still make out the blurring wall; he swam down to the ledge and looked in. He had expected to find a small alcove in the wall, but what he saw gave him hope; a deep cave extended off into darkness. All he needed it to do was curve upwards ten feet and he might be able to find a pocket of air, maybe even enough to wait out the guards. If he could find a cave to breathe in, fine. If he could find another escape route, all the better.

He swam back up to the surface. The native watched him with curiosity as he drew another deep breath and dove down again, this time making his way below the ledge and into the cave. He swam with slow, deliberate strokes, doing his best to conserve oxygen. The darkness came on quickly, and he rose up and felt along the ceiling. It was rising. He caught his scalp on a stalactite, and the surprise of it caused him to suck in some water. The water filled his nose and ran down the back of his throat. He blew out some air and, with nothing left in his burning lungs, turned and swam back out of the cave and up to the surface. Coughing out water and drawing belly deep breaths, he blew the burn out of his lungs. Feeling dizzy, he remained floating for a moment.

"You have no way out, amigo," the native called down to him. "You will die, but continue if you like. I would like to go home."

So if I do disappear, you'll leave. All I need is a pocket of air big enough to breathe in for an hour or so.

Rafi drew several deep breaths, loading his bloodstream with oxygen and dove down again. Swimming back into the cave, he stayed lower, clear of the unseen stalactites hanging down like claws from the roof of the cave. He swam along until his lungs began to burn, at which point he floated upward. His hand brushed a smooth, hard stalactite, and he followed it up to the ceiling. The cave had risen enough that, as he touched the ceiling, the light from the entrance disappeared from view, and he could see nothing. Nothing but water, no gap. But it must rise further down.

Weighing the options of turning back to get more air or exploring deeper, he decided to drive on just a few more feet before going back. He dropped down below the stalactite and swam on. A nascent burn in his lungs caused his diaphragm to begin twitching. He tried to quiet the impulse as he swam. He rose again and found only water and stone. No air pocket. Diving down again, he began to feel his heartbeat throbbing in his chest. The desire to breathe became more intense. He would have to turn back. Just a few more feet and he would. He swam on and his sweeping hands hit a stone wall, a dead end. Now the need to breathe began drawing a desperate energy across his shoulders. He let out some air with a flurry of bubbles to fight the sensation.

He rose up and hit the ceiling of the cave. He had to breathe, needed air. He dove down and swam in the direction he thought he had come from but felt unsure. Several times he ran into stalactites in the darkness and had to dive deeper, but his desperate lungs wanted him to rise, and he had to fight the impulse. With a few more kicks, he saw the light from the entrance of the cave. His diaphragm yanked at him and drew water into his nostrils. His chest heaved with a cough, and precious air blew the water back out his nose. Feeling dizzy and somewhat confused, he swam on toward the opening pulling at the water with his weakening arms. He was almost to the mouth of the cave. Kicking with his legs, he hit another stalactite with his shoulder. More water came into his mouth and nose and he coughed up the last of his air. Now his belly pulled in constant yanks on his lungs. He willed his arms to pull through the water, but as his muscles ran out of oxygen to burn, they responded only half-heartedly. Then he was out of the cave and looking up at the blue sky bending beyond the surface of the water. He could see the ragged edges of the rock ledge and the native's head, a warping, dark disk extended into the blue of the sky.

Rafi wanted to rise to the surface, but with no air in his lungs he had no buoyancy, and he had nothing left in his arms and legs, which merely pawed at the water. He began to sink. His belly yanked at him.

He screamed at himself in his mind. *Push yourself. Get up there.*

His arms rose up and pulled down, and his legs swayed back and forth, but still he sank. The surface drifted away. His belly yanked again and the water rushed in, filling his mouth and nose. He tried to cough out the water, but there was nothing to replace it but more water, and it drew deeply into his lungs. As the last of the air bubbled up away from him, he felt himself go limp, disconnected. He had heard that once the initial terror passed, drowning was a peaceful way to die. As he resigned himself to death, and as the survival instincts of his body faded, he found that peace and floated calmly downward.

While he had given himself over to dying, something felt wrong. He could still see, was still conscious. He could feel his ears pressurizing, could feel the water growing colder. One eardrum ruptured with a shearing pain and then the other.

He approached a reddish-orange layer, which hung suspended in a broad, undisturbed sheet. Sinking through it, he caught the taste of rotten eggs in the back of his mouth. He drifted still downwards, the light now tinted red.

The light faded away, and he sank until his back thumped onto the floor of the cavern. He could not direct his vision, his eyes passive, taking in what lay before them. Yet Rafi could still see the walls stretching up away from him. Not see them exactly. It was more an awareness; he could feel the boundary where the liquid ended and the stone began. The stone seemed to glow with a faint moonshine. A cloud of debris rose up around him and blocked out the walls. Then, finally and to his relief, he felt what he had hoped for.

He felt himself disconnecting from his body, rising away from it. His awareness rose up through the darkness toward the light. He rose through the layer of orange cloud, and the light intensified. He passed through the blur of the halocline and came into the brightness of the day. He slid above the surface of the water without disturbing it and up and out of the maw of the pit. His sudden vision of the breadth of the world made his heart glad. He continued rising, the forest and then the island descending below him. His mind became unfocused, unconcerned with the things he had known.

At that moment Rafi felt himself connecting to his genetic lines, could feel each generation drawing him close. He felt his father's bloodline, a fire forged in cold glens and misty crags. Through his mother he felt the nations of Assyria and Babylon, back through Sumer to the beginning of recorded time. However, as he drifted among clouds so white they deepened the blue, which hung in perfection above their curved pillars, he thought of a beautiful face with gem-blue eyes. His ascension slowed and stopped—he floated.

He could not remember her name, but knew she had been someone loved, someone who faced grave danger. He understood he had failed her and felt that failure like burning coals on skin. Grief and regret crested through him, and the burden drew him away from his ancestors. He felt himself beginning to sink back down toward the small island far below. As he descended, his memories of Erica, the gold, and the cartel came back to him.

He dropped through a cloud, the whiteness blotting out the blue sky, and felt sure this was wrong. He would not be able to help her but could not stop the descent.

Please don't let this happen.

But he was uncertain who he offered the thought to and found no response.

The island rose up to meet him.

This cannot be happening. It cannot be my fate.

His descent continued. The forest came up to him and there, below him lay the gaping mouth of the pit, its waters reflecting the clouds above. He dropped down below the tree tops and into the mouth of the cavern, in among the limestone walls and under the surface of the water—his corpse pulling him back down into the deep, drowned earth. The triangle of light faded again, and he descended through the blurring halocline, down through the orange layer of muck, and down into darkness. Terror rose as he approached his corpse, yet still he drifted into the cold. He felt the deadness nearing. It touched him, drew him in, and he joined with it; the bones, muscle, and skin locked around him—still and silent and motionless. He could feel the body already stiffening, could feel the jaw hanging open. Unable to marshal the dead joints, he lay in his corpse as if a coffin and, in his mind, screamed.

CHAPTER 18

Erica found herself in a comfortable bedroom with bright sunlight filtering in through an open window. Recognizing it as the room from her dream, she turned to the corner where she had seen the visage of Rafi but found only an empty chair and a fern on a pedestal.

The gossamer drapes floated on a breeze coming through the open windows, and she felt her skin go cold despite the heat of the day. She walked to the windows, which had been framed into the walls on either side of the bed, and pushed the drapes aside. Fat, white clouds had risen up in towering columns against the blue sky. She looked down into the courtyard of the old Spanish mission, its archways coated with fresh, earthen plaster. The Land Rover that had brought her to the compound sat parked between broad-leafed, potted plants. Palm trees threw shifting shade across the courtyard and her window. The window had no bars, but a man wearing a worn hat looked up at her from the cobble stones below, a pistol on his hip.

She turned to the two doors. The closed door to the hallway had been reinforced with a solid-steel plate. The bathroom door stood open, and the chrome fixtures sparkled with sunlight. Walking in she found the drapes pushed outward, framing the open shape of the window and the lines of metal bars. Looking at herself in the mirror, she found a wreck of tangled hair and red eyes. A mixture of dried mud, sweat, and tears lay streaked across one side of her face.

She considered cleaning up, but the thought of herself in the shower naked made her feel far too exposed. She pulled open a drawer, found a brush, and returned to the bedroom. If not already, Rafi would soon be dead, and she knew nothing could stop it. She felt numb and understood it was her ability to wall herself off from grief that would save her now. She sat on the side of the bed, and as she began brushing the tangles from the ends of her hair, considered how best to kill Antonio Camejo.

...

Hours had passed, and the sunlight filtering through the windows grew ruddy with evening shades. Erica went to the window and looked out to where the walls of the compound ended and the light-blue ocean waves broke on a stony shore. On the broad lawn near the ocean, a circular table had been set with fine dishes and silver serving trays glinting in the setting sun. A breeze tugged at the tablecloth, wrapping it around the legs of the table. No one sat at the table, but remnants of a meal remained on the dishes. As she watched, servers came out and cleared them away. The lock on the door behind her released with a clank.

She turned as Camejo entered with the African and the native. Camejo wore a light-cotton shirt and white slacks. His shoes were some type of reptile hide as was his belt.

"My dear, you are a mess," Camejo said with a smile. "I would have thought you would have cleaned yourself up by now."

"Not all women are so shallow as to have that be their first reaction, pendejo."

The smile faded from Camejo's face, and he crossed his arms.

You don't like that? Good.

Erica looked at Camejo's hands. On his left wrist, he wore a silver Omega watch with a deep-blue face. On his ring finger he wore a ring in the shape of a human skull, no lower jaw. Diamonds in the skull's eyes burned with orange and red fire as he moved his hand.

"Please sit." Camejo held out his hand to a small table with two stiff-backed chairs.

Erica stared at him.

"No? Be uncomfortable if you wish." He walked to the chair and sat. He held up his hand to the native. "Tell her."

The native looked at Erica with his dark eyes and said in a light voice, accented so heavily that Erica had to pay close attention to understand, "Tu amante, he is dead. I see him drown, sink down into el pozo." He stared at her, his face blank. Rafi's death meant nothing to him.

Rafi's death. Erica felt a horrific sadness burn into her chest, as if hot lead had been poured into her lungs. The intensity of the sensation frightened her.

Rafi's dead.

Unbidden, the vision of Rafi lying in the darkness at the bottom of the cavern came to her. She saw his arms suspended slightly above the floor of the cavern and his hair floating around the crown of his skull. His face was slack with death, and his vague eyes stared upward. His gaze shifted and locked on her. She started and shoved the vision aside, looking back at Camejo. She thought she would be able to control the feeling in her chest, push it down. Just one more failed romance in her life, nothing more than her destiny. But the shock of her vision of Rafi dead was too much for her. The grief and terror of losing him welled up in her heart, and her jaw trembled as her vision blurred with tears.

Do not do this. DO NOT let them see it.

She gritted her jaw so hard she thought she might break her teeth and, mastering herself, glared at Camejo.

"Mi querida," Camejo said, "You try to be so strong. I see this, but sadness is wrong. You were too good for him, and you can still save yourself. My offer stands for you: plomo o plata... lead or silver. Give me what I want, and I reward you; make me wait, and I punish." He ran his index finger over the skull ring and smiled at her. "Here is how the next twenty-four hours will pass. You are free tonight to bathe and sleep. Food will be brought for you. Tonight and tomorrow you are my esteemed guest. You may even take a walk down by the ocean after breakfast if you wish. I am offering you these twenty-four hours as a gift because I am a reasonable man. Consider the truth of it. You have stolen from me, have made me do violence to another human being, and yet still I offer hospitality."

Camejo stood and walked to Erica. He put his hand on the side of her face, wiping away some of the dirt with a gentle sweep of his thumb. "I understand you are confused. You do not know who to trust." He leaned close to her, his face a few inches from her. She did not like him that close, wanted more distance from him, but felt that she should remain still and be a wall.

"I can see that you are afraid," he said. "I want this to be over for you too. You can be my guest for many more days if you like. We can be friends, but I must have the gold."

She considered telling him off or telling him that only Rafi knew where the gold was, but she knew that, if Camejo didn't have the gold and thought she couldn't get it for him, she was as good as dead. If he did get the gold, there would be no reward for her; she'd be a fool to believe otherwise. The only thing keeping her alive was the gold, and she had to keep the stalemate going as long as possible.

Camejo put his arm around her, and she felt the warmth of his hand on the small of her back. He pulled her close to him. The musky smell of his aftershave mixed with humid sweat overwhelmed her, and she found herself drawing short breaths trying to keep his scent out of the deeper regions of her lungs.

"After twenty-four hours," he said, "if you haven't given me the location to the gold, I will no longer be your host. Please do not make me do that. You will like me much better as a host."

With that he turned and walked out of the room. The native smiled at her, and she hated him, wanted to shoot him like she'd shot Alex. The African walked out of the room after Camejo, but the native stood staring at her a moment longer. His eyes traveled down to her waist and back up. The African stood at the door, looking back at the native.

"Come," he said to the native.

The native winked at Erica and walked out of the room. The African, as he left, gave Erica one last look, and there was something in his eyes, or the lack of something. It wasn't a look of malice or lust, but forced emptiness.

...

After the door clanged shut, Erica went into the washroom and stared at the tile shower stall. She balanced her feeling of exposure with the feeling of the grit across her salted skin. She looked at the free-standing, claw-foot tub and then at herself in the mirror, her brushed hair looking greasy. Finally, she gripped the tub's white handled faucet and twisted it. The faucet gave a squeak and fresh water poured from the barrel of the tap. She let the water warm before sealing the drain. A bath would be quieter. She could hear if someone came into the room.

After she had drawn the bath, she undressed and lowered herself into the hot water. She lay there, looking at the faucet for some time. A drip of water hung from the fixture and would not drop. That's how she felt right now. There was something in her that needed to happen, some grief or anger, and it would not let go, could not let go right now. She could see the colors and light of the room in the drop.

Closing her eyes, she thought of Rafi sitting at the coffee shop in West Palm Beach. She remembered him tugging Alex's body up on the gunwale of the small boat and saw him swimming in the pit, covering his head with his forearms as the gunshot went off. With that the thing in her broke free and fell into her heart, and she sobbed for Rafi. Her arms and legs trembling, she cried until her stomach muscles hurt.

When she had calmed again, she lay her head back, knees up out of the water, and let her ears sink below the surface. There she could hear a humming and the clink of the drain plug chain when she shifted her weight. She listened and found that she could hear something in the water, something that sounded almost like words. She thought perhaps she was listening to voices in the room beneath her. She closed her eyes and listened into the water, focusing on the sound. The sound rose up and a guttural voice said, "Erica, don't leave me down here."

She sat up with a start, the water splashing around her and spilling over the edge to the tile. As the water in the tub quieted, she thought she heard something in the other room. Standing from the tub, she wrapped a towel around herself and walked to the doorway. She heard shuffling in the bedroom. The metal door clanged shut as she looked around the corner. Walking into the room, Erica found that clothes had been set out for her. She looked them over—jeans, a collared shirt, and silk pajamas, all the correct size. She looked back to the door. She truly was a guest for tonight, a guest in a room with a steel-plate door. Unsure what to do, she stood for a moment with water dripping off her legs. Touching her face, she felt the grit of the dirt and went back to the tub, took off the towel, and lowered herself back into the water. This time, she did not allow herself to relax, but went about washing herself.

When she had finished washing, drying, and dressing in the pajamas, the sun had faded and darkness lay beyond the curtains. She sat on the bed, feeling herself sink into the thick mattress. She had intended to stay awake, to think about what she needed to do, but tiredness overwhelmed her, and she lay back. In a few moments, she had drifted off into a dreamless sleep.

Sometime late in the night she woke. The wind had picked up and now lifted the curtains in great sweeps of white fabric. She sat up. A man sat in the chair in the corner, just beyond the square of moonlight on the floor.

She didn't think she was dreaming but even so felt that it was somehow not real.

"Who are you?" She asked.

The man gave no answer.

She continued to stare at the figure, but could not quite get her eyes to focus on it. The dark hair hung wetly about the face. The shoulders were strong, and the legs athletic, and she saw a long tear in the thigh of the man's pants. She shifted to the edge of the bed and put her feet into cold water. She lifted her feet with a start and looked down, finding that the entire floor ran with a sheet of clear water.

She looked back at the man. He sat with his face turned away, seemingly shamed, his shoulders hunched.

"Rafi," she said, alarm rising in her voice, "is that you?"

He didn't move but let out a low groan. The animalistic sound lacked sanity and made Erica unsure if she should speak again. Pulling her feet back on the bed, she glanced at the locked door and the window. She considered the broken ankle she might have from falling from the second story, weighed it against staying in the room with the man. His head turned and Erica saw Rafi's handsome face, gone pale and gaunt.

The jaw did not move, but she heard a whisper in her head, "You... left... me..."

She began to turn her head from side to side.

The whisper came again. "You... left... me... to... die..."

The whisper held the traces of Rafi's voice, but came into her mind without color, without life, as if listening to wind through trees.

Still, she found herself responding. "I'm sorry Rafi. I had no choice. I—"

The head turned fully now, and dark, dead eyes stared somewhat past her, not locking on correctly, not truly seeing. The voice growled now, "You left me to die down here."

"No," she yelled at the apparition. "I had no choice. They took me away from you. It was them…"

She slid to the far side of the bed and stood. Here the floor was cool and dry and she looked down at it. When she looked up the room seemed different. The chair in the corner sat empty, and the drapes only lifted a bit from the windows, riding a soft nighttime breeze. She reached over and turned on the lamp beside the bed, casting yellow light against the walls and long shadows across the floor. She climbed over the bed and turned on the second lamp, cutting down the shadows. Moving back to the center of the bed, she held her knees, not daring to move.

CHAPTER 19

The stiffening in Rafi's joints, which had begun as a delicate ache, now grew fiery as rigor set in. In his guts, he felt the blister of rot as microbes turned against his body.

Through the intense pain, he became aware of something high above, something he felt he wanted, warm blood and a quick heartbeat. It skitted near the mouth of the pit, and he yearned for it. Its quick motions and sparkling light made him feel as though he were starving. As his focus on the thing intensified, he disconnected from his body and felt a rushing relief from the rot and rigor, and he drifted upward, freed from skull, guts, and groin. Yet, he could feel his corpse below, as if chained to him with iron links. Against the weight of that chain, the brilliant spirit shuffling at the underbrush high above drew him onwards.

The corpse-chain grew heavier and heavier the farther away he drew. When he reached the water's surface, he barely moved at all, dragging himself toward the bright thing with all his will. As he came up over the lip of the pit, he saw that long, evening shadows lay in among the trees. Searching for that skittering heart, he found it—bright and glittering—as it shuffled under leaves just at the edge of the clearing. Its brilliance renewed his will, and he crossed the clearing, fighting the great weight binding him to his corpse. The heart ran like a chainsaw as he approached. Sniffing and scrabbling under the roots of a tree, he found a little, gray mouse. He felt himself touching the spirit of the mouse, felt its clear light warming him. The mouse let out a crushed squeak, and its legs went rigid. He began to pull at the light, as if sipping at it, and the mouse screeched and fell on its back, biting at the air.

Rafi felt sorry for the little beast, but gluttony for the brilliant light overpowered his regret. He pulled at its soul, trying to pry it out of the body, but it would not come free. The little thing resisted, fighting to keep its spirit planted in muscle and skeleton. Bracing himself against the brilliance of the mouse, he wrenched again. With too much focus on the mouse, the weight of the corpse-chain hauled him back toward the pit. He froze, stabilized himself, and called to the mouse. Lying on its side, it began to spasm. He felt its legs, felt the muscles along its back to its tail, and he reached its front paw out, then the other, and brought it up onto its feet. He drew it out from under the tree, front claws digging into the dirt and back feet dragging. He slid away before it, over the ledge, and as he slipped below the surface, it tipped over the edge in a morbid cartwheel, which ended in a plinking splash. He sank back down into the dark cold, the mouse just above him, and when the body drowned, he reached out and pinned the little soul to the flesh, preventing it from rising away.

The effort had made Rafi tired. He felt stretched thin and wanted rest. The tiredness made him glad when he reached the resting spot of his corpse even as its pain meshed into him. He lay in the pain and perceived the small spirit sinking down to him like an ember falling out of the sky. It landed in the silt beside him, its energy burning hot, and he pried at it again, and his power here made it simple. The soul rent free, and he felt the brilliance merge with him in a thermic swath, scintillating and calm. Its energy gave him strength but had been insubstantial, and he wanted more. Directing his awareness up again, he searched the mouth of the pit. He wanted to drift up away from himself, to hunt further, but without something to draw him out, he could not disconnect himself.

A cool-blue energy landed in the trees near the pit. It felt lighter to him, calmer, less intense than the mouse, something graceful. He began to drift up toward it, but the thing spread itself wide, and with an azure rush, flew off. His corpse pulled him back down into the pit and locked onto him.

He lay there for some time, feeling for something to consume. Finding nothing, he felt his mind bending with frustration and sorrow. He found himself thinking back over his life, but he couldn't remember things quite right. Memories slid away just as he had their essence. He recalled the home he shared with his father in Arbil, but when he tried to remember his father's face, the eyes blurred. He thought of Erica, and a vision of her sleeping came to him. She lay on a banistered bed on top of the quilted covers wearing silk pajamas showing the curve of her leg and hip and the fullness of her breasts as she breathed in and out. She was so beautiful and so at peace...

A horrific sadness rose in Rafi's chest. She was out there, still at risk, and all he wanted was to be with her. Rafi felt a maddening regret. He should have convinced her to leave Brandon when she first came to his shop and never let her go back home. Anything would have been better than this. They could have travelled to Northern Iraq, gone into the mountains and lived in a small house with goats standing on a hillside in the shade of old pine trees.

As he imagined her sleeping with her hair spilled across the pillow, he knew how much he still loved her and found himself sitting in a chair on the far side of the room. She stirred and sat up. Peering into the darkness, her eyes landed on him, and he looked away, fearful that he should seem horrific to her.

"Who are you?" She asked him.

He wanted to answer, wanted to get up and go to her, hold her again, but he could only sit in the chair feeling as though he were encased in heavy, cold water.

He saw fear in her eyes and wanted to tell her that everything would be all right, but it would not. He lay dead at the bottom of a pit, and she was a prisoner of... he couldn't quite remember whom. Unable to keep his mind focused, the room darkened. For a moment, he found himself back in the depths of the pit. He turned his thoughts back to Erica and returned to the room. She had swung her legs off the bed, and as her feet touched, she recoiled with disgust... or perhaps fear.

"Rafi," she said, her voice quiet, "Is that you?"

At first he thought to soothe, but his grief and fear coagulated into anger. He tried to speak, but couldn't and growled with frustration. He willed his mind to clear and found his voice, not through the flesh of his throat, which lay deep in the earth, but from his mind, clawing its way into hers. He thought, "You... Left... Me..."

She began to shake her head.

This made his anger peak, which gave him strength. "You... left... me... to... die..."

She shifted away from him toward the far side of the bed. "I'm sorry Rafi. I had no choice. I—"

"You left me to die down here."

She held up a hand and opened her mouth to speak, but something shifted and Rafi was back in the blackness of the cave. Far above, he sensed a fat spirit rooting in the bushes near the mouth of the pit. Drifting upward toward its bandit-like energy, he felt a great sense of contentment and hyper-awareness. As he came up over the edge of the pit, he saw it sitting between two plants, eating a large insect. The raccoon lowered its meal and its black-bead eyes looked toward him, searching. It turned to run just as Rafi touched its soul. The raccoon froze and let out a wailing screech. That made Rafi's anger flare. The raccoon was his and should submit. The animal turned on stiff legs, walked to the edge of the pit, fell in, and sank down.

Rafi found his corpse and the rotting pain, but he kept his attention on the fat, warm spirit coming down to him. When the raccoon settled nearby, he pried the round energy loose from the skull and spine and savored it. He felt stronger, and the pain in his joints and the troubling sense of rot lessened.

Thinking of the bug the raccoon had been eating, he realized how much life lay just outside the pit. He felt for them and sensed their archaic energy scattered all about the forest, but that energy did not have enough light to draw him up, so he lay in the dark pit, three hundred feet deep in the gullet of the earth, waiting.

CHAPTER 20

Erica spent the rest of the night hyper-aware, the slightest sound pulling her from sleep. As the light of dawn grew in the room, she lay watching the sky turn blue beyond the gauze of the curtain. When she considered what she had seen in the night, she felt sure it hadn't been a dream, and that left only one conclusion, she was losing her mind. She hadn't been overly emotional at Rafi's death. Perhaps the stress of it had come back to her in delusions. Now sunlight broke in through the bathroom window, and from where she lay, she could see the white enamel of the tub glowing brightly.

She rose from the bed and changed into the jeans and white shirt. As she finished zipping up the pants, the lock on the door clanged, and the sudden sound flooded her with adrenaline. The door opened, and a short woman came in butt-first. She turned, exposing a tray of food, and walked toward the glass-topped table. Her dark hair was rolled into a tight bun, and she wore a light-blue maid's uniform. Glancing at Erica with flat eyes, she set the tray down and walked back toward the door.

"Good morning," Erica said.

The woman gave Erica one iron glance and walked out of the room, leaving the door hanging open. Erica watched the gap. She expected it to snap shut at any moment, but it remained open. She waited for the woman to return. She did not. After a few more heartbeats, which brought lightness to Erica's shoulders and the strength to run into her legs, she walked toward the door. Its open promise felt like a trap.

She ran her finger down the rough-cut, metal edge of the door and leaned her head out into the hallway. The African stepped in front of her.

In his broad, West-African accent, he asked, "What ah you doing?"

"I was just looking down the hallway."

"Hoping to escape?"

Erica thought to accuse the woman of leaving the door open, but then thought better of it. If the woman was being careless, it was nothing, but if the hard look she had given Erica was a cover for someone who might be willing to help her later, she could not expose her.

"I can't escape," she said.

The African nodded and pointed into the room. "Eat. Then I will take you to the lawns by the ocean. There you can rest and consida' your situation."

Erica kept an eye on him as she walked back to the food. Feeling hunger coiling in her stomach, she picked up a thick slice of bread. Biting into it, she looked back to the African, who still stood in the doorway. After a moment, she realized she had been stuffing her mouth full of food, and midway through a tortilla filled with potatoes and eggs, she stopped and drank off half the glass of milk. The African stared at her as she ate but not with menace.

Her mouth full, she asked, "Why are you staring at me?"

The African's expression struck Erica as doubtful, not what she'd expect from cartel muscle, and he looked away from her to the window.

"Come on," she said, "If you have something to say, out with it."

His eyes, pure-white contrasting with pitch dark irises focused on her, and he said, "I am sorry."

"Sorry? What for?"

"I have a strict agreement with Camejo. I deal wit men in the trade. You were not drug runnas, and so I should not have been involved in his death."

Erica waited for more from the big man, but he only stared at her.

"That doesn't change the fact that he's dead."

The African nodded.

"You don't like working for him do you?"

"I have no problems with it."

"Telling yourself you have no problems is a lot different than enjoying it."

The African pushed the door closed, locked it, and walked over to the window, drawing the curtain aside. "Today is beautiful. You should enjoy it."

"It might be my last?"

The African stared out at the ocean in silence.

"Rafi was a good man you know."

He made no response, and in that silence, Erica thought she sensed regret.

"What's your name?" Erica asked.

If he gives me his name, there's a chance.

The African half-turned and glanced at her, but said nothing.

Erica walked up to him and held out her hand, "I'm Erica, and if you're going to kill me, I'd like to at least know the name of the man who is going to do it."

"I am Sedar, and I will not hurt you. It is not what I am paid for."

"It seems like that's what you're paid for."

"I am paid to deal with dangerous men, not people like you."

"You don't think I'm dangerous?"

"You do not seem so, but I have heard otherwise. It is not important. Today you ah safe, but tonight, if you have not revealed the gold, you will be hurt, not by my hand, but anotha's."

"You could stop it."

The African laughed and said, "Perhaps, but I would not. I have many obligations to my people. Senegal is very poor with little opportunity, so my family depends on the money I make here. I will not give that up for you. Your best plan is to give up the gold."

"But if I do that, I'll still be in danger."

Sedar's eyes searched hers for a moment. "A wise thought."

• • •

She spent the day on the lawns of the compound, which looked out on the Atlantic Ocean. Sedar maintained his distance from her, and brushed aside her few attempts at conversation. The woman from her room set lunch out on a table under a white pergola. As Erica ate, she scanned the borders of the compound, noting where guards stood, which ones remained vigilant and which drifted into boredom. She had no idea what to do with what she learned, but it was easier than thinking about Rafi.

In the later morning a small boat bobbed out onto the ocean. One of the men in the boat raised a gray cylinder. A cord trailed from the cylinder, and another man took hold of the cord's end. Smoke began curling away from it. The first man threw the cylinder in a broad, end-over-end arc. It splashed into the water, and after a moment, the sea lifted in a great disk, which ruptured, spraying water out onto the men in the boat. They raised their hands and shouted as the boat turned and motored to where the explosion had occurred. They began scooping nets into the water.

"Are they fishing with dynamite?"

"Yes."

"Why?"

"Because these ah children playing at being men."

"And yet you help them in their games."

Sedar looked at her, his eyes still calm, and said, "I love my wife and son more than my own self."

"The ends justify the means?"

He took a folded paper from his pocket and handed it to Erica. She opened it to find a child's drawing in crayon. It was of a small house with a misshapen door, a dark woman, and a young boy. The boy held his hand up under a round, yellow sun. Something had been written in what looked like French.

Sedar said, his voice becoming more intense, "In Senegal it is not so easy to change your fate, but because of these men, my wife and son sleep in a comfortable home. It is my fate to serve my family in this way."

"But doesn't Antonio become angry when you refuse certain... tasks?"

"At first yes, but I am too valuable to him otherwise. These men," he held his hand out toward the men still scooping fish out of the ocean, "do not have my sense of purpose."

As the sun crested past noon, Sedar took her back to her room. Remaining in the hallway as she walked into the room, he closed the door, and the lock clacked. There she remained with her thoughts as the afternoon wore on to evening. When the door clanked open again, Antonio, the native, and another man she had not seen before came into the room.

She found herself wishing Sedar was with them. It seemed that he had made good on his promise to not be present during this part.

Antonio held his hands out. "It is time for a decision. The gold... please."

Erica stared at him.

I've got to figure out how to buy some time.

"No?" He gave her a broad smile as if somehow relieved of a burden. "Then you are no longer my guest, and now I will make you give me what I want." He walked over to the window and pushed the drapes aside. The diamonds in the skull's eyes glinted in the setting sunlight. "It is an unfortunate outcome. If you had helped me, I would have let you go free." He turned back to her. "But... I prefer it this way. I have given you the opportunity, so without regret, I now get more than just the gold."

He tipped his head to the men, and they approached Erica. She backed away from them until her thighs touched the bed, and she knew what the first night would be. Her skin crawled, but she had been around long enough to know her choices, take a beating and be raped, or be raped. She couldn't fight off three men. With one she might be able to claw out an eye, maybe crush a testicle or smash a nose, but she wouldn't come out well against three.

If she just let it happen, would it be all three? She considered that Antonio wasn't the kind of man to share. It might just be him. Or perhaps he would just let his dogs have their share. Her heart raced. Fight or take it? She would take it, just let them do what they wanted. The less she fought, the less of a beating she would get.

She felt the native grip her wrist.

Just take it.

But as the other man reached for her wrist, she slipped his grasp, clawed across the native's face, and kicked at the other man's groin. He turned as she kicked, and her foot hit the meat of his thigh. The native made a grunting sound, holding his face as he turned away from her. The other man snatched both her hands and spun her around.

"Don't damage her," Antonio said, walking up beside them, "or you will reduce the price we can command for her. Now tie her down."

The man pulled her to a chair, not the bed. The native came over, his face bleeding from four thin trails, two above and two below his eye. He punched her in the stomach; his stony fist hit her spine through her guts, and pain disgorged itself, filling her torso from hips to throat. She leaned forward and dry-heaved. With her stomach muscles locked up, she couldn't breathe, and darkness began to fold in around the edges of her vision. Despite the pain, she forced herself to suck in air, and the sick sensation slowly flushed out of her chest and belly, leaving a sharpness where his fist had struck.

"That was due," Antonio said, "but no more games. Secure her."

The two men tied her hands to the chair's arm rests and her ankles to its legs.

"What are you going to do?" Erica let slip. She had wanted to be silent, to stonewall them, but as she felt her ability to move binding away, she became unsure.

Antonio stroked her face and said, "Mi querida, it is not what I will do to you that will make you tell me about my gold." He took a chair from the corner of the room, the one she had seen Rafi in the night before, and sat. "You are a beautiful woman. You are just a bit too old for my tastes."

With disgust Erica remembered the photo of Antonio with the young girl on the beach.

He motioned to the native, "Bring her in."

The native walked out of the room.

"You see," he patted his knees, "I understand you probably better than you do yourself. After years of this type of work, I have learned so much about people's true nature. Some will beg, others will last hours, a very few die without breaking, a very few."

The native came in gripping the bicep of a beautiful, young girl with copper-black skin. She couldn't have been more than sixteen years old, perhaps younger.

"Ah yes," Antonio stood, "here she is." He walked to the young girl and held up his hand, presenting her to Erica. "This is Hanna, the daughter of a man who works for me."

Hanna's eyebrows tilted with worry when she saw Erica.

"Don't worry," Erica said to the girl.

An attempt at a smile fluttered across Hanna's face.

"Yes," Antonio said, "Do not worry about her. She will sit comfortably," he raised his hand to the other man, who dug through a case and came out with a small slip of leather, buckles hanging from it, "while you are compromised."

The girl's eyes went wide. "No sir, please. My father... he—"

Antonio cut her short with a stiff slap across her face. "Mi querida, talking back will make it worse. Your father has lost too many of my shipments, so he must pay through you. In this case, I have the opportunity to make two of my debtors pay at one time." He stroked his hand across Hannah's face where he had slapped it and then down to the small curve of her breast. She tried to back away, but the native twisted her arm behind her, shoving her forward. The other man set the leather thing in Antonio's hand.

"Now," Antonio held the thing up to her, "if you let me put this on you without a fight, it will go easier. But if you fight, I will hurt you again. What do you think?"

He waited for her response.

She stared at him, her lower lip trembling. Tears spilled from her eyes, running down her neck to the collar of her shirt.

"So sweet and innocent." He gripped her by the back of the head, yanking her forward, and strapped the leather muzzle over her mouth, tugging the buckles tight. "You see," he said to Erica pointing at a faint scar, which ran along his left temple, "I learn from my mistakes." He motioned to his men as he said, "Tie her down."

Hanna's breath rushed through her nostrils as the two men shoved her forward and bent her face down on the end of the bed, her feet still on the floor. She screamed through the muzzle as they wrapped a rope under the bed and tied the ends to her wrists, hauling it tight.

Erica said, "If you do this, I am going to kill you, all three of you, in a worse way than you can possibly imagine."

At this the native gave her an angry stare, but the other two laughed.

Antonio said, "My dear, I do not need imagination when it comes to death and violence. I need only look into my memory. This, for example, is a masterpiece of my understanding of you. You are strong enough to hold your secrets. I would have to destroy your beauty to take them. I know this even if you do not. However, I think you will not allow an innocent to suffer."

The two men spread the girl's legs out, tying each ankle to a leg of the bed.

Antonio said, "You will not allow young Hanna to go through this."

He gripped the girl by her long braids and twisted her head so she faced Erica. Her eyes were red with tears, and her cheeks puffed against the muzzle. "Now my sweet, tell this woman, with a nod of your head, are you a virgin?"

The girl nodded.

Antonio released the girl's hair and sat on the side of the bed, his hand on the small of her back. "You see? You have the opportunity to preserve her."

"And I die after I tell you where the gold is." Anger flushed Erica's face as she said it, not because she would die, but because Antonio was right. She would not keep herself safe at the expense of the girl; he had beaten her so easily.

"No, mi querida," Antonio said. "We have already discussed this. You will be sold like an animal. I must make a profit for all my trouble. You will not be hurt, at least not in a way that will scar your body, and you will service countless men, seven days a week each day of the year. It is not so bad when you consider that you are already a whore. She though," he patted the girl's butt, and the girl turned her head away from them, "can go home, unscathed."

"The coordinates are wrong," Erica said.

"Ha!" Antonio shouted out standing up from the bed. "You see men? I can break the strongest will without effort. Learn well. Understanding is key. We must be intelligent in our work." He walked up to Erica, "What are the correct coordinates?"

"Rafi mixed them up."

Antonio took the scrap of paper from his back pocket and held them out to her. "How?"

She looked at the scrap and tried to remember what Rafi had said but couldn't recall even the first step in the changes he had made.

She looked at the girl, who lay with her face turned away from them, her shoulders trembling. Erica felt a sense of dread as she said, "I can't remember."

"Cannot or will not?"

"I want to, I will… just give me a minute."

Antonio looked at his watch. "I give you sixty seconds."

Erica stared at the numbers. Rafi had changed the minutes and the seconds. Transposed the seconds? Some up, some down.

Dammit, Erica, you have to remember this…

But as the minute passed, she couldn't, and when Antonio said, "Your time is up," she knew the gold was lost not only to Antonio, but to her as well.

She looked back at the girl as she said, "I will remember, please. Just give me some time."

"You are stalling."

"No, I—"

"Enough of this." He moved to stand behind Hanna and took a blade from his pocket. Crouching by the girl's ankle, he gripped the fabric of her pant leg and slit it all the way up. The girl shouted something beneath the muzzle as her leg and panties became exposed. He gripped her other pant leg, cut it up the back, and pulled the splayed jeans out from under her. Lifting her shirt, he cut it open, exposing her dark, smooth back, which tremored with her crying.

"Don't," was all Erica could think to say, "I swear to God I'll kill you if you do that."

Antonio did not look at her as he smiled at her threat. He slid his knife up under the girl's white panties, saying, "Oaths to God will do you no good here. Even He cannot save you pitiful creatures from me."

CHAPTER 21

Rafi lay in the darkness, the burning in his joints increasing; the heat of the disease made him desperate to rise away again. The cold water pressing in on him, filling his nose, mouth, and lungs, did nothing to ease the fire. Along with his joints, his skin began to smolder and his belly went taught, distending with the rot inside him.

He had to get away, screamed for it in his mind, but couldn't let the scream out, so it stayed with him, bottled up in his mind. High above, he sensed the sparkling energy of life, and as his spirit disconnected from the corpse, he felt the rushing relief of separation—no pain, only lightness. The predatory need for what scuffled in the undergrowth above overwhelmed him. The life felt primitive, somewhat dim, but large and with enough intensity to draw him up. He rose up with more power and speed now, and he wished he could move more slowly, wished he could spend more time separated from his corpse, but the desire for the thing and the fear that it might escape drove him on at a great rush.

He rose up out of the water, over the edge of the pit, and saw the snake. Reaching out to it, he felt its reptilian energy and instinctual mind. The snake curved into a half circle and rolled belly up, muscle tremors passing down its length in waves. It went still. Rafi wanted to draw the snake into the pit, but it wouldn't move. He stayed with the snake, feeling its strange mind, but could not lever his way into it. Yet the snake could not escape him. At that moment, he sensed the bright heat of a large rodent farther away.

His spirit leapt away from the snake, but the moment he left it, the rodent moved too far away, and Rafi lost the connection. His corpse began to draw him back toward the pit. In desperation, he sought the anchor of the snake and found it moving away into the underbrush. He gripped it, and the snake writhed and went still again. Holding the snake, he extended his awareness out into the world. He sensed the soul-heat of many animals around him, but none were close enough to move to. He felt as though he were hanging on a wall, the soul of the snake his only handhold. Out here in the light of morning, freed from the pain of rot and the darkness of his grave, he could see with clear vision, could feel the world glowing with a streaming energy all around him.

The spirit of the snake began to feel strange to him. The warmth of it, a deep violet, darkened and faded. A rush of energy dispersed into the surrounding world, and only then did Rafi realize that he had been gripping it too tightly. It had suffocated. With only the cooling flesh there, he had nothing to hold, and he slipped away from it, down into the mouth of the hole, under the surface of the water, and back into the depths.

...

Rafi lay in his corpse for some time, pain clawing its way into the pores of his bones, before he felt a brilliant heat high above. It faded away but then returned, and his soul leapt away from his corpse. He did not wish to hold himself back now but rose up out of the hole and crossed the stretch of forest and gripped the fat hutia. Rafi felt the rodent's mind; faded with age, the animal had ignored the instinct to stay in its burrow in the daylight, almost as though it had given up. He folded himself into its mind and felt its heat, weak and old, but with more than enough energy to serve. With ease the mind became his, and the animal turned and walked to the pit, fell into the water, and floated head down. Squeezing the belly, he forced its air out, and it sank down. He drifted down before it and joined with his corpse, the blistering pain coming to him again. When it landed in the muck near him, he pried the soul loose, drew it in, and felt a delicious cooling of the burn. The pain in his joints faded to a tolerable ache, and the distension of his belly lessened. His left index finger twitched, which startled him.

...

Throughout the day he captured several other small animals, mostly mice. He happened on a few other snakes but had the same experience with them. A few birds landed in the trees near the pit, and when he clutched them, they fell from their perches and dragged their wide-splayed wings through the dirt and fell in the pit. But the hollow-boned birds would not sink, and he had to give up on them. When he released them, he felt each soul drift free.

Each time he rose up, the day had worn on, and soon evening came on. The darkness of night brought more hutia out. He fed on them, growing stronger. When the stars had turned a quarter arc in the sky, he could move all the fingers of his left hand, and the pain of rotting had faded to almost nothing. Yet, when he wasn't hunting, he still felt the desperation of being locked in the corpse with the dark water pressing on him. He dug the fingers of his left hand into the hundreds of years of silt; sifting through its soft layers kept him calm.

As the night wore on, he began to think about Erica again. He missed her and wanted to be with her, wanted her to be with him. He imagined her soul glittering with blazing rainbows as if sunlight through a diamond and felt hunger, and that hunger troubled him. Still, he contemplated how a person's intricate soul would feel and the strength it would give him. He had to get someone near his grave.

He lay thinking of Erica's bright spirit for some time. He thought of the last time he had envisioned her in that unfamiliar bedroom. Now he felt as though he could see the bedroom again, see the drapes billowing in arcing curves. In the darkness, he saw the bed, empty with its covers disheveled. Beyond the bed, in the corner, he saw a crown of blonde hair.

Erica.

Her head rose, and she looked at him.

CHAPTER 22

When Antonio had finished with the girl, he dressed and left the room, his men leaving with him. The girl lay in the nude, still tied to the bed, and in the quiet of the space, Erica could hear the girl's grief in the tremor of her breathing. Erica had tried to pull herself free from the chair, but could not. She tried to think of something to say to the girl, but knew nothing would really help.

"It will be all right," she paused for a moment before settling on, "someday."

The lock clanked and the door opened. The native entered and untied the girl, pulled her up, and took her from the room, leaving her shredded clothes behind. Another man came in, untied Erica's arms, and left the room, leaving her to free her own legs. At that moment she felt sorrow and self-pity rising up, felt as though she might cry, but instead she screamed and hit her thighs with clenched fists.

I won't let that bastard break me.

She felt her skin crawling, as if what she had seen had happened to her, and she went to the bathroom and showered, scrubbing her skin raw. When she came back out into the room, no one had set out pajamas for her.

No longer a guest.

She looked at the silk pajamas she had worn the night before but instead put her jeans and the shirt back on. She felt the need to be ready should some kind of opportunity arise. Sitting on the bed for a moment, she felt uneasy being connected to it. As she stood, the lights in the room clicked off, leaving her in darkness. She looked to the door, but it remained closed.

She felt exposed in the darkness of the room, at risk, her back out in the open, so she went to the corner between the bed and the wall, sat on the hard tile, and stared at the metal plate of the door. She had been there for some time, not sleeping, her butt going numb on the tile. She sat holding her knees looking at her toes as what had happened to the girl began to play through her mind again.

She blocked it by imagining Camejo dead. Imagined what he would look like. She began to play scenarios through her mind as to how she would kill him. But the girl came back to her again, and the belief that she had failed the girl haunted her. If she had only been able to remember the changes Rafi had made.

She felt angry—angry at herself and angry at all the men she had known for either being evil or useless. All but Rafi. She thought of Abram and considered how she would make him pay if she could. She thought of Brandon's head caved in. She thought of Alex's look of shock and anger when she had shot him.

That's what I'm going to do, kill each one, but not fast like I did Brandon. The next one I'll let drown.

Erica... a whisper, not heard as much as sensed in the corner of her mind, interrupted her thoughts.

She looked up. Rafi's apparition sat in the far corner of the room. The visage made her uneasy, but after what had just happened, even the spectral image of Rafi was some kind of comfort. She wanted to speak, wanted to get up and walk over to him, to see his face, but she felt a flush of fear at what she might see and what he might say. The dead tone of his voice in her mind felt wrong, as if it was some kind of sin to even listen to it.

Erica... the thought came to her again, sending a chill down her spine, *what have they done to you?*

She tried to speak, but could not, so she only let the thought go through her mind: *Nothing, I'm fine.*

No. Not fine.

I'm fine Rafi. She put her face in her hands and thought, *I'm either dreaming or losing my mind.*

Why would you think so?

She looked back to the apparition, now finding her voice. "Because you're dead. This isn't real."

Tell them to come to me.

She closed her eyes and drew a deep breath.

Tell them to come to me. I will give them what they deserve.

The voice in her mind grew in strength, no longer a whisper, but a low, stiff version of Rafi's voice. Keeping her eyes closed she drew another breath, exhaling slowly.

She thought to herself, *You've got to keep calm. Don't lose it now.*

She heard nothing for some time and continued her slow breathing, drawing each breath through her nose and letting it out through her mouth. Opening her eyes, she looked at the chair, hoping to see it empty, hoping to have control of her mind now. Yet there Rafi sat, looking out from under his draped, wet hair. As before, his eyes did not quite meet hers but missed at a dead angle, as Brandon's had. His skin seemed grayer than before as well, but not quite as gaunt, less rotten.

Surprising herself, she found her voice and screamed at the apparition, "Leave me alone! Go away!" She gripped her knees tighter to herself.

Don't do this. Don't let yourself go crazy.

You are not crazy.

"If I'm not crazy, why am I talking to a dead man?" She regretted asking it the moment it was out. She was playing into her own mind, letting the fantasy take over. Closing her eyes, she heard a squeaking, wet footstep and then another. She looked up. Rafi was walking toward her. Gripping her knees, she pushed her back into the wall.

"Please don't Rafi... please. Just go. I can't take this."

I can help you, Erica. I can take them, punish them, but you have to bring them to me.

In the dim light, she saw the water come drooling across the floor in an unbroken sheet, preceding him as he walked. It touched her toes, wrapped around her feet, and soaked into the seat of her jeans. She stood and pressed her back into the corner of the room. Rafi continued toward her.

I can take them down with me. It will make me stronger. In time we might still be together.

He walked around the corner of the bed, the animated cadaver's chest sunken, shoulders slumped, and head set wrong. The terror she felt became tinged with sadness. Rafi didn't stand like that. He had been so... vibrant.

He entered the space between the wall and the bed, blocking her in. She thought for a moment to jump over the bed, but as she looked at his eyes, not quite meeting hers she found she couldn't move. She drew quick, shallow breaths as he walked right up to her. The smell of death hit her, mold and rot, but she understood somehow that it wasn't Rafi's body that had rotted, not yet, it was the smell of the water, the reek of the depths of the pit he had drowned in. The stench surrounded her, spread across the tile, soaked into his clothes and hair, and into her jeans.

Her voice a whisper, she asked him, "What do you want?"

Bring them to me. I can make them pay. I will consume them.

His eyes remained misaligned with hers, and she was glad of it, afraid of what she might see in them.

Bring them to me.

She nodded and forced out a whisper, "Okay, I'll try. I will. I'll find a way."

Then he was gone. She leaned back against the wall and slid down to the dry floor. She felt her jeans. Dry as well.

...

She stayed in the corner the rest of the night—at one moment her eyes scanning the room, the next her head on her knees dozing. When dawn had come on enough to burn the darkness away, she stood and sat on the bed. Despite what had happened there, the softness of the mattress called to her, and in her exhaustion, she lay back. As she stared at the ceiling, sleep pulled at her eyes. She didn't want to fall asleep, but the fear and abuse had taken its toll, and she drifted off into a wonderful emptiness.

...

Hearing a clank, she opened her eyes. She looked around the room, her mind still half in the underworld of sleep. The door swung open, and her chest flushed with a fast heartbeat. The adrenaline brought her to clarity, and she sat up on the bed, shoving herself backward, getting her back against the headboard.

Antonio walked in, followed by the native and another man, short and thick across the shoulders and neck.

Antonio smiled. "Did you sleep well, mi querida?" He took the chair from the corner and moved it to the bed. Erica stared at it as he brought it near her. She felt something hopeful in that chair now, something good in Antonio sitting in it.

Antonio sat. "You look like hell itself, mi querida. I do not think you slept well. It would be unwise to not keep up your beauty. If your value should falter, I will be compelled to use the old way of things, fingernails, eyelids, lips. Do you understand me?"

She stared at him.

He held his palm out and set his other hand in it, inspecting his fingernails. Then he rubbed them together. "Now is the time for you to begin to talk. Although, I have to admit," he leaned forward in the chair, "After last night, I hope you don't just yet. Another night, another girl. It is wonderful for me." He smiled. "How did it feel for you, to allow that to happen?"

Anger burned in Erica at that, and she had to force herself to let it go. She had weighed the next few moments in her mind, measured them out against the risk. "What you did last night is no different than how you came into this world, your mother tied to a bed."

Antonio stared at her, not appearing to have understood her.

Erica watched him for a moment before saying slowly, "Your mother is a whore."

His face flushed red, and he came out of the chair and onto the bed. She brought her hands up. He shoved them down, slapped her, and gripped her neck, cutting off her air.

"You low-rent puta," he said, speckling her face with warm spittle. "How dare you."

She shoved his hands aside, sucked in air and said, "You're a pig."

Antonio fairly growled the next words. "Every night for the rest of your short life, you will regret this."

She smiled at him. "...just a sack of shit in a silk shirt."

Antonio bared his teeth and backhanded at her face. She fell away from the blow, and his fingertips flicked her cheek.

"Perra," he said through gritted teeth, grabbing her shirt and pulling her forward, "give me my gold."

"You're desperate," Erica said, "because they're going to skin you alive if you don't get it. Am I wrong?"

He punched at her, but she slipped it and received only a glancing blow along her ear. The next caught her full in the face, and a cracking sensation filled her skull as she went bright-blind for a moment. Blood poured from her nasal cavity into the back of her mouth, and she sputtered. When her vision returned, she saw she had sprayed red speckles across Antonio's white shirt.

"You filthy whore," he yelled at her, the veins in his neck and across his forehead rising. "This shirt is worth more than your life." He hit her in the left side of her ribcage and then on the right, then left, and then right. An open palm cracked across her face.

With each blow Erica felt herself breaking down, wanting it to end, but she had to hold on, let it be bad enough that he would believe he had broken her. She sputtered more blood, and Antonio screamed at her, "Tell me where the gold is you filthy whore. Tell me or, and I swear this on my mother's grave, I'll have dogs raping you by the end of the day."

"Stop," she said and meant it. "Please stop."

Antonio held up a fist, which trembled with his anger, and he spit the words at her, "Tell me."

"I don't remember the changes to the coordinates fully. I remember some though, but not all."

He slapped her again. "That won't save you. We cannot find the gold with just a few of the changes. What are the minutes and seconds of the position?"

"I don't know."

He slapped her again.

"I have no idea."

He held up his hand, ready to slap again, and said, "You are making this worse."

"That's all I know." She raised her hands, hiding under them. "Please, you have to believe me. I just can't remember it all."

Antonio shoved her arms aside and raised his hand again.

"Stop... please."

He hit her again.

"Please no more."

He raised his hand again, and a thrill of fear went down her back. He brought his hand down, cracking it across her face and a well-spring of endorphins rose up on the pathway the fear had cut down her spine. She felt dizzy and her face burned. She turned her head and spit out more blood.

"Please, I do know it... not the exact numbers... but they're written down."

Antonio's hand hovered mid-strike, and he stared at her. "Where?"

"On a second slip of paper. The correct coordinates."

Antonio smiled at her now, sincere and warm, his anger suddenly forgotten. "Good. Where is this note?"

"In Rafi's shoe."

CHAPTER 23

Antonio shoved himself off the bed, kicked the chair over, and spit on it. He glared at her, and she saw in his frustrated anger that he believed her. The victory blanched just as she felt it because she had no idea if the visage of Rafi in the night had been real, a dream, or her mind coming loose. She had gambled on it being real and felt she was probably a fool for having done so. It had only bought her a scrap of time, which would run out all too soon.

"We go *now*." Antonio motioned for the native to deal with Erica and left the room.

The native walked over to the bed, grabbed her arm, pulled her off the bed, and shoved her forward, out of the room.

In the courtyard, Antonio climbed into the driver's seat of a Land Rover, and the native pointed Erica to its open rear gate. She climbed in. When the native stepped away, Erica found Sedar standing a few paces from the Rover, his expression blank. She stared at him as he climbed into the back with her.

He did not look at her but took a white cloth from his pocket and held it out.

She took it and began to wipe the blood from her upper lip. "Thank you."

With a quick motion of his hand, he indicated she should be silent.

The native climbed into the passenger seat. The door closed with a flat, aluminum thump, and Antonio pulled the truck out of the courtyard, down the gravel road, and out onto the highway. After a short drive, they arrived in a worn-down, waterfront town. Men sitting in stained resin chairs set out on the dirt space in front of a sheet metal-roofed house watched with callous eyes as the Land Rover passed.

Antonio pulled the truck up to a shop, which had a cracked front window held in place with a lightning swath of duct-tape. Above the window, a weathered sign read, Escobar's Diving. Antonio tipped his head to the native, who went into the shop. In a few moments, he emerged followed by two men carrying scuba tanks. They each had dark-brown skin. The younger man had thick, blue-black hair. The older man's had thinned with age, but the muscles of his back showed through his red shirt as he lifted the tanks and set them in the back of a dented Toyota pickup.

They went back into the shop and emerged again carrying heavy, mesh bags. As they set the bags in the truck, Antonio backed the Land Rover into the street and drove away. Erica watched the buildings go out of sight among the trees. After a few moments, the Toyota came into view behind them and, turn after turn, caught up. The truck came close enough that she could see the men well and, looking them both over, decided they weren't evil like Antonio, merely apathetic, which was of no help to her.

She turned her attention to Sedar. He glanced at her, and she continued to watch him.

He looked directly into her eyes. "Why do you stare at me?"

"You're from Senegal?" Erica asked him.

At first he said nothing, just gazed at her with his obsidian irises, his body shifting in subtle jolts with the motion of the Land Rover. "Why?" he asked.

Erica shrugged off his question. "I just wonder who you are. What was your mother's name?"

He looked away and said nothing more.

The Land Rover turned off the road, dropping down the gravel shoulder to a two-rut trail into the forest. As the Rover crawled its way down the trail Erica began to feel uneasy, something primal, as if a predator were stalking her, its eyes golden among tall grasses. Her legs glittered with nervous energy, and she shifted them, tried to let the feeling go, but the closer they came to the pit, the stronger the feeling became.

Sedar looked out the windshield, his eyes concerned.

...

Rafi lay in the depths, feeling for life. With each small animal taken, his left hand had become more and more animated until he could move his left arm. He felt the ache of rot in his elbow and shoulder as he bent them, but moving them gave him release from the sense of being trapped in the rest of his corpse, so he continued to shift his arm, bend his wrist, and flex his fingers.

As he curled each finger, touching the tips to his thumb one at a time, he sensed another spirit come within his reach, something stumpy and earthen rooting in the brush. He lifted away to go take it just as a brilliance came into the edge of his

217

awareness, four souls, dazzling in their depth and color. He paused, hovering in the darkness just above his corpse. They came directly into his circle, right toward the mouth of the pit. He felt each spirit, searing with power. One burned with anger, another with nervous energy. Still another felt a troubling regret, and then he felt the fourth. At first it pained him to feel the light, like the shock of mountain water. He watched her approach, the others forgotten in her scintillating spectrum. He felt a profound love for her and coveted her light as it shifted in deep hues from violets, through blues, and into gem-stone reds. He had asked something of her... tried to remember what it had been. He thought through each animal he had drawn down into the pit until he came back to the memory of her in the bedroom and him asking her... to bring them to him.

He moved his attention reluctantly away from her and to the others. They did not have the same intensity for him but still had so much blinding energy that he feared what would happen when he tried to take control of them. Being this close felt as though he were standing too near a bonfire, its heat at once painful and yet tantalizing after being in the cold. Another pair of spirits came on behind the first four, and Rafi understood how well she had done. She had come to save him.

Despite the voracious desire to rise up to them, he settled back into his corpse and waited. Let them come, and take them one at a time.

...

Eduardo Escobar stopped his pickup beside the Land Rover and stepped out onto the hard-packed dirt. He walked around to the back of the truck, keeping his eyes off the woman in the back with the swollen right eye and blood at the corners of her mouth. It wasn't his business. He worked for Antonio because the money was right, and money made the world go. He had hurt no one and could do nothing for those who had been hurt; he made his money and went on with his life.

If Antonio needs something from the pocket of a man's body at the bottom of the Sacred Blue Hole, then I dive the Sacred Blue Hole. I have no connection to the death.

Antonio came around the cab of the truck and said, "Make sure to get everything in the body's pockets and shoes."

Eduardo, now unpacking his gear, nodded without raising his head.

He turned to his dive partner, the darker skinned Mayan, Pacal, and motioned for him to get the tanks from the back of the truck.

If luck is with us, the body will have fallen straight down to the bottom of the main cavern. If so, we will be down and up in no time.

Pacal set the tri-mixed tanks in front of Eduardo.

"We are going deep today," Eduardo said to Antonio as he began to assemble the tanks in a triangle of two mains and one emergency pony bottle. "The bottom of the well is just over 300 feet. It is a straight shaft, so what you need should be at the bottom. It will be no problem." He looked to Pacal, "Can you bring my B.C. as well?"

Antonio held up his hand, "Take care to not miss anything."

Eduardo glanced at the cartel boss and wondered if he could handle a cave collapse. He had seen many men show their true selves in the depths.

Pacal set the buoyancy compensators beside the tanks, and Eduardo attached his B.C. to his tank setup. He stood, walked around the back of the truck, took a red reel of guide line from his bag, and attached it to his B.C. If the body was in the main shaft, they should not need the line, but even up and down can become confused in a silt-out, and if they had to search side caves it would be essential.

Pacal inspected Eduardo's tank setup and gave an okay with his hand. Eduardo attached the tanks to his B.C. and screwed the first stage yokes of each regulator to the tank valves. Twisting the valves, he checked the pressure on his computer and fitted each of the three regulators into his mouth and breathed in. He received a smooth flow of air from each. The emergency regulator buzzed a bit on exhalation, but it would not be a problem.

As he helped Pacal with his setup, Antonio asked, "How long will this take?"

"Patience will be needed today, Señor. Even though we are diving ten-seventy tri-mix, and even if we only spend a few moments at the bottom, we will need perhaps an hour of decompression time near the surface. He pounded a stake into the ground near the well, tied a cord to it, attached the other end to a pair of tanks with regulators, and lowered them into the water. The tank faded some sixty feet down into the darkness.

"Air for decompression time," he said in answer to Antonio's quizzical look.

Antonio waved Eduardo's words aside. "Just bring me the scrap of paper in his shoe, and be careful not to smear the ink."

As Eduardo and Pacal walked back to the truck, Pacal said, his voice higher and his words clipped in the Mayan way, "If the ink smears? If the paper cannot be read?"

Eduardo gave a subtle shake of his head and said, "The goal today, is to get down, get what he wants, and get back up."

"I do not like this. Who will be blamed if he cannot read it or if we find nothing?"

Eduardo shrugged.

"I do not like doing business with this kind of man," Pacal said as he walked away from the truck with his wetsuit, fins, and mask.

Eduardo followed him. When they had their gear on, Eduardo stood at the edge of the hole and stared into the dark water. In over three decades of diving, he had learned to trust his instincts, and at this moment, he felt something unlucky in the air.

He looked at Pacal. "How do you feel?"

Pacal stood looking down into the hole. He rubbed his smooth face, and said, "Not good."

Eduardo looked over his shoulder at Antonio, who leaned with his elbow on the Land Rover, and then back down into the water.

"It should be an easy job. We go down and get the paper from his pocket and we make one thousand U.S." He said it more to ease himself than to convince Pacal, but it did nothing to improve how he felt. Looking back over his shoulder at Antonio, he said, "This is not feeling right, Señor Camejo. I do not think we should dive today."

"What?" Antonio pushed himself away from the Land Rover and walked over to them, anger in his voice. "Por qué no hoy?"

"There's a bad feeling to this. I—"

"Eduardo, you are a friend," Antonio said. "As a friend, I tell you I need this. I need what is in that man's shoe. It is critical."

Eduardo looked at the still surface of the water, at his reflection hovering over the lip of rock. If Antonio had threatened him, been rough, he would have walked away. He'd been through enough and wouldn't be pushed around. He looked over to Pacal. Pacal shrugged at him. Eduardo looked back down into the well of water. He could see the sides of the limestone walls in the clarity of the water, could even see the ledge of the first side cave. He knew the hole well; it would just be straight down and back up, only an hour of decompression. He imagined how that would go. Hanging in the maw of the cavern with nothing to do but breathe, the mind could play tricks. The hairs on his forearms tingled.

"You're a cautious man, Eduardo," Antonio said. "That is why I do business with you. You have always helped me when I needed it. I need this now. I will make a better deal, yes? If you get me what I need, you will have a bonus... double my first offer."

Eduardo looked at Pacal again. One thousand dollars each was a lot of money.

Pacal said, "Just down and up for that? Even if everything goes wrong, I can hold my breath long enough for that much money."

Nodding, Eduardo said to Antonio, "You are a generous man. We will dive."

With that, he looked over Pacal's gear, and Pacal did the same for him. He lifted his mask to his eyes, adjusted the strap, and put his regulator in his mouth, inhaling the dry air. Looking down into the water, an electric uneasiness filled his chest and tingled down his spine. He put his mind off of it.

A quick two thousand dollars.

With that thought, he gripped the low-pressure valve, adding air to his B.C., held his dive computer and safety spool to his chest with one hand, and his mask with the other and stepped off the ledge. With a fluid motion he brought his legs together just as his heels struck the water, which crashed over him. He floated to the surface. Resting back on the air in his

B.C., he kicked away from the center to give room to Pacal, who jumped in just as Eduardo had. The crash of water filled the space and faded, the water slapping in echoes against the limestone walls. Pacal turned to him and put his fist on the top of his head and Eduardo did the same. All okay.

Laying face-down in the water, Eduardo looked into the depths of the cavern. His eyes traced down the far wall to where it faded to blackness, and he drew slow breaths through his regulator. When he exhaled, bubbles roiled around his ears and neck.

Just down and up again.

Taking the guideline reel from its D-ring, he swept his fins and floated over to the side of the wall. Finding a thick root, he tied the end of the line to it. He turned to Pacal again and gave him an okay sign. Pacal returned it, so Eduardo pulled his dump valve and dropped below the surface of the water. He equalized the air pressure in his ears and, as he sank, turned on his side to look up at the sky, warping beyond the surface of the water. He let the spool turn freely on his finger, and Pacal followed him just a few feet above.

Descending below the lip of the side cave, he looked into the wide, dark gap. He unhooked his pistol-grip light and drew it out on a coiled line. Pressing the rubberized switch, he played the broad beam across the canine-like stalactites and stalagmites. He aimed the beam deep into the cave, and it ended on the distant, dead-end wall in a broad, blue circle, lined with the uneven rings of the dive-light's lens imperfections.

He turned and found Pacal hovering beside him, waiting. Eduardo lay horizontal again and let himself drift downward. Pacal's flashlight beam flicked on behind him, illuminating more of the well below. As they descended, the cavern walls further down lost their clarity, blurring with the halocline, the layer between fresh and saltwater. There, the cave opened up in a broad shelf. Dropping below the blur of the halocline, they returned to crystalline visibility. Down further, lay a red swath of hydrogen sulfide excreted from bacteria. They passed down through the layer, their skin absorbing the toxin. As they passed he felt his lips tingling and the scent of rotten eggs bloomed in his sinus cavity. He tipped head-down and kicked to drive through the layer quickly. Passing beyond it, he turned sideways again and aimed his light back up, watching Pacal emerge from the cloud, followed by a swirl of red fog. Returning to his descent, he played the light along the limestone walls, which were broken here and there by side caverns.

At regular intervals, he equalized the pressure in his ears and tapped his low pressure inflator, adding air to his B.C., slowing his descent. Patience and slow going were important here. If he touched the bottom, or even kicked a fin near it, he'd raise a blinding cloud of silt. Eduardo looked up at Pacal, who hovered beside the guide line above him. Beyond Pacal, he could see the towers of bubbles from their regulators leading the way to the surface. He panned the light downward and instead of a dark maw, he saw the pattern of his dive-light on the cavern's pale floor. He dropped closer and played the light back and forth, illuminating a waxy hand.

The feeling which had continued to worry at his mind crested to a panic at the sight of the hand. He felt as though his regulator was not giving him enough air, and his ribs did not seem able to expand enough to draw a full breath. For the first time in decades, he looked up and wanted to race to the surface, but at three hundred feet that was not an option. From this depth the bends would likely kill him without decompression. He hovered for a moment, drawing slow breaths, and looked at Pacal, whose diving mask framed his worried eyes. Eduardo gave him the okay sign and Pacal held his hand flat and tilted it back and forth in the 'something's wrong' signal. Pointing at the body, he rolled his finger in a 'let's get this done' motion.

Eduardo nodded his agreement and flicked the switch on a second, larger light that let off a wide-beam floodlight. Letting the new light float freely at his side, he descended toward the body, which lay in the shifting circles of his and Pacal's dive lights. The blue light gave it a supernatural pallor. Eduardo felt his chest fluttering and measured his breaths to the best of his ability. The body lay with its hands strewn at its sides and one leg folded under.

He stopped his descent with a touch of air and hovered a few feet over the body. The feeling of panic rose to terror. The desire to ascend became unbearable, and he looked up to find Pacal turning upright and kicking his fins as he rose away from Eduardo. Pacal looked down and motioned for Eduardo to follow him. With his attention on Pacal, it seemed as though he could feel the body beneath him... looking at him. He turned to find the dead eyes, which he had thought had been off at an angle, staring into his.

Screw the money and screw Antonio.

He tried to look away from the eyes, to begin his ascent, but found he could not. He failed to maintain his elevation, drifting down close to the dead face. He wanted to sweep his hands, to shove himself away from the body, but his arms would not move. Adrenaline coursed through his chest, but still his arms hung in relaxed arcs at his side.

The corpse's left arm fluttered in a current of water and, trailed by silt, floated up toward Eduardo's chest. Another current of water caught the hand, flushing it open, and as the hard fingers scraped along his BC's straps, the fingers clamped down, locking onto him. The corpse's other hand floated up, and the fingers drifted open and gripped the regulator. Eduardo's relaxed jaw allowed the regulator to slip from his mouth.

Eduardo's wanted to hold his breath, but he felt his mouth opening and his belly begin to pull. Water drew into his nose and mouth, passing along his tongue, down his throat, and filling his lungs. Everything fell to darkness. Yet, in that darkness he sensed a hunger smoldering nearby, blistering him with pain. He felt his soul, not drifting free as he felt it should have, but being torn away from the flesh and consumed one blazing piece at a time.

CHAPTER 24

Rafi basked in the heat of the soul as he absorbed it. His cold heart filled with a luminous energy, beat twice, and fell silent again. The sensation thrilled him, and he wanted more. His arms had more strength now, and he shifted the diver's body aside. Feeling the second soul rising away, he disconnected from his corpse and flashed up after it.

...

Erica had been taken from the back of the Land Rover and stood beside Antonio now, who had passed the time telling her what he had personally experienced in the Middle Eastern brothels. She might not face too much pain, he assured her, if she cooperated. It was always worse for those who were difficult for their handlers. They would inject her with heroin, and when the addiction took over, she would cease caring. She would bring high rates and might be fortunate enough to find a private setting, servicing only a small group of men rather than an endless line of those unknown. When her beauty had faded she would be set free, an addict and most likely infected.

He looked over her face, touching the swelling he had created, and said, "I don't think you'll suffer any permanent damage." He lifted her chin with his index finger. "It will do my heart good to know that I helped you find your place in the world. Nothing but a—"

Splashing water and screams interrupted him. As Sedar crouched down at the edge of the pit, Antonio gripped Erica's arm and dragged her with him. She looked over the edge with them and saw the younger diver. He tried to begin climbing, but the weight of his tanks prevented it. He threw off his mask and clawed at his harnesses, all while yelling out several times, as if in a cry for help, "Está ahogando!"

Erica saw animal terror in his eyes and wanted to run, not caring if it meant they would beat her again. But instead of running, she lay down in the dirt at the edge of the hole and reached out to the diver. Some fifteen feet still separated them, but she had nothing else to offer.

The diver finally managed to fully disconnect the straps of his B.C., shouldered them off, and let the assembly fall into the water. He tried to climb, but something stopped him. He pushed off the wall, falling back into the water, and pulled his fins off his feet, tossing them aside. As they sank in slow rotations, he began to climb the rock wall, keeping his eyes on hers, as if drawing strength from her. The look in his eyes terrified Erica, but she remained with her arm extended.

In quiet, pleading words, as if between just them, he said, "El fantasma ahogó Eduardo."

He had come all the way out of the water and in a few more yards would have Erica's hand. She heard a scuffle of dirt and rocks beside her and looked over to find Sedar lying with his hands on the ledge. Erica felt something coming up out of the depths, but could see nothing in the clear water. She pulled her arm back and moved into a pushup position, fighting the desire to run. The diver, still in the barrel of the hole, seemed fully exposed to whatever she sensed rising up around him.

The diver, still looking into Erica's eyes, stopped climbing. The veins in his neck and on his face stood out. He sputtered, saliva spraying the rocks in front of him, and his arms began to tremble.

His breath seething through his teeth, he said, "Ayúdeme," and fell. In the short moment before he hit the water Erica could see his fingers locked in claws, the tendons straining at the flesh. He hit the water, and the noise of it crashed around the mouth of the pit, echoing up. As the turbulent water stilled, she saw the diver's face warping below the surface, his body sinking down. His eyes remained on hers. Bubbles erupted from his mouth, and he sank more quickly, vanishing into the depths.

An arm wrapped around Erica's waist, and she was off the ground, over a shoulder and moving fast. She couldn't take her eyes off the limestone ledge. That wide gap in the forest floor below the ledge of rock seemed to call to her. Even as it drew her, she wanted be away from it, on the other side of the world, but at that moment even the other side of the world didn't seem far enough.

The forest spun, and she could no longer see the hole. The rear doors of the Land Rover interrupted her view of the forest as they slammed shut. Sedar sat beside her, gasping for air. The Land Rover's tires spun in the dirt as it reversed. Leaping backward down the rutted trail, it bounced off rocks, and tree limbs cracked on the rear doors. The transmission howled.

She turned to look out the windshield and found herself facing Antonio, his arm braced over the passenger seat as he looked out the rear windows and drove.

"Get your head out of the way woman."

She leaned to the side and through the windshield saw the limestone ledge moving away from them. The native ran down the sandy ruts after them. She looked to Sedar, who also watched the native chasing after them, and saw in Sedar's eyes that he had no use for the man.

...

When they got back to the compound, Antonio leapt out of the truck. He came around the back, threw open the doors, gripped her by the hair, and dragged her out. She staggered to keep up with him as he led her into the mission, up the stairs, and down the hallway. He threw her into the open doorway of her room. She fell, and he followed her into the room and kicked her in the thigh. The sick sensation that came on with the white-hot pain made her wonder for a moment if he had broken her femur. Her lower leg and foot went numb.

"Explain to me what just happened." He kicked her again.

She shouted back at him, angry that he should expect her to explain something she was equally unsure of, "I have no idea."

"This was your doing," He got down on his knees beside her and gripped her hair.

She'd had enough and punched him in the throat as hard as she could. He fell backwards as his hands came to his throat, and he let out a wet wheeze. His back arched up, and he rolled to his side, coughing so violently that it made his feet kick at the floor.

She screamed at him, "I have no fucking idea what just happened!" She sat up and leaned closer to him, her numb leg sticking out to the side. "Do you get that? Are you smart enough to understand that?"

Sedar, who had followed them into the room, stepped close to her, and she looked at him. He stopped short.

She said, "Do you understand it? I don't know; I don't fucking know what just happened." But in her heart she really did know, and it scared her more than anything she had experienced yet in life.

Sedar nodded at her and looked to Antonio, who still lay on the floor wheezing. He walked up to Antonio, lifted him to his feet, and walked him hunched over and gasping for breath, out of the room. Another guard pulled the door shut, and the lock clanked.

...

The native ran down the forest road as fast as he could. He shouted curses at the Land Rover as it disappeared in its own dust cloud. He sprinted, and his lungs burned, but a wild fear swirling at his back drove him on. Soon, his legs felt like rubber and his feet began to catch on roots, but he ran.

...

Rafi felt the other spirits leaving, but the brilliant soul floating down to him took over his attention. The body floated into the silt-dimmed light of the first diver's lights, and he gripped it, feeling the beauty of the soul trapped in the flesh of the body. The edge of the soul had a crystalline wall on it, flexible and scintillant. He pressed his will against the energized wall and felt it go weak. He drew at it, pulling it thin. When it split open, the soul screamed out, and its fear lit him with an incandescent thrill. He drew its energy in, and the heat of it caused the aching in his joints to fade away. Strength flourished through his corpse, and he sat up, shoving the body aside.

Still unable to move his legs, he sank his hands into the silt beneath him and his hips shifted. It felt wonderful. He shoved himself again, just for the sensation, and silt rose up around him darkening the diver's lights. He wanted to be free of the pressure of the water, wanted to be up on the surface, to feel the world around him. Breeze, he missed the light touch of breeze the most.

CHAPTER 25

The native ran down the rutted trail until the stitch in his side felt as though a blade had been shoved under his rib. He slowed to a quick walk. Behind him he felt the thing that had taken Pacal laced into the air, pressurizing it. The pain in his side had diminished, and when he saw the gravel shoulder of the highway through the trees, he began to run again. The pain in his side came on again, but he kept running. The pressure behind him pulsed and rushed forward. Glancing over his shoulder, he saw only the sandy ruts in the underbrush, the thin trunks of trees, and their dusty leaves. Yet, he felt it coming at him, welling through the forest, up the rutted path. He looked back at the smooth blacktop of the highway and sprinted, growling against the pain in his side. The thing chasing him seemed to crest and, with one last lunge, swirled around him, acid-hot and hungry.

Despite his will to carry on, his legs slowed to a walk and then stopped. The muscles of his thigh quivered and clenched, and his leg yanked him sideways. His other leg trembled and his shoe slid around in the dirt, facing him back toward the pit. He took a stiff step, then another. He tried to scream, but his jaw would not open, and his lungs would not drive air to his throat. His breath flowed in smooth, deep draws through his nose. At first his legs stepped forward like rigid poles, but as he walked, whatever had him grew more skilled at moving him, and soon his legs and arms swayed in an easy rhythm. While he had long ago dismissed his grandmother's stories of skinwalkers and chupacabras, he now understood the truth; this went well beyond the cruelty of men. In the grip of what he believed to be the Devil himself, he did something he hadn't since he was a boy living in the hills of southern Mexico; he prayed.

Dios te salve, Maria. Llena eres de gracia: El Señor es contigo. Bendita tú eres entre todas las mujeres. Y bendito es el fruto de tu vientre: Jesús...

He could not remember what came next and felt hopelessness weigh down on him. It wouldn't do him any good to remember. He didn't want salvation of his soul; he wanted salvation of his life. He rounded a bend and saw the pit. The grip of the thing went iron, and his breath wheezed in his throat. He thought through his life, the violence and greed, and as he neared the edge of the pit, tears began to pour from his eyes. He understood the Devil's intentions just as a goat understands the jaguar.

With only a few more feet to the edge, he began again.

Dios te salve, Maria. Llena eres de gracia: El Señor es contigo.

Two more steps and he would fall.

Bendita tú eres entre todas las mujeres.

One more step.

Y bendito es el fruto de tu vientre: Jesús.

His foot came out over the air, and he tipped forward into weightlessness. The air rushed for a moment, and he crashed into the water and, in a slow rotation, faced upward. The sun wavered beyond the turbulent surface, and he began to buoy upwards. Hope sprang up in his heart, but the Devil crushed his chest, and air tumbled out of his nose and mouth, roiling upward. He sank down, away from the surface, away from the air and the light.

Santa María, Madre de Dios, ruega por nosotros pecadores...

His belly trembled as his lungs burned for air, the darkness growing as water slipped into his mouth through pressed lips.

...ahora y en la hora de nuestra muerte.

As the walls of the cave faded into darkness, his belly yanked at his lungs and his nose, mouth, throat, and finally his chest filled with water.

...

Erica sat on the bed in the darkness, knowing she wouldn't sleep. The image of the diver falling into the water, his fingers hooked, wrist tendons straining, kept forcing its way back into her thoughts. She tried to put him out of her mind, but each time her thoughts began to wander, his eyes—wide with terror—returned. The predatorial hunger, which had pulled him off the wall, had also been Rafi. She could feel him woven into that dark voracity, not as she had known him in life, but primal and half-insane. She shouldn't have brought those men to him. By doing so, she had fed into something monstrous.

But he had only been able to hold one person at a time...

She heard a sound and looked to the open window covered by the still drapes. Fear tingled up her back, but she had been so terrified at the pit that it almost felt as though she had burned something out. The tingling along her spine spilled into her arms, crested as gooseflesh, and then faded. She kept her eyes on the window, half expecting the apparition to come drifting in. Laying back, she kept her eyes on the window and listened to the night. She could hear the ocean waves on the shore and two men talking in the courtyard as she drifted off into a dead sleep.

...

In the heart of the night she dreamt of a dark place; something held her, pressing in on her body. Moving her hands, she felt the dragging swirl of water and opened her eyes. She found herself down somewhere in the barrel of the pit. The walls hung in great, melted sheets of stone, in one place smooth, in another hanging with uneven stalactites. No light made its way from above, but she could still see the walls, glowing with a silver, moon-like illumination. Her hair billowed around her head and face. She tried to sweep it out of her vision, but more drifted in from the other side. She began to sink down, deeper into the gullet of the pit, and her hair floated up away from her. Not breathing and not troubled by it, she looked down to where the dim walls went black.

After a few moments of descent, the floor of the cavern materialized out of the darkness. Here and there boulders lay in the brown detritus of the floor. Rafi sat upright in the center, and as she descended, his head tilted up, his hair floating away from his face as he looked at her. Her feet touched down, sinking into the soft silt. She settled to her knees in the pillowed layer of rot, and a cloud of it drifted up around her waist.

She sat only a few feet away from him, and as he looked at her, she knew that her imagination hadn't created this. She would not have imagined him this way. She would have imagined someone rotted, the eyes beginning to fold in, the flesh puffing. The thing before her looked like Rafi as she had known him, his face handsome and his eyes deep, but in those eyes she saw a disturbing knowledge of what lay beyond death.

You've come to me.

She shook her head. She tried to talk through the water in her mouth and throat.

Rafi's lips drew into a slight smile. As he stared at her, she found she could not look away and felt his eyes drawing her to him, felt herself leaning forward. Her heart surged.

This is only a dream.

Yes, you are not here... yet.

The smile pulled at his lips again and broadened until his teeth showed; his hair floated around his head in a dark halo.

We can be together again.

Erica wanted to be away from him, wanted to swim up, but her legs wouldn't respond.

No. You cannot leave. Not yet. Let me just look at you a moment longer. His dead eyes penetrated hers. *You are so beautiful Erica. The brilliance of your soul is like pure, blue flame. You are amazing. I want you.*

She probably should have felt fearful at that but found only anger. Too many men had seen her as something to possess.

No. Rafi's hand floated up, palm out. *Don't be angry with me.*

Why not? Will it hurt your feelings? At that moment, she felt her legs twitch, and she pushed herself up and stood in the silt, a cloud billowing up around her knees.

No. Don't go.

Does my anger block you out of my mind? Do you need me to be afraid of you?

No. I don't need fear. I can take at will. But not you. I want you to give yourself to me.

No. Erica reached up and pulled her arms downward, cupping at the water. She kicked her legs and rose up off the cavern floor. The silt billowed away from the pressure wave of her kicking, floating in all directions, obscuring Rafi's outstretched legs and lifting up around his chest.

He lifted his arm, reaching out toward her. *Don't go.*

She began swimming away from him. *I was falling in love with you, Rafi. I really was. But I'm not letting you do this to me. This makes you no better than Brandon.*

His thought tremored with anger, *No. I'm not him.*

Rafi, you've lost your mind in death. You have to realize that.

The voice growled now, *No.*

Her arms and legs stiffened. No longer able to swim, she again drifted downwards.

You will not leave me.

But you said you wanted me to give myself to you. What about that?

I cannot bear to lose you again.

Erica's mind raced. She had to figure out a way to get him to let her go.

You cannot escape me.

She thought of him sitting in the coffee shop in Palm Beach, where she had asked him about the safe. She remembered his sincere eyes as he said, "You have far too many troubles, Erica." She remembered the waitress blushing as he smiled at her, which caused horrific sorrow to flush through her. This was all her fault. Without her, he would be sitting on that comfortable couch in his shop, perhaps with the waitress beside him. She looked at the animated corpse before her. She had to put this right, not just run from it, and with that, an epiphany crystallized itself before her. She put the thought out of her mind before it had fully formed, before he could have it.

I've destroyed you Rafi. I'm so sorry.

He did not reply.

But I don't want you to be trapped down here, Rafi. It's my fault that you're here. Let me help you.

I do not need your help. I will simply take another after you.

But you can't take my soul with my body so far away.

Rafi's grip tightened on her, and she felt as though her ribs were bending.

Please Rafi, let me help you. It's my fault.

I will not allow you to leave again.

She had to risk what she had guessed at.

I know that you can only hold one at a time, so you can't draw another down here and feed unless you set me free. You have to let me go, but I promise you, I will bring someone else. I'll help set you free. That was sincere; she wanted Rafi out of this tragic mess.

He lowered his eyes, and his thoughts went quiet with sadness. *I need you Erica. I would rather hold you here and be trapped myself than lose you again.*

You'll begin to rot again without new souls. You can't have me this way. They'll keep my body locked up.

You will lay in a coma, and they will give up on you, throw the flesh aside. Then you will be mine.

We can be together, Rafi. She felt regret for the lie and quickly pushed that regret out of her mind before he could sense it. *We will be together.*

He sat in silence, and his grip on her lessened.

I'll bring you Antonio.

He looked up at her. *Yes. That is good. I want him.*

Will that set you free?

No. Not yet. Perhaps just one or two more after him.

I'll bring them to you.

He nodded at this, and his grip lessened a bit more. She began to float up.

I need to be able to communicate with you. Can you read my thoughts when I am at the compound? Will I be able to reach you from there?

Only when you are in the dream state. When you are awake, I need you closer.

How much closer?

I can reach the edge of the highway. There I will be able to hear your thoughts.

In that he had trusted her too much, and she knew with enough luck she could escape Antonio and set Rafi free.

His grip on her let go, and she swam upward with casual strokes, fighting the urge to race away. When she had risen to the place where her dream had begun, the limestone walls grew dim, and she fell into darkness.

She woke in her bed and the desire to cough up water overwhelmed her, but she drew a breath, and the air filling her lungs calmed the cough. She felt dry bedclothes beneath her and, rolling off the bed, went to the window. Out over the ocean, the glow of dawn hung across the sky.

I won't sleep again until I'm free.

CHAPTER 26

The sun rose. Its beams broke into the room and tracked down the walls to mid-morning, and no one came. She would wait no longer. Walking over to the door, she hit the metal plate with the side of her fist. She hit it again and again, the booming of the metal trailed by the clank of the lock. She didn't bother to shout out, knew that it would sound desperate, and she was done playing that part. She hit the door again.

When the side of her fist began to hurt, she hit the metal with her left hand. At that moment, she heard an angry voice on the other side, and the lock clanked free. She stepped back as the door opened. Sedar walked in, eyes narrowed.

"What is your problem? You want anotha' beating?" He said it, not as a threat, but in disbelief of her actions.

"No," she said, walking around him and pushing the door closed, "I want your help."

"Have you lost your..." But he fell silent as she held her finger to her lips.

"You aren't an evil man. I know that much."

He stared at her, still angry, but listening.

"You won't take part in my beatings, or in the girl's rape, but allowing it is nearly as bad for you."

He set his jaw and stared at her.

"What if it was your wife in my position? What would you do?"

He said through his teeth, "She is not."

"Do you think I'm an evil person?"

He said nothing. She began to speak again, and he slapped her. She shouted out in surprised shock but did not doubt him for it. She knew violence, and a man as big as Sedar, hitting with anger or the will to punish, would have hit much harder. He hadn't intended to hurt her. The sting of the slap was already leaving her face.

"You ah a fool to think I would help you," he said as he gripped her upper arm and pulled her close. His mouth near her ear, he whispered, "I apologize. There is always someone listening. If you cross me... know that I will kill you. Now what do you want?"

Her face brushed his rough stubble as she whispered into his ear, "I have over ten million in gold. There is a monster out there and one in this house. I need your help to stop both."

He whispered, "Why should I take a risk on you? How will you support my family?"

"You hate working for Antonio, for evil men. Work for me. I'll match his pay. You can support your family and do something right in the world. It doesn't have to be a compromise."

"How do I know you will keep your word?"

"I'm taking the same risk on you."

At this he let her go and looked around the room. He leaned in on her and whispered. "What do you want me to do?"

...

Erica sat in the evening light waiting. She had spent the day in her room, no one coming or going. Hunger scrabbled at her belly, making her light-headed and angry. She paced the room for hours, feeling the stress of expectation squirreling across the back of her neck and shoulders. Her hands trembled with that energy. As night came on in earnest, she considered that Sedar might have changed his mind. At midnight she found herself sitting on the side of the bed, hungry, exhausted, and stalked by failure.

After midnight, the night grew quiet. No sounds came from the courtyard aside from crickets and the occasional rustle of palm fronds. She looked out on the dark courtyard. One Land Rover sat parked in the center. She heard an approaching engine, and a second Land Rover pulled in and parked next to the first just as she had requested. Getting out of the Rover, Sedar walked over to the courtyard guard, who nodded at him. Sedar embraced the guard, and Erica heard a wet sound. Sedar set the body down and walked out of view. Erica could now see only the guard's legs beyond the ledge of the second story. The legs slid out of view.

After a few moments, the lock on the door rasped quietly open. The hinges creaked as the door opened. Sedar entered and pushed the door closed. He handed her a bundle of clothes: black dungarees and a T-shirt. Taking the clothes into the bathroom, she dressed and returned to the bedroom. She put on her white canvas shoes.

Sedar motioned for her to follow him and walked out of the room.

When she entered the hallway, he leaned close again and said, "I thought you might want to be with me when we take him."

She nodded and, for the first time since she had been with Rafi in Nassau, felt a sincere smile pull at her lips.

He walked ahead of her down the hallway. Moonlight coming in through the window at the end of the hall threw a crossed pattern along the floor. They walked toward that moonlit window through the darkness. His black shirt and dark, muscular arms, head and neck became nothing more than a silhouette in front of her. When he reached the end of the hallway, he turned right and led her down another long corridor. A guard sat in a wicker chair in front of a set of double doors. He stood and his eyes moved from Sedar to Erica, a question forming just as a knife, glinting in Sedar's hand, slid into the guard's chest at heart level. The guard opened his mouth and let out a muttering exhalation as his body went slack. Sedar lowered him to the floor beside the chair. He opened the doors and walked in.

"Who's there?" Antonio asked from the darkness.

...

Antonio lay in a fitful sleep. He would begin to drift off, and Pacal would materialize before him, eyes terrified, hands clawing at the rock. He fell into the water and sank down. Each time, Antonio woke with a start. He cursed himself for weakness. He had seen many men die. This should be nothing to him. When the fear of death faded into death itself, it had always seemed peaceful to him. The men and women he had killed or watched die would sob and scream and beg, their faces covered with tears and snot. When their gasping went quiet and their eyes still, nothing remained but a soft, relaxed body.

That peace had given Antonio comfort. Not because he cared about the men and women dying before him, but because he feared his own death. In seeing that peace after death, he believed there was something good on the other side, something not to be feared. Pain and anguish were things for this side.

But what he had seen in Pacal's eyes had not been the peace of death. When a man drowns, at least in Antonio's experience, when he breathes in the water, he loses consciousness and finds his peace right away. But Pacal's eyes had stayed alive, terrified. He had not died correctly. Something horrific had happened to Pacal's and Eduardo's souls, and that knowledge caused Antonio's heart to beat shallow and quick.

He shoved the thought out of his mind. He did not worry about things like this, would not allow it. He began to drift off to sleep again, his eyes folding shut in the dark room, and he felt the dizzy lightness of sleep carrying him off. In that half-dream state he saw the surface of water bending before him, reflecting his own face. Beyond his reflection he saw Pacal sinking down. Antonio woke with a start, cold sweat soaking his head, neck, and the fabric of his pillow.

Muttering a curse, he rolled over and considered what to do about the thing in the pit. He felt that if he did not deal with it, it would someday come for him. He would travel to Nassau and find a priest to exorcise it. Then he would be able to rest easy. His door clicked, opened and two figures walked in, the first much larger than the second.

He squinted into the darkness of the room. "Who's there?"

The larger one leapt at him. He reached under his pillow and took hold of the gun there, but the man was already on him, pinning his hand and the gun down, and he could not reach the trigger. A rag covered his nose and mouth, and his shout for his guards came muffled through its rough fabric. In shouting, he had let out all of his air, and he felt the fast-evaporating coldness of a chemical on the rag. He turned his eyes and saw the blackness of his attacker's arm. Sedar. So Sedar had betrayed him. He kicked his legs.

"Hold his legs down," Sedar said.

Antonio felt someone climb onto his legs, his knees bending backward painfully. Beyond Sedar's shoulder he saw a crown of blonde hair. The woman. After all his speeches about his wife and children, Sedar had fallen to the charms of this whore. He pushed at Sedar's arm, but could not overcome the African's strength. He felt his lungs burning for the need for air, but knew what would happen if he inhaled, so he held his breath.

He heard the woman say, "Antonio, you're not going to just die. I'm going to feed you to that thing in the pit." Then she asked, "Did you get the dynamite?"

"Yes," Sedar said, "I prepared it just as you asked."

Antonio's need for air overcame him, and he drew deeply through the rag. His sinus filled with chemical fire as the world melted away.

...

He woke lying on his back, disoriented. Canvas above him, trussed with black bars, bumped and shifted. He seemed to be in a vibrating tent. In confusion, he sat up and found himself in the back of one of the Land Rovers. He looked to the front of the truck; the seats were emtpy. On the dashboard he saw the green, illuminated 'D'. The truck idled itself down a two rutted trail in the forest. Looking at his hands and legs, he wondered why he not been restrained.

He crawled between the two front seats just as the truck veered off the trail, crashed through the bushes, and slammed to a stop on a tree. The engine bogged and died. Pushing open the passenger side door of the truck, he stepped out onto the dirt and rocks of the two-rutted trail. He looked up, through the canopy of leaves to the stars.

What strange plan is this?

He looked back to where the Land Rover had come from. Through the trees he made out two headlights, not far off, glowing through the thin trunks.

Looking in the direction the Rover had been headed, he recognized the trail to the pit. As he realized it, something brutal and overwhelming came rushing at him. He turned to run, but his legs went stiff, and he fell. He landed on his side and white-hot pain lanced through his shoulder. He lay with his face in the dirt, his forehead pressing into a rock. His hands, moving with their own will, scrabbled up beside his shoulders and pressed into the dirt. His arms pushed him up, and he sat upright. Hot wetness flooded down his face from where his head had hit the rock, and he smelled the copper tang of blood. The blood ran into his eye and down into his mouth. The taste, mixed with his fear, soured his stomach.

His hands braced themselves on the ground and his legs shifted, standing. His legs turned him and began to walk him down the road. He tried to stop himself and screamed out in his mind, but his lungs and mouth did not respond. He continued to walk at an easy pace down the trail. The sudden urge to pray arose, but he knew that would be foolish. He would not find forgiveness for all he had done and was unsure if God existed at all. Yet what held him now made him very sure the Devil lived.

He turned a bend, and the ledge of limestone came into view. Clouds faded in over the moon, darkening the mouth of the pit, and he tried to fight again for control of his body. The more he fought, the tighter the thing held him. His foot stepped out over nothing, and he fell forward. The crash into the water came so quickly that he did not have time to brace himself for it, and in his mind he cried out his mother's name. He floated face down, the darkness of the water overwhelming him. The air crushed out of his lungs, and he began to sink downwards. He could see nothing in the blackness but felt the water drifting by. As he sank downward, the wall scraped along his right side, causing him to rotate. Turning, he saw the distant shimmer of the night sky beyond the small, crooked opening of the hole. The turn continued and he rotated back into blackness.

He drifted downward for a long time, not breathing, not dying, just sitting in his own skin, unable to move, feeling his sanity cracking at its weakest points. His mind wandered back over his life. From his poverty stricken youth in Venezuela, he saw the corrugated metal roof of the shanty where his mother had raised him. He saw himself kicking an inflated goat's stomach around the dusty street. As he saw himself growing up, he knew the memory was coming and tried to force it away, but it came to him all the same. He stood over his childhood friend holding a pistol to his forehead. Both of them were near manhood, and his friend sobbed as he pleaded with Antonio. He had not intended to become addicted and knew it was wrong to lighten the shipments, but he had developed a taste for the cocaine. He begged Antonio for another chance. He would never use again. His final words had haunted Antonio through his years.

"Please do not tell my mother I died like this."

As the memory passed, Antonio saw himself wearing his first suit, white and cheap, but it made him feel strong, as though he had been graced with knighthood. He walked down the street with his head held high; women glanced at him, looking away with a blush when he caught their eye. He had felt drunk on himself in those days. He moved through the memory of his second kill, and then onto her. He had found her enchanting, but she wanted nothing to do with a cartel man. Her father had told him to leave, so he had his men beat the father. Antonio had taken her, and the experience had been thrilling. He drifted further down into the pit, facing each pleading face, each scream of rape, each death tremor, up to Rafi drowning in this water. Last he saw the woman Erica watching as he took the young girl.

As that memory came to a close, he was left with only the water drifting by as he sank face first into blackness. Ahead of him, he felt the evil growing, and he thought his heart should accelerate with fear. Yet his heart no longer beat, and he found himself in a profound stillness. He felt regret then for what he could have been. He could have been an honest man. He could have helped his friend. He could have found a woman to love, and raised a family, and saved his soul. He felt himself come side by side with the Devil. He could see nothing but felt it there as it began to burn at his soul, corroding as acid on metal. Large chunks of himself began to tear away and float out and be swallowed whole. The pain, profound beyond a physical agony, caused him to scream out in his mind, but his body lay still and docile as the beast consumed him.

CHAPTER 27

Erica watched the taillights of the Land Rover idle away. She willed the truck to stay on the trail, to get as close to the pit as possible. To her relief the truck followed the ruts in the road and curved away into the forest. Out of view, she heard it crash though bushes and thump into a tree. The engine died. Just as she wondered how long Antonio would remain unconscious, she heard the door open.

She had felt Rafi whispering at the edge of her senses, like the echoing pain from a burn, and now the night seemed to grow darker as if something had siphoned off the starlight. She looked up, expecting clouds over the moon, found it hanging free in the sky, and understood that the perceived darkness did not come from a lack of light, but a void which pulled at the energy that animates all living things. That darkness tugged at her, as a river eddy on shore tugs a swimmer toward the torrent.

Stepping backward, she felt a hand touch her shoulder and looked back at Sedar, who kept his eyes on the forest.

"Do you feel him?" She asked.

He gave one nod.

Footsteps out among the trees caused her to worry that Antonio might escape the trap. He fell with a scuffle of dirt and rocks. The forest lay in silence for a moment. She heard shuffling and a long scraping followed by steady footfalls moving away from them. Rafi had him, and she felt a thrill of success, but her belly fluttered when she considered what must come next. She touched the heavy strap of the bag over her shoulder. She wanted to believe that she would succeed but felt only doubt and loneliness.

This had to be done. Antonio's soul might be enough to loose Rafi on the world. She imagined his corpse walking along the road toward Nassau, consuming as it went. He must be put to rest, and as she had brought him into this mess, she had to be the one to do it. If she failed... She put the thought out of her mind.

Sedar opened the door of the second Land Rover and sat in the seat. They waited for a long time, Erica leaning on the side of the truck listening to the forest. She didn't know exactly what to expect, but had to believe that she'd know when he had finished with Antonio. She heard a faint splash out in the darkness. They waited longer, the crickets signing, and the moonlight silvering the branches hanging out over the road. Something pulsed through the trees. That burning energy, which had touched at the edge of her senses, now swelled past her.

Her stomach felt weightless and her arms and shoulders tingled.

It's time.

She turned to Sedar and said, "Wish me luck."

"Ah you sure this is right?"

"It has to be done."

He regarded her for a moment before saying, "I give my family's fate to you. I would not do so if I doubted you."

She looked into the forest, drew a deep breath, and began walking down the rutted trail. Above her, moonlight filtered through the bladed leaves of the upper canopy, illuminating the nearest rows of thin, crooked trees, which only a few yards away, dematerialized into a black thicket. The sense of fear, the feeling of a predator staring at her, became stronger with each step. She wanted to run, wanted to jump in the Land Rover and be gone from the island, never set foot in the Bahamas again. She imagined living up north, in Sweden or Norway, as far away from this place as she could get.

The swell of energy from the pit had been diffuse, but as she walked along the moon-glowing sand of the trail, she felt it focus and race up at her through the trees, pushing a wave of dread in front of it. She stopped on the trail.

What if he's too strong?

The dark energy swirled around her and locked into her muscles, and as her jaw clamped tight, she knew it was too late for doubts. Quivering with the foreign energy, her right thigh tensed and pulled her foot forward. She had planned this, needed it to happen, but as her left leg twitched and slid forward, she fought him for control of her body. The energy constricted around her and for a moment would not allow her to breathe.

His voice came into her mind, as if through the leaves rustling in the night breeze. *I have you now. Do not fight me. We will be together.*

As she began walking, panic overtook her for a moment as if she floated in a glass-smooth river as its waters bent between two great rocks, beyond which nothing could be seen but sky as the river dropped away over a cliff.

Be brave, she told her herself. *Stay calm and it will come out fine.*

He responded, *Yes, just let this happen.*

Anger flared in her, but she stopped her specific thoughts before they could fully form.

One of her shoes jammed between two roots, and her foot pulled free from it. She continued walking and, after a time, a stick stabbed into the sole of her foot. Her weight pressed down, and the stick sank into the flesh, up between the bones, tenting the skin along the top. A shock of pain lanced into her thigh, and her head went light with endorphins; however, she moved on, and as she brought her foot down again, she felt the stick shift.

Her lungs drew in air, and the muscles from toes to shoulders flexed and relaxed, but she had no control. Her heart beat in a slow, calm rhythm. She stepped again, and the base of the stick cracked free, twisting at the section still jammed in her foot.

A poisonwood unfolded from the darkness ahead. As she walked by, its lower branches dragged along her neck and arm, catching on her shirt. She feared that the bag might become tangled, but the fabric of her shirt pulled taut and ripped open at the side, freeing her.

She passed into a darker section of the forest, and the trees faded into blackness. As her eyes gave her less, she became more aware of sounds: her feet shuffling in the dirt, twigs cracking, the breeze filtering through leaves.

Her neck and arm burned where the poisonwood had brushed, yet her thoughts stayed on the pit. She had no idea how far she'd come or how far she still had to go. At any moment she could fall.

Soon the mineralized scent of cold, stone-leached water tinged the air and grew stronger with each step. Walking out of the trees, she entered the moonlit clearing where the tombstone glow of the wall hovered above the gaping maw of the pit.

Not yet.

She needed to be closer, had to be right at the edge.

Two steps away she closed her eyes and imagined Rafi sitting at the café in the shade of the palm trees. He smiled at her, warm and alive.

I love you Rafi; with all my heart I love you.

And she did. Letting go of all fear and instinctual self-preservation, she allowed herself to feel nothing but great joy in having known him. She took one more step, and her body went still as Rafi's grip on her slipped. She could not take control back from him, but neither could he move her. As she focused on her body, her muscles began to quake again. Her foot, now only a few inches from the edge, slid forward. She returned to Rafi at the café, but her foot continued to slide, so she thought of him on the beach at sunset. She thought of embracing him, of her cheek resting on his strong shoulder, the rough feel of his shirt, the scent of his neck. Her foot stopped moving.

Erica, you must come to me. I must have you.

She ignored the thought, knew reacting with fear or anger would give him power over her again. She thought only, *I love you Rafi.*

With sad resignation, he responded, *I love you as well. I always have.*

With that she felt him slip far enough away from her to allow her arms to move. She drew the four sticks of dynamite from the bag and held them out. Sedar had bundled them together with duct tape around an electric blasting cap. A thick, yellow wire extended from the top of the four-stick bundle and ran into the bag. At the bottom of the sticks, Sedar had attached several lead fishing weights. She felt her legs quivering again, and for a moment she could not move her arms.

It's all right Rafi. It is going to be okay.

I am afraid.

At that her heart broke, and in that upset, he locked onto her and dragged her foot forward. It came out over the edge and she began to fall. If she had allowed herself to be afraid or angry at his control, he would have had her, but she let her heart stay calm and thought of him again, alive and loved.

I forgive you Rafi.

With that thought, his control slipped, and she shifted her weight, falling onto her back with one leg hanging over the edge. She sat up and took a large spool of the yellow wire from the bag. Hanging the spool off her finger so it would spin freely, she threw the dynamite over the edge. There was the risk that the dynamite might hang up as it descended, but it was a risk she had to take. The spool spun on her finger.

When about half of the three hundred feet of wire had played out, it stopped. The dynamite had caught on the wall. She pulled the cable up and let it go. The spool spun freely again, until all the cable had played out. At the end of the wire, she found the capped battery. She uncovered its terminal as Sedar had shown her.

Just before she connected the bare, copper wire to the lead, she heard Rafi in her mind. *I am sorry Erica.*

I forgive you Rafi, I just hope you can forgive me. This is all my fault.

He did not respond, and with that lack of forgiveness, tears blurred her vision and ran down her face. Letting out a heaving sigh, she touched the wire to the lead. The ground shook, and the water heaved, belling up. The surface shocked, going white, and settled into waves.

What she felt next gave her hope for the world and every living thing in it doomed to die. She felt an immense wave pass upward, like the pulse of a heart, and as it passed her, she felt a great sense of joy and peace pass with it. She knew it was him, set free from his obliterated corpse. She lay back on the ground looking up at the moon drifting behind clouds and felt solace in his final passing, but through the solace, the grief of losing him settled over her. It did not overwhelm her, did not cause her to break down, but lay in her heart as a deep fissure that she knew she'd carry with her the rest of her life.

She stood and looked down into the pit, now just a hole in the ground. The waves were calming and would go still soon. She turned and left it, limping back down the sandy ruts to Sedar.

When she sat down in the passenger seat, Sedar said, "I felt the release. You have been successful."

She nodded as she looked back to where the pit lay obscured among the poisonwood trees. "I just don't understand why this happened."

Sedar started the Land Rover and pulled out onto the highway. "My people, the Wolof, believe that strength is the ability to face pain and loss with a calm heart. Only then can the spirit find peace in an unfair world. During my initiation to manhood my grandmotha visited me in the mbarr and told me ghost stories—spirits who became caught up in vengeance or could not face losing what they had in life. Your man, may he find peace, might have sought revenge for his own death or been unable to let you go."

"Why would he try to kill me then?"

"Because the difference between love and possession can be confusing to a desperate heart."

Erica nodded at that and turned her thoughts to what came next. She crossed her leg and looked at the sole of her foot, at the hole where the thick splinter had imbedded itself. "First, I think I need a hospital. Then we pay a visit to Abram Malevich."

CHAPTER 28

Abram Malevich woke as the crowning sun broke into his window. He pushed the comforter aside and sat up, his lower back and knees protesting the motion. Sitting for a moment, he allowed the dizziness brought on by his old heart to pass before he pushed himself to his feet and wandered into the bathroom. He brushed his teeth, showered, and wrapped a towel around his thin waist.

Wiping the steamed mirror with his hand, he looked at himself. How had he come to be so old? He pulled the knobs of his shoulders back, but his once-proud Soviet chest remained withered. He felt tired. Lathering his face, he shaved and, when he finished, looked again into the mirror only to find that he had cut himself. He dabbed at the cut with a towel, and blood bloomed there again. He felt it wouldn't be a good day.

After drying his head again, he dressed and placed a scrap of toilet paper over the cut. It soaked through and stuck to his skin. He walked into the living room, the hardwood flooring cool on his bare feet. As he entered, he considered that he would have tea and read a novel. The morning would be better. He felt fortunate to have survived so many years, to have found such a peaceful finale to his days.

"Do you ever think about him?" A woman's voice asked from the corner of the room.

Abram's heart punched at his sternum as he turned. In the corner of the room he found a woman sitting in his easy chair. Rafi's blonde. To her right, looking out the parted blinds, stood Antonio's bodyguard Sedar. He looked to the end table by the couch, to the small, teak box where he kept his pistol. The box lay open, its interior empty.

"What is the meaning of this?" He asked Sedar, feeling angry that the African would enter his home unbidden, but Antonio must have his reasons.

"Don't worry about him," the woman said, "Worry about me."

Abram looked back at her. "I'm not worried about anyone, particularly a woman." As he looked at her, with sunlight in bands across her face, he saw that she had a freshly blackened eye and a red rash across her neck.

Abram looked to Sedar. "What is Antonio's game? Why have you brought her?"

"Antonio is unaware of our presence here," Sedar said in his deep voice, "and he will not know."

Abram looked back to Rafi's woman. She wore black dungarees with cargo pockets and a dark gray T-shirt. She had tucked her pant legs into black, thick-lugged boots, and her breasts curved the cotton of the T-shirt nicely.

"Did you ever think of him after you betrayed him?"

Abram looked to Sedar and then back at the woman. "You're Rafi's woman, yes?"

"No. I was never Rafi's. I was never anyone's." She stood and walked over to him with an ever-so-slight limp. Even with her baggy pants he saw the shape of her figure, curving and beautiful. Despite his age and the circumstances, he found his heart accelerating at her approach. He looked her over, from the shape of her hip, up her thin waist with its flat stomach, to the perfect curve of her breasts, and into her blue eyes. Despite the rash across her neck, she was stunning, but he no longer had patience for beautiful women with their vanity and insecurity.

"No," he said to her, "I have not," which was dishonest of him. He had felt the horror of betraying Rafi more than anyone else in his past. Over the last several nights he had been tortured by terrible dreams filled with screams in dark, closed spaces. The dreams ended with Rafi emerging from the ground, digging out of it, finger bones worn through. His tiredness was largely due to these dreams.

But he gave the woman no indication that he cared. "You are the one to blame for his death. You brought him in," he held his hands out toward her breasts, "tempted him."

He turned to Sedar, "Why is she not with Antonio?"

Erica held up her hand, "You are talking with me."

Abram shook his head at this pugnacious woman. "No. I am talking with Sedar." He turned to speak to Sedar again, but Sedar shook his head.

"My employer will speak with you."

"Is Antonio nearby then? Is he here?" Abram looked back, over his shoulder to the kitchen. The woman touched his chin, turning his head back to face her. He shoved her hand aside and slapped her, but she did not react. Sedar stepped forward, and she held up her hand stopping him.

Abram smiled at her. Now the tables were turning to where they should be. The weaker sex should not push him. He'd lived through too much. "I want to speak with Antonio."

"You will soon enough," she said.

"I will speak with him now."

"But you can't just now, because he's dead… by my hand."

Abram looked at her, not believing it at all. He let out a small, dismissive laugh, but when he looked at Sedar, the African's steady gaze stilled him. The woman took something from her hip, and he looked to her and found her holding a dark, military blade. A small silver line ran down the edge of the blade where it had been honed sharp.

He now understood that he had misread the girl and that would cost him. How high the price remained to be seen.

"So you finally learn to be quiet," she said, "but too late."

She whipped the blade at him and he felt a deep numbness at his throat. Reaching up, he touched the cut, which ran from one side of his neck to the other. Looking at his hand, he found it bright with his own blood and felt wet heat on his chest. As he breathed in, his throat bubbled. His head felt dizzy, and the floor became unstable. Lowering himself to his knees, he coughed, spraying red across the wooden planks of the floor. Looking up at her, he felt his neck separate, and a stream of blood pulsed away from him. He looked into her blue eyes. He wanted to tell her, not that he was sorry for how he had lived, but how fitting that such a beautiful woman should end him after all he had done.

Feeling himself tipping, he put out a hand to hold himself up, but weak and slippery, it came out from under him. He fell to his side. She stared at him with those blue eyes, and he felt transfixed by them, considered them the last beautiful thing he would ever see. He would not do well in death if the churches held any truth. He wished he did not fear the old stories, but he did; he always had. The fear had just never been strong enough to overcome the advantages of convincing the young women to go south with him. He felt the room going dark, and she looked away from him. He felt fear in that, did not want to lose sight of her eyes, not the last beautiful thing.

Please let me look at them until I'm gone.

But the words bubbled in his ruined throat, and she did not look back. She had turned to Sedar, and Abram felt a terrible jealously in that. She rubbed the side of her face where Abram had slapped her. He began to drift away. As the room fell into darkness, he heard her say to Sedar, each word growing more distant, "I'm tired of being hit."

Sedar's voice came as if from far away, echoing up a narrow, dark canyon. "Pain is inevitable, but as you find your true strength, it will no longer enter your heart."

CHAPTER 29

Erica and Sedar left the house via the back door, walking through a narrow passage between tall hedges to the street. The Land Rover sat beside the curb a few blocks down. They walked along the sidewalk, its cement blinding-bright after the dimness of Abram's house.

"And next?" Sedar said in a machined tone, the brutality he had just witnessed seeming to have no impact on him.

Erica still felt the strangeness of having killed the man. It wasn't horror, although she hadn't expected that much blood to pour from the withered, old man. It was the heartless purpose with which she had killed him. In her mind three people held fault for what had happened to Rafi. Antonio and Abram had paid their price.

"Ah you all right?" Sedar asked her.

She came out of her thoughts. "I'm sorry. What?"

"I asked you what is next. What do you wish to do now?"

"I need to get the gold secured."

As they approached the Land Rover, she opened the passenger door and sat down. "Does the Nassau library have Internet access?"

Sedar shrugged his shoulders at the question as he started the engine. "We will soon know."

•••

Erica walked out of the library holding a yellow paper with a phone number written diagonally across it. Sedar stood at the front of the Land Rover, heat shimmering off its roof.

His expression did not change when he saw her. "Did you find what you needed?"

"The library has a fax machine," she said, feeling herself picking up on his stoic, military style and liking herself that way. This change was right. There would be no more afternoon coffee and designer jeans, no more luxury cars. Now her life would be do or die. The cartel would never let her live for what she had done, so she had to take the fight to them. But first she had to grow her wealth and her ability. Making a fist, she inspected her knuckles, wondering how effective a fighter she could become and felt a smile draw across her face.

She asked Sedar, "Can I use your phone for an international call?"

Sedar handed her his phone.

She took it and dialed the number on the yellow paper. The phone rang, clicked, and a man answered in a professional, British accent. "Grand Cayman National Bank, how may I direct your call?"

"New accounts please."

•••

They went to the marina, a field of antennas and white hulls. To her relief, she found that no one had moved Rafi's boat. They recovered the remaining cash and Rafi's Berretta, which she slid into her right cargo pocket.

She stood for a moment looking over the boat before turning her gaze out to the harbor, to a departing cruise ship. It towered over the squat lighthouse, which stood at the harbor entrance on the flat, gravel tip of Paradise Island. She had come inevitably to a dead end and hesitated to even discuss it with Sedar for fear of how he would react.

She ran her hand over the top of her head and let her pony tail slide through her fingers. "Okay," she said, drawing a deep breath and letting it out, "here's the problem."

Sedar sat down on the rear bench, the boat tilting. He said nothing, simply waited for her to speak.

"I don't know where the gold is... exactly."

Sedar stared at her for a moment, his expression giving her no hints to his thoughts, before saying, "And where is the gold... approximately?"

"In the ocean."

"The ocean."

"I know it's to the east of here, but not exactly where."

"To the east..."

Sedar's eyes narrowed, his jaw muscles contracted, and the corners of his mouth drew outward in a grimace. Erica braced herself for anger, but instead he broke into sincere, belly-deep laughter. He laughed so hard it seemed he could not breathe. Erica stared at him in amazement, as if his onyx-carved effigy had finally come to life before her.

When his laughter faded away, he sighed, pressing a tear from his eye with the side of his index finger. "I suppose this is my fate. Still, it has been worth it. I had no idea how much of myself I had compromised in working for him. Income or no, I feel—"

"The GPS," Erica said and moved in one, quick step to the helm. "I can't believe I didn't think of it before." She pressed the unit's power button. "Rafi set our location with an alarm, so if the anchor came loose during the night, we wouldn't drift off. The alarm's location is the place we dropped the gold."

Sedar stood beside her now as she looked over the GPS's menu and carefully pressed a button. The last location stored came up, out in shallow water to the east.

...

They spent the evening on the boat. Sedar had insisted they each sleep in two hour shifts, while the other sat on the back, keeping quiet watch. As dawn glowed beyond the masts and the bridges, she had managed six hours of sleep and he four. She told him to catch up. The bank in the Caymans would not open until 9 AM anyway.

As he slept, she watched the cars on the street, the sidewalks quiet before the cruise ship crowds came in, and she felt an intense promise in the day.

The heat had already begun to rise when Sedar emerged from the cabin. He stood looking out on the street as an old Nissan minivan rolled by, windows dirty and springs in the rear sagging and creaking with each bump. She looked over Sedar—tall, broad shouldered, and intimidating—and felt glad to have him with her today. She had dangerous men to dance with.

The clock on the boat's helm read 9:03 AM.

"Can I use your phone again?"

He handed it to her, and she dialed. A woman with a British accent, tinted with the musical cadence of the islands, answered. "Grand Cayman National Bank, how may I direct your call?"

"May I speak with Charles Blake?"

"Will you hold?"

"Yes."

The line clicked, and classical music came on. Erica looked out on the street again. An athletic man and a beautiful, young brunette stood looking over a rack of shirts. He held a dress out to her. She hugged him and kissed the side of his face.

The phone clicked in Erica's ear and a man said in a refined English accent, "Charles Blake. How may I be of service?"

"Hello. This is Erica Morgan. You faxed me documentation to open an account. I signed those documents and mailed them overnight air to you."

Mr. Blake said, "Yes, I have it here. Let me see... Yes, everything looks very good." Keys clicked in the background. "Will you be wiring funds today?"

"Yes, this afternoon."

"That will be fine. As we discussed, a three hundred thousand U.S. dollar minimum is required to open a private account."

"The wire should be somewhere over ten million."

Without pause Blake said, "Of course ma'am. Would you like me to call you on this number when the transfer is complete?"

"Yes."

A few more keys clicked.

"Everything is in order Ms. Morgan. The account is created and waiting for your funding."

"Thank you." She hung up the phone.

...

Erica leaned over the edge of the boat, tilting in the calm ocean. Forty feet down in the crystalline water, two divers floated above the coral.

One of the divers began to rise, the bubbles from his regulator preceding him. The diver's black hair and masked face broke the surface. Rolling onto his back, he swept his fins, coming up to the stern, and set a small metal detector on the wooden slats of the fantail. He reached back into a mesh bag at his hip, lifted a gray square from it, and set it beside the detector.

Removing his regulator, he said, "That's either gold or lead by its weight, and I don't think you'd have us out here pulling packets of lead up from the sea floor."

Erica didn't like the diver's tone nor the look in his eyes. *There's no use trying to hide it though.*

"It's gold," she said, "and there are forty-three more bundles of it down there."

The diver nodded, pushed away from the boat, fitted his regulator, and sank below the surface. Erica leaned over the gunnel, watching the diver descend. The other diver had begun his ascent, and they stopped beside each other and shared hand signals. The second diver rose, handed over two bundles, and descended again. His lack of questions troubled Erica.

"They're up to something," Erica said.

"The promise of wealth is a demon," Sedar said, "which unchains the fool in weak men's hearts."

Erica looked back down into the water. One rose up, set two more bundles on the fantail, and descended again. She handed the bundles to Sedar, who stacked them beside the others on the deck.

Seven bundles now. Almost two million in gold right there.

Sedar remained crouched as he held the last bundle, weighing it.

"What about you Sedar? What will the demon do to you?"

His dark eyes lifted to her, and he set the bundle down. "I am not a weak man."

A diver rose and set three more bundles on the fantail. As he submerged again, she handed each to Sedar, who stacked them neatly aside.

He moved to the helm, turned the helm seat sideways, and sat down facing her. "The gold is cursed somehow, and I wanted nothing to do with it. And yet, when you tell me you will use it to do something right in the world, I think to myself, this will break the curse."

A diver rose with a torrent of bubbles and splashed his metal detector on the fantail. He set two bundles on the wooden slats and drifted back under water. Sedar's eyes were on the horizon.

Erica watched him for a moment. "You were saying?"

He looked at her, his eyes focusing in from far away. "I've done many things I am not proud of, but what I have done, I did to drug dealers and users—to unscrupulous and violent men. I did not participate in those things I could not agree with, as with your beating and the girl's rape."

She flushed at his casual reference to what Antonio had done to the girl, but the bastard had paid his price. Hanna may have been through hell, but unlike him, she still had air in her lungs.

Sedar said, "I think you will do something profound, and I would like to see what that is. You see, I always believed that

Allah would come to me one day and tell me when he'd had enough of my bending his will. He would give me a sign to go home and live in peace. I think you ah that sign," he laughed, "but I do not think it will lead me to peace."

Erica nodded, "Not to peace I'm afraid. To war."

"And what war did you have in mind?"

A diver rose, removed his regulator, and set his metal detector on the fantail. "I found a big pile of them." He refitted his regulator, gave a thumbs up, and leaving the metal detector on the back of the boat, descended into the clear water again.

"You and I both know the cartel won't stand for what we did."

Sedar, his eyes on the stacks of gold, nodded. "So we go for the heart in Venezuela. If we kill the master, the dogs will not be fed." He indicated the stacks of gold with his hand. "You will need more money than this for such a thing."

"I know," Erica looked out on the western horizon. Beyond it lay the U.S. "I need to figure out a way to turn this into a lot more money." She looked at Sedar. "You have any ideas?"

Sedar let out his sincere belly-deep laugh again. "You I like, Erica. You have no plan, just an idea, and yet you leap in as if you know exactly what you are doing."

"Seriously though," Erica said, "do you have any ideas?"

Sedar's eyes went absent as he looked out past her. He sat for a few moments in silence before saying, "I may have a few."

The divers continued to rise with bundles of gold. The first diver took his metal detector back down, and the intervals grew longer. When both divers rose together, the first one said, "How many do we have?"

"Forty-three. There should be one more."

Both divers submerged and came back up several minutes later. They set their metal detectors on the fantail and removed their regulators. The first diver pulled himself up onto the slatted wood.

He removed his goggles and looked over his shoulder at Erica. "We've found it all. If there is another bundle, I don't know where it could be."

"So," Erica said, "You were able to quickly find all forty three bundles, yet when it comes to the last, you search for only a few moments before claiming it can't be found?"

The diver looked down into the water and glanced back at Erica. "Yes. It isn't there."

Erica looked at Sedar. "I believe our friend is lying to us."

Sedar stood from the helm, gripped the diver's tank, hauled him in, and shoved him against the gunnel. The man drew a blunt-nosed diving knife from his forearm, and Sedar gripped the man's wrist, slamming his hand against the railing. The man hollered as his knife fell into the water. Sedar drew a blade from his pocket and held it against the diver's neck.

"That gold," he said staring into the diver's eyes, "would be worth what?"

"About a quarter million," Erica said.

The other diver pushed himself up onto the fantail, and Erica drew Abram's pistol and motioned with the barrel for him to drop back down into the water. The diver let go of the fantail and pushed off the boat, floating a few feet away.

Sedar said to the diver, "This gold is cursed my friend. Those who steal it end badly."

The diver gave as much of a nod as Sedar's blade would allow.

"But I think we should make a deal," Sedar said, looking to Erica.

Erica nodded.

"If you retrieve the last bundle," Sedar said to the diver, "we will give you one of the plates. That is still valuable and is surely worth more than…" he let the blade shift on the man's neck, nicking the skin, "…dying."

Erica turned to the other diver floating behind the boat, his flippers drifting back and forth. "Go get my last bundle." He nodded, fit his regulator, and descended. Erica watched his dark outline descend straight down and rise right back up. He set the bundle on the fantail and pushed off the boat again.

"Very good," Sedar said. As he stood, he jerked the diver to his feet and threw him overboard. The diver fell back-first into the water, disappeared, and bobbed back up spitting water. Erica threw the diving mask to him as Sedar cut open the last bundle of gold.

He drew out one of the plates and tossed it at the diver. The diver reached for the gold, bobbled it, and it flipped out of his hands and into the water. Chasing it under the surface, he rose holding the plate, a big smile on his face.

Erica sat at the helm, fired the motor, and shouted over the burble of the idling engines, "That's the best money per hour you've ever made."

The diver nodded.

Erica edged the throttle forward, pulling away from the divers.

The diver waved his arm in a desperate arc and called out, "You can't just leave us out here."

"The shore is right there," Erica yelled, pointing toward the beach and low trees. "Give yourself some rest. You've earned it. We'll send someone for you tomorrow, when the gold is gone." She shoved the throttles forward and left the two divers diminishing at the end of the white-foamed trail of their wake.

Erica turned to Sedar and shouted over the wind and engines, "Do you know a Bertram Webber?"

Sedar nodded and asked, "Why?"

"It's the only contact I have to move the gold. Just before I killed him, Alex Castellanos wanted me to go to him, said Webber could help us." She felt a small shock at how casually she admitted to the murder. But it had been self-defense hadn't it? She thought back to that night on the boat, to Alex sitting in the rear seats. Looking over her shoulder at the rear seat, she felt calm. She had removed a blemish from the world. Brandon, Alex, Antonio, Abram, she was on a roll and why stop now? The head of the cartel snake would be next, but she had a lot to learn, a lot to plan, and other ideas. She thought of the girl tied down before Antonio... Hanna... frightened to death, powerless to stop the rape, and she considered what Abram had said about moving young women... She looked back at the stacks of gold.

So much work that needs doing.

"Are you all right?" Sedar asked her.

"Yes, I'm fine. What were you saying about Webber?"

"I know him. Was this Alex you speak of one of Antonio's men?"

Erica nodded. "They worked for the same cartel. Alex was lower on the food chain though. He supervised drug mules in Florida."

"Strange that he would recommend Webber then."

"Why's that?"

"Webber has a... contentious relationship with the cartel."

"So you know how to contact him?"

"Yes."

CHAPTER 30

The streets of Nassau lay in a haze of sunlight. Erica walked with Sedar past the shop fronts, the harbor to their left. A breeze came in over the water, but it did little to cut back the afternoon heat. She felt sweat between her shoulder blades and, for a moment, imagined herself sitting on a beach in a white Adirondack chair. A cold drink sat on the arm of the chair, its sides beaded with condensation. An umbrella fluttered in the breeze over her cutting out the sun as waves broke on a reef out beyond the peaceful cove. She came back to herself, overheated in boots and black cargo pants, her neck salt-crusted from ocean spray, a gun thumping her thigh as she walked, and her heart pressurized with expectation. She would rather be right here right now. This is her.

They turned the corner and the café came into view. A group of four ebony-dark men sat at a patio table wearing pale, tailored shirts and slacks; their eyes roamed the street. When they caught sight of Erica and Sedar approaching, they stood.

Sedar sat down at the table, but Erica remained standing. This role reversal—Sedar the negotiator and Erica the muscle—electrified her. She drew a deep, slow breath through her nose to calm herself.

"What do you want?" asked one of the men, possibly Jamaican by accent.

Sedar said, "If you sit, I will tell you how to make a good deal of money."

They did not sit. The one man said, "You are Sedar Morel, one of Camejo's dogs. We do no deals with—"

"Camejo's dead," Erica said.

The man looked to Sedar. "Is what she tellin' true?"

Sedar gave a slow nod.

The men sat down. Erica remained standing a few feet behind Sedar, her arms crossed.

"Thank you," Sedar said. "I must speak with Webba'. Can you bring him here?"

The Jamaican's eyes narrowed with irritation. "What? What kind'a bait up is this? Webba' don't meet with riff raff—"

Sedar's voice went louder. "And what if the money was so easy, that he cut you in for a share?"

The four men looked at each other, and the talkative one smiled at Sedar and said, "Well look at you, full a' yourself and boasie. What's it about then?"

"When Webba' is here, I will offer details."

"No, no, no." The man said. "I don't put my neck out without knowing somethin'."

Sedar remained quiet for a moment before saying, "I have something of value that I need converted into cash. I do not have time. Webba' has time and cash. I have the commodity, he has the means. He profits and perhaps you do too."

The talkative one looked at the others and each gave him a short nod.

The talkative one said, "Okay, daddy." He placed his hands on the table palms down and leaned toward Sedar. "Webba' may be in town. It might be your day. But pray on this, if it isn't your day, it'll be mine. You seen?"

Sedar nodded.

The talkative one stared at Sedar a moment longer and then drew a phone from his pocket and dialed. He held the phone to his ear and everyone waited, the sounds of the harbor filling the silence. The talkative Jamaican looked at Erica, his eyes tracked down her figure as he said, "Here's Deval. I need ta talk ta Webba'... because man, just give 'im the clottin' phone." Deval paused for a moment and then said into the phone, "Hey bossman, I got here Antonio's pira Sedar." He listened for a moment. "Yeah, that's 'im." His eyes went back over Erica's body. "He got some kinda smokin' hot special forces girl with him."

Erica's heart accelerated at the 'special forces'. She had never been more complimented in her life. She had to fight not to let a smile show on her face.

Deval continued, "They sayin' Antonio's dead." He looked at Erica. "Were you the ones ta do it?"

"Yes," Erica said.

She saw Deval's confidence flicker at that, and he looked away as he said into the phone, "Yes." He listened, and then said, "He sayin' he needs help and you could make big money being the one ta offer it." He listened one last time and hung up the phone.

"What is the verdict?" Sedar asked.

"He say that any man... or woman, who brought Camejo down is worth meetin'. He'll be here soon."

They sat in silence but didn't have to wait long. After a few minutes, a black Mercedes rolled up beside the café. A stocky man with dark, curled hair and a Grecian profile got out of the car. He looked over Sedar, Erica, the street, and scanned the roof tops.

The man looked back at Erica and pointed at the cargo pocket on her right thigh. "Will that stay put away?"

"If yours does, mine does."

The man nodded at this and opened the rear door.

A man, perhaps mid-sixties, classically handsome with silvered hair and wearing a well-tailored suit stepped out of the car. He walked over to the men, motioned for Deval to rise, and took his place. Erica stepped back as Deval stood and moved. She noticed that Webber's body guard moved when she did, keeping a clear line of sight to her.

Webber said to Sedar, "The woman behind you is your new employer, is that right?"

Sedar smiled. "Who says so?"

Webber returned the smile, amiable and friendly, and said, "No one. I can see it in her eyes, and you, Sedar, are not an entrepreneur. You're a salary man. You do as you're told."

Erica said, "I think Antonio might disagree with that assessment."

Webber's eyebrows rose. "Is that so? Well, I'm not often wrong, but it has happened from time to time over the years… Well… now that the players are known, why have you called me here?"

Sedar said, "We have a valuable commodity to move. You move valuable commodities."

Webber drew a tri-folded handkerchief from his breast-pocket. Keeping it neatly folded, he pressed it across his forehead and slid it back into the pocket. "We should dispense with vagueness. We are all friends here."

"Are we?" Erica asked him.

"Perhaps," Webber said, measuring her with his balanced gaze. "If you truly have killed that fool Camejo, you are a friend... for now."

Erica nodded at this. "We have some of the cartel's gold."

Webber held up his hand. "Gold owned by the Maracaibo Cartel?"

Erica did not know the answer to this and looked to Sedar, who gave a short nod.

Webber asked Erica, "You do not know the name of those you have stolen from?"

"I've been too busy staying alive."

Webber smiled. "You," he pointed the knuckle of his index finger at her, "are a fighter. I can see as much." He looked to the Jamaicans sitting around the table with him. "Look into her eyes." Webber looked at her, not with narrow aggression, but with cautious curiosity, as if he were looking over the edge of a cliff to a sea crashing on jagged rocks below.

He turned to one of his men. "Do you see it?"

The man shook his head 'no'.

Webber touched the man's shoulder and lowered his voice. "Then she would have you." He ran his thumb across his own neck in a cutting motion. "Look at her." The man turned his head to look at Erica and his gaze did not caress her body as was so often the case, but stayed on her eyes.

As the man stared at her, Webber said, "She is an apex predator."

With all eyes on her, she felt her face flushing.

"But not yet experienced," Webber said and raised a quick hand. "But do not take insult. You will go very far." He laughed again, so sincerely it drew a smile out of Erica.

"And there it is," Webber said, holding his hands palm up as if to warm them in sunlight, "the sun breaking out, and all my years fall into my young heart. That is her most dangerous weapon." He looked at his men. "Even the scales of Grendel could not withstand that smile. Hmmm?"

His men stared at him.

"Achh," he said, flipping up his hand with irritation, "I am surrounded by brutes. Not a poet among you."

But she knew the story and said, "Not Grendel. Antonio was the monster feeding on the weak." She tapped her sternum. "I ripped his arm off."

At this Webber clapped his hands together. "So we have before us the bear, the Beowulf. You see, men? As intelligent as she is beautiful. I wouldn't give any of you ten minutes alone with her before she had you in her spell."

At that Erica felt a rush of fear. Is that what she'd been doing? Had she somehow seduced Rafi without even realizing it? She blamed herself for his death, but how much choice had she given him? Had she been greedy enough to steal him from his life? But no, she hadn't done anything. She thought of Sedar. He had shifted over so quickly...

Webber smiled, his teeth straight-edged. "And even now you are only beginning to realize what you have. I've known women like you before, have fallen prey to them, and I would knowingly do it all again."

"Enough of this," Erica said.

"Of course," Webber said. "We have business to do. How much gold do you need to move?" His eyes glittered with a merry excitement, as if he couldn't wait to get his hands on the Maracaibo Cartel's gold, as if it would disgrace them.

"Five hundred pounds, give or take."

The smile faded from Webber's face. He sat still for a moment before giving a short nod and drawing his phone from his pocket. He tapped on it for some time before placing it face down on the table. "At Market prices that is worth nearly thirteen million in U.S. currency. I will give you seven."

Erica felt a strange mix of relief at having an offer and frustration at the low amount. "Seven million?" she asked, hearing too much of that frustration in her tone. "That's a six million dollar commission."

"No," Webber said. "I will not be able to sell it at full value. That is for the final merchant."

Erica looked to Sedar, who sat expressionless, waiting. She looked back at Webber and said, "That's too low. You sell it to your people for maybe eleven million and profit a quick four? I'll let you profit one million. I'll take ten."

Webber laughed at this good-naturedly. His men seemed unsure at this, perhaps not used to him being so jovial. "That is bold. You need me, cannot live without this deal, and yet you barter. I should get up and walk away, but the enemy of my enemy is my friend. I will offer you eight."

"Ten."

Webber's eyes went grave now, business only.

"Look," Erica said. "I'm not going to buy a villa with this money. The Cartel... the Maracaibo... they're going to come for me."

Webber said in a dismissive tone, "So you will use the money to run."

"No," Erica said, angry that he'd think that. Stepping up to the table, she placed her hands on its worn, metal surface. Webber's body guard moved within a few feet of her.

Erica looked at the bodyguard, and then at Webber. "I won't run. If I do that, I run my whole life. I'm going to build that money up, hire a private army, and cut the head of the Maracaibo snake so I can live in peace."

And then I'm going to go after as many bastards in this world as I can until they cut my head off.

"Ten." She said again. "You get to unleash a curse on the Maracaibo and make a million dollars in the process."

Webber's smile returned. "I won't make anything worthwhile at ten, but," and he held up a finger to highlight his point, "it isn't about money every day is it? I think you will go and fight, and win or lose, you will at the very least cut their knuckles."

Erica nodded.

"Ten million then. Perhaps I can push my buyers a bit and make a small profit."

Erica noticed an unhappy look on Deval's face. No profit for Webber, no finder's fee for him. That irritated look let Erica know Webber was probably being straight with her.

"Now," Webber said as he stood from the table, "we need to see this gold."

His men began to stand, and Erica held up her hand and said, "Only you and I go. No one else."

At this Webber stared at her, and she gave him her warmest, most beautiful smile and said, "I'll even throw a boat into the deal."

CHAPTER 31

Erica sat in the cramped berth of the boat with Betram Webber while he looked over the stacks of gold. He took out a pocket knife, opened a stack, and took out a plate. He cut into the plate with the knife. The gold peeled away. He shaved into it a few more times.

"I have seen people put lead inside the gold." He set the plate on the stack and folded the open duct tape back together. Setting the bundle aside, he cut open another bundle. Erica watched in silence, letting him do his inspection.

When Webber had cut half of the bundles open, he looked up at her, took his handkerchief from his breast pocket, and dabbed it across his forehead. Taking off his suit coat, he folded it and set it across his knees. Erica saw he had begun to sweat through the armpits of his shirt. A bead of sweat dripped down her forehead as well, and she wiped it away.

Webber said, "I hope you do not have a problem with me inspecting all the packages."

Erica shook her head. "There's a lot of money on the line. You should take your time."

He slapped his hands on his knees and stood in a crouch, his head touching the low ceiling. "I've seen enough then. You are not nervous. If you were trying to rob me, you would have shown it in your eyes. I've got to get out of this furnace." He stepped through the open hatch and onto the deck.

Erica followed him.

The air coming in off the ocean had finally dropped some of its oppressive humidity, and it draped her with coolness.

"Do you have your account numbers?" Webber asked her.

She nodded and handed him a slip of paper. He looked it over and dialed his phone.

After a moment, he said, "Yes, this is Bertram Webber, I need to speak with Gustav Schapp. Yes, of course." He looked over the harbor, casual, but Erica could see in that casual awareness a lifetime of caution. Webber had lived a long time playing a hard game. She doubted how long her own life would last, but with what she had planned, she didn't really care. That realization shocked her. She didn't care if she died young as long as she was doing the right thing when it happened. Better to burn out chasing something true and right.

"Yes, Gustav, Betram here. I need to wire some funds please. Yes, of course." He waited for a moment before turning the scrap of paper over and reading from it, "Grand Cayman National Bank." A pause. "Yes." Another pause, then Webber gave the man named Gustav the routing and account numbers. "Wire ten point five million to the account please." He listened and then said, "Yes, ten million, five hundred thousand U.S. dollars."

It took Erica a moment to realize he had just added half a million to their negotiated price.

Webber glanced at her and smiled, "I don't need the money dear. What I want is to see you succeed. I think you'll make good use of every dollar. I consider it an investment."

She nodded at him and wanted to thank him, but couldn't speak; a mixture of excitement and fear held her still. Men like Webber had often been gracious to her, but they only wanted one thing. She looked at her chest, along the curve of her hip, and down to the black cargo pants and boots. Webber didn't see her the way other men had, but it wasn't Weber that was different was it?

I'm not acting a part. I am this.

She knew that as truth and knew she would follow it to her grave. The world had given her enough shit. Now it was time to give it back.

Webber said something about a confirmation code into the phone and gave a series of numbers and letters. Erica felt the weight of the gold coming off her, felt as though her feet did not quite touch the dock. She had secure currency in a bank. She was rich.

"Yes, goodbye," Webber said into the phone and turned to Erica. He held out his phone to her along with the scrap of paper. "You'll want to confirm with your bank."

She took both but could only nod at him. She tried to keep her face grave, tried not to show him the lightness she felt.

Webber stepped closer to her and took her by the shoulders. Then he said something that would stay with her the rest of her life. "You're powerful. It's written all over your face. But it will only come out if you believe it's there."

She felt herself flush at that; her heart thumped in her chest, and her legs went electric.

I'm powerful. Yes. Finally found it.

She smiled at him, took the phone, and stepped off the boat. "A bit of privacy," she said, and he nodded and waved her away.

Walking down to the end of the dock, she looked out on the water, blue and chopped in the afternoon wind. She dialed the number written on the slip of paper.

"Grand Cayman National Bank," A woman with a British accent said, "How may I direct your call?"

At first Erica feared she would be unable to speak. Her mouth felt dry. She looked over her shoulder and saw Webber standing down the dock, beside the boat with the gold. Looking toward the street, he waved his hand. She saw the four Jamaicans then, walking toward the docks. Sedar was supposed to have kept them at the café.

"Hello?" the woman on the phone said.

"Yes, sorry. I need to speak with Charles Blake."

"May I ask who is calling?"

"Erica Morgan."

"Will you hold?"

"Yes."

The phone clicked and classical music began to play. Erica looked back out to the ocean and then to the Jamaicans who were walking along the dock toward Webber. Erica guessed that she had been whitewashed, but she kept the phone to her ear. The music kept playing.

"Come on Charles," she said, "pick up the damn phone."

The Jamaicans walked up to Webber. Webber pointed to the boat. They would start unloading the gold, taking it to the Mercedes, which she saw parked on the street by the marina entrance. She had to have the confirmation first. Had Webber simply lulled her into his confidence to locate the gold and take it? She feared something else then, not that the gold was at risk, but that all the respect the men had shown her, Webber's body guard, Webber himself, the comment on being powerful, had been intended only to build her up so she would trust them enough to fulfill a hustle.

The music in her ear played on, and she felt the skin on the back of her neck crawling.

Where's Sedar?

She scanned the street and found nothing.

The Jamaicans jumped onto the boat, and one of them leaned over the helm. She felt for the keys in her pocket, still had them. Despite that, after a few seconds, the boat started. The men untied the cleats, threw the lines up, and the boat pulled away.

No.

She began to walk toward the boat, toward Webber, who stood watching the boat leave. Two of the Jamaicans remained with him, standing on either side. One turned and watched her approach. The boat was about to pass her, and she thought perhaps she could run up a side slip and jump onto it as it passed, but the Jamaicans on the boat ignored the harbor speed limit and throttled the boat full-on. Leaning back, it ripped out from between the docks, leaving the other boats tilting and scraping at their moorings. A man sitting on the deck of his sail boat, yelled at them. Rafi's boat turned and pulled into the harbor, out toward the open ocean and Abaco. She felt it all falling apart again. She couldn't have come that close.

As the boat's engine faded she heard from the phone, still held to her ear, "Is anyone there? Hello? Ms. Morgan?"

Her chest flushed with adrenaline. She didn't want to know now.

A half-million extra. Just enough to win my trust completely.

Why had she walked away from the boat?

"Hello?" Charles Blake said into the phone.

Erica shook her head and closed her eyes. Feeling dizzy, she opened them and stared at the planks of the dock, still tilting with the wake from the speeding boat.

"This is Erica Morgan," she said.

"How may I assist you?"

"I..." she paused. She didn't want to ask, couldn't hear him say the account was empty. With her voice quiet and her throat dry, she said, "I need to check on a wire transfer." She felt nauseous and considered hanging up the phone.

Blake said, "Yes ma'am. Allow me call up the account."

She heard keys tapping.

"Hmmm..." Then silence and more keys tapping. "That's strange."

She knew why it was strange. Someone calls in asking to see about a wire transfer and there's no money. Now he has to explain there's no money. People probably freak out then. She felt like she was going to. She looked back at Webber. He stood looking at her, one man on either side. They looked ready for her to lose it, ready to pull her gun and shoot. They would get the draw on her. One of the men put his hand in his pocket.

The keys tapped more in her ear, and Charles Blake said, "No."

"No, what Charles?" Erica asked. What would she do? She had been ready to take on the world, and now it would end, standing on this stupid dock, trapped. Looking back at Webber, she knew she'd take him with her. They'd kill her, but she didn't care. She wouldn't just walk away from being burned...

"There it is, yes," Blake said. "I apologize, another account kept coming up because I had not refreshed the screen. I show ten-point-five million U.S. dollars having been transferred to you a few moments ago. The funds are confirmed."

Erica's mouth went dry, and she felt she could barely breathe.

"Hello?"

"Yes, sorry," she said in a whisper. The anger and fear blurred together, and a hot tear spilled from her eye and ran down her cheek. "Did you say it was there?"

"Yes Ma'am, ten-point-five million dollars U.S."

"I- It's confirmed then?"

"Yes, fully funded."

She looked at the scrap of paper in her hand. She couldn't quite remember the next step. She looked over the scrap and saw the second account number.

"I need—" Her voice caught on emotion and she fell quiet.

"It can be overwhelming at times," Blake said. "Did you need to transfer some of those funds to the second account?"

"Yes," she said, still in a whisper. Now tears flowed freely down her face. She was free, had survived it.

"What amount would you like to transfer?"

In that moment the money wasn't half as important to her as Webber's sincerity. There had been no hustle, no obsequious lies.

"Transfer ten million to the second account," she said, her voice stabilizing. There was probably no need to do the transfer, it had been to assure the bulk of her funds were in an account that Webber did not have knowledge of, but Webber seemed to be on her side. Still, caution would be wise.

The keys clicked and Blake said, "There you are, the transfer is complete."

"Thank you, Charles."

"I am glad to be of service, Ms. Morgan."

She hung up the phone and walked toward Webber. As she approached she felt herself growing in stature, felt her shoulders going back and her legs flowing beneath her. Walking up to him, she took gentle hold of his face and gave his left cheek a light, soft kiss. She drew away from him and saw that his face had flushed.

She smiled at him and said, "Thank you."

Webber's sincere, broad smile broke out across his face as he said, "A pure jaguar." He took her hand, kissed it, and walked away saying, "Come men. We have business to attend to and should not stay long in her company. She'll bewitch us again and cost me more money."

Erica smiled at that. Webber lifted his hand, and the door of the Mercedes opened. Webber's body guard got out followed by Sedar.

CHAPTER 32

That night she dreamt of the black cave again, but the unseen chamber felt devoid, echoing and empty. She crossed the pool, her hands outstretched, feeling for the far wall. When she reached it, she felt along the damp stone until her fingers found the passageway the beast had come down. She made her way up that passageway with slow, careful steps in the blinding dark. Soon, she saw light glowing far down the passage. Shadows along the rough walls of the passage stretched toward her. As she neared the light, it shone with the spectacular brilliance of a summer sky.

She walked out of the cave into a meadow. A river ran through breeze-bent grasses, and beyond stood the rose-colored granite of mountains speckled by fir trees and delicate flowers. The sun-warmed air smelled of pine pitch. In the shadow of a nearby tree she saw a man looking out on the mountains, his shoulders strong under a white cotton shirt, and the breeze pulling at the easy curls of his dark-brown hair.

"Rafi?"

He turned and smiled, holding out his hand to her.

She walked up to him with caution and touched his chest, holding her palm there, feeling his heart pulsing and his breath rising and falling.

"Rafi—" she began, but a sob cut her short.

He took her in his arms and she rested her head on his shoulder, kissing his neck once.

"Please tell me this isn't just a dream," she whispered, feeling her tears dampening the fabric of his shirt.

"I am here," Rafi said, and she felt the vibration of the words in his chest and neck.

She held him tighter, gripping his shoulder and back with her hands.

"I'm so sorry—" she began, but again her voice failed her.

Rafi hushed her, his hand stroking the back of her head. "I came to tell you I am free, that all is well."

She let her head rest fully on his shoulder. "I love you so much Rafi."

She woke holding her pillow, the case wet with her tears.

"No... not yet," she said as she buried her face in the pillow, but she knew the dream wouldn't return. She cried then, not from regret or loss, but from having been forgiven.

• • •

Erica looked into the beveled mirror of the hotel bathroom and liked what she saw. The damage Antonio had done to her face was healing well. She ran her fingers through her newly-cut hair and thought it looked very... Nakita. She smiled at herself, not due to her outward appearance, but from the sense of reconciliation from her dream.

She found Sedar in the Atlantis' pillared lobby wearing a dark-blue silk shirt and gray slacks. He looked up at her, and as she approached him, he stood and gave her a professional nod.

"Do you have the tickets?" she asked him.

"Yes."

She walked past him, out of the hotel lobby, to a black Lincoln Continental waiting to take them to the airport.

She sat down in the soft seat of the car. As Sedar settled into the seat beside her and closed the door, he said, "You have not told me where we ah going."

"I said Paris."

"But that's not the final destination."

Erica nodded at that. "We're going to Israel."

"Why?"

But Erica did not answer. She was deep in thought, laying plans for the rest of her life.

...to make an end is to make a beginning.
The end is where we start from.

-T.S. Elliot

Bestselling author Jason Andrew Bond grew up in Oregon and currently lives in Washington State with his wife and son. He holds a Bachelor of Arts in English Literature from the University of Oregon and an MBA from the University of Colorado. When his first novel *Hammerhead* unexpectedly reached bestseller status, he dedicated twenty-five percent of his profits to disabled U.S. veterans. Mortal Remains is Jason's second novel, which will be followed by *Hammerhead Resurrection*. Jason takes a hands-on approach to writing. When SCUBA research couldn't wait for summer, he found himself certifying in Puget Sound's frigid January waters. Outside of writing and his family, martial arts are an important part of his life. At eighteen years of age he entered an Aikido dojo for the first time, and has since trained in Jeet Kune Do, Tae Kwon Do, Shudokan Karate, Goshin Jutsu, and Brazillian Jiu-Jitsu.

For more about the author, future novels, and events, please visit:

www.JasonAndrewBond.com

Made in the USA
Charleston, SC
20 November 2012